The Scratchling Trinity

Boyd Brent

Author contact: boyd.brent1@gmail.com

D0293325

Table of Contents

One
Max Hastings

London, England, 2016

Max Hastings was leaning low over the handlebars of his bike, and pedalling like he'd flipped out. The distance from his school to his home was two and a half kilometres, and Max *had* to smash his personal best time. The reason was written on a scroll of parchment, held closed by a black ribbon and jutting from his blazer pocket like a piston powering him towards a new school-to-home record. He sped up his drive, leapt off his bicycle and sprinted, arms flailing, towards the front door. Once through it, he darted into the living room, unclipped the strap on his bicycle helmet, and cast the helmet onto the couch. Max was twelve years old, of average build if a little on the chunky side, with a shock of white-blond hair that grew every which way except the way Max would have liked. Max drew the scroll from his pocket, gunslinger style, straightened his back, and announced his extraordinary news to his parents: 'I've finally *won* something!'

Mr Hastings looked at Max over the top of his newspaper. 'There must be some mistake,' he said.

'That's what I thought when Miss Hale announced the name of the re-cip-ient.'

Mrs Hastings, who was holding Max's one-year-old sister Maxine, put the baby down in her walker. 'Congratulations, Max! So what have you won?'

Max gazed at the rolled-up parchment in his hand. 'It's a grand prize, Mum. They picked *my name* out of a hat during the last assembly of term.'

'You've broken your duck, then?' said his astonished father. 'If memory serves me correctly, you've never won anything in your life. Not even when you went through that annoying competitions phase.'

'I know, Dad. I was there.'

'So *what* have you won, exactly?' asked Mrs Hastings.

'No idea.'

'Well, then, I suggest you untie that ribbon and find out.'

Max glanced from the parchment to his mother and back again. Mrs Hastings placed her hands on her hips. 'Whatever is the matter with you?'

'It's just so ...'

'So what?' said his father.

'Official-looking.'

'Which must bode well for the prize,' said Mr Hastings, putting down his newspaper. 'Give it here, son. I'll open it.'

Max shook his head. 'I'll do it.' He untied the ribbon and unfurled the parchment. His lips moved slowly as he read it, and his brow furrowed.

'Well?' pressed his mother.

His father leaned forwards in his armchair. 'What are you the recipient *of*?'

'Of a life-time membership ...' murmured Max.

'A life-time membership of *what*?' said his mother testily.

Max read the words slowly. 'The Ancient Order of Wall Scratchings.'

'Of *what*?' said Mr Hastings.

'Of *wall* scratchings,' repeated his mother helpfully.

'But what does that even mean?' mumbled Max, his eyes glued to the parchment for some clue.

'Oh, for pity's sake, give it to me,' said his mother, sliding it from his hand.

Mrs Hastings scanned the parchment. 'Oh, my goodness. Max has been invited to a private viewing of their wall scratchings tomorrow, at Mansion House!'

Mr Hastings cleared his throat. 'What? The place where the Lord Mayor of London lives?'

'Yes!'

'There must be some mistake,' asserted Mr Hastings.

Mrs Hastings shook her head. 'No mistake. The Ancient Order of Wall Scratchings, Mansion House, City of London, London.'

Max sighed. 'Trust me to win a grand *booby* prize. Tomorrow's *Saturday*, not to mention the first day of the Christmas holidays. I'm not going.'

'Not going?' echoed Mrs Hastings.

'Why would I? Since when was I interested in *wall scratchings*? I don't even know what they are!'

'They're scratchings on walls, presumably,' said Mr Hastings, happy

6

to apply his keen insight to the problem at hand.

'Well, whatever they are,' said Mrs Hastings, glancing at the parchment in her hand, 'it says here that they have the world's largest collection of them.'

'Not helping, Mum,' said Max. He went to the dining table and opened his laptop, muttering absently to himself as he typed *the ancient order of wall scratchings* into the search engine. He sat back in his seat and breathed a sigh of relief. 'Just as I thought. There's no such place. It doesn't even exist! ... What are you doing?' Max asked his mother.

'There's a phone number on here. I'm calling them.'

'But—' said Max.

'But nothing. I intend to get to the bottom of these ... these *scratchings*.' She tapped her foot impatiently as the phone rang at the other end of the line.

A woman with a cut-glass English accent answered. 'Thank you for calling the Ancient Order of Wall Scratchings. How may I help you?'

'My name is Mrs Hastings, and my son Max has just won a free membership to your organisation.'

'Hearty congratulations!' said the woman.

'Be that as it may, there's no mention of you on the internet. No mention whatsoever.'

The woman drew a deep breath. 'Ours is an ancient organisation, Mrs Hastings. As such we frown upon all modern conventions.'

'Alright. But your address appears to be the very same as the Lord Mayor of London's.'

'That's right.'

'And the Lord Mayor?'

'What about him?'

'He's happy to share his residence with your organisation?'

'The Ancient Order of Wall Scratchings has been located at this spot for over a thousand years, Mrs Hastings. Since the year 1065, to be exact. The first Lord Mayor didn't move in until some seven hundred years later, in 1752.'

'*And?*'

'And since then we've had no complaints from any Lord Mayor in office.'

A man's voice came on the line. 'Max is going to benefit greatly from membership, Mrs Hastings,' he asserted.

'*Max is going to benefit greatly from his membership,*' repeated Mrs Hastings, as though in a trance.

'And he'll meet a great many important people.'

'*And he'll meet a great many important people,*' echoed Mrs Hastings.

'People,' the voice went on, 'who will be able to help him in his chosen career.'

'He wants to test video games for a living,' murmured Mrs Hastings.

'*Help him in his chosen career,*' said the man, raising his voice.

'*Help him in his chosen career,*' repeated Mrs Hastings obediently.

'Tell Max he's welcome to bring a friend tomorrow. Goodbye.'

'Goodbye!' said Mrs Hastings, putting down the phone. She turned to Max. 'You're welcome to take a friend tomorrow,' she said, grinning terrifically from ear to ear.

Max scratched absently at his left cheekbone, just below his eye, where there was a birthmark that looked as though someone had signed their initials in black ink. 'O-kay. Are you alright, Mum?'

'Never better,' she replied. Mrs Hastings's smile then did the seemingly impossible and grew wider still. Max had never realised his mother had so many teeth.

Two
Eric Kettle

Yorkshire, England, December 1st, 1840

Inside a carriage drawn by two horses, a frail boy sat shivering beside a giant of a man. The man was expressionless and granite-faced, and indeed any onlooker might have thought him cut from granite. The only clue to his being flesh-and-blood was the smile that curled his lips whenever the carriage hit a pothole and the boy yelped. The man took up most of a bench designed for three adults, squashing his young companion against the carriage door like an item of worthless baggage. The boy's name was Eric Kettle, and Eric looked so fragile that he might break in two every time the carriage lurched over a bump in the road – of which there were a great many, and many more potholes besides. Despite these hardships, Eric's saucer-like brown eyes gazed with extraordinary hope from a face gaunt with hunger.

It was gone midnight when the carriage came to a halt at its destination: the St Bart's School for Boys. The school was a crumbling mansion that rose from the Yorkshire countryside like a vampire's abandoned lair. The carriage door was opened by the driver, who was hidden by an entire closet's worth of coats, scarves and gloves. The brute heaved himself out of his seat. 'Fall in behind, sir,' he grumbled at his young ward. Eric followed as quickly as his shivering legs would allow. He hugged himself for warmth, and stumbled towards the promise of heat beyond the door that now opened for them. Once through the door, Eric wondered if it hadn't actually been warmer outside.

They'd been admitted by a pale and hungry-looking boy swaddled in a threadbare coat several sizes too large. He was carrying a paraffin lamp, and, without uttering a single word, he illuminated their path across a cavernous entrance hall and up a sweeping staircase. Two flights up, he lit the way down a long corridor before finally stopping outside a door, on

9

which a gold plaque read: *Headmaster. Augustus Mann.* Augustus took a key from his pocket and unlocked the door. He turned to the boy carrying the lamp, now hastily lighting a candle by its flame, and snatched the lamp from his grasp. The boy scurried off on bow legs, and Eric watched the candle light until it disappeared from sight at the end of a corridor. 'Fall in, sir!' came the gruff voice of Augustus Mann, from inside the study.

The headmaster placed the lamp on a desk piled high with books, and pointed to a spot on the wooden floor before the desk marked with an X in chalk. 'Stand there, arms at your sides, chin held high. That's it. And stop your shivering.'

'I'll try, sir, but it's just so ...'

'Say the word *cold,* and as God is my witness, I'll thrash you where you stand. Perhaps you think that I should light a fire for you? Waste good wood? Is that what you think?'

'No, sir.'

'Speak up when I address you!'

'No, sir!'

'No what?'

'No, I don't think you should waste good wood on me, sir.'

'Spoilt! That's what you've been. Spoilt to the core.'

Eric shook his head. 'They work us very hard at the orphanage, sir.'

The headmaster sat down and opened a folder on his desk. 'It says here that your father went off to seek his fortune the day after you were born. Wherever he went, he must have liked it there.'

Eric smiled. 'Do you think so? Why do you say so, sir?'

'Liked it more than he liked *you,* anyway.' Eric's smile vanished as the headmaster grunted and went on, 'I see your mother went looking for him soon after, and whether or not she found him, nobody knows. Never seen nor heard from again. But whatever she *did* find, she must have preferred it to you.' The headmaster observed Eric through narrowed eyes. 'What is it about you that so vexes others, *boy*?'

Eric's gaze dropped to the ground. 'I'm sure I don't know, sir.'

'After so many years in an orphanage, I dare say you thought your ship had come in, with your name chosen from a hat to receive a scholarship to attend a fine Yorkshire school of good repute. Thought you'd get yourself a proper education, eh? Those abominable do-gooders, passing their laws that say the likes of *me* must look with charitable eyes upon the likes of *you*. The paltry compensation I will receive for your keep will barely cover my costs.'

'I'm very sorry, sir.'

'You will be. The fact is, you are worth more to me *dead* than you are alive – a fact that doesn't bode at all well for you,' said the headmaster, rising from his chair and turning to face a collection of canes hanging on the wall. He stroked his grey moustache thoughtfully, smiled, and then reached for one.

'Please,' implored Eric. 'I don't know why my parents left me. I did nothing wrong. I was just a baby, and that's the God's truth, sir.'

The headmaster turned and swiped the cane back and forth to gauge its suitability. 'I would strongly advise you not to take the Lord's name in vain. Not in this establishment, *sir*, or God help me …'

As Augustus Mann made his way around his desk towards him, Eric closed his eyes and willed himself back at the orphanage. It didn't work, although the heavy blow that struck his face might almost have launched him back there. Eric's legs gave way beneath him, and he collapsed to the ground, groaning and clutching a cheek that felt savaged by a thousand bee stings. Augustus Mann loomed over him, cane in hand. 'Down at the first lash? Pathetic! That is what you are, pathetic. Is it any wonder your parents left you?' The headmaster yawned, ambled back around his desk, placed the cane back on its hook and walked towards the door. 'You can spend the night there on the floor, like the dog you undoubtedly are. Although I can assure you that your life expectancy is considerably shorter than a dog's. A truth I intend to take *considerable* comfort from,' he yawned. Augustus Mann stepped through the door, closing it and locking it behind him.

Eric dragged himself into a corner, where he huddled miserably for warmth, trying to remember a legend he'd heard some years before at the orphanage: *If a child of kind heart and noble mind is ever in mortal danger, all he needs do is scratch a message of help into a stone wall, and help will find him*. Eric fumbled down his side for one of the safety pins that kept his clothes from falling apart, and with it he scratched the following words in tiny letters into the wall: *If ever a boy was in mortal danger, it's me. Please, if anyone's there, help me!*

Three
Saturday

London, England, 2016.

When Max Hastings woke up the next morning, he smiled in anticipation before remembering he wouldn't be spending the day playing *Heroes and Zeroes* online with his best friend Ash. *We have to go and look at a load of wall scratchings*, he thought glumly as he stretched. Max's mother had called Ash's mother, and now Ash was being forced to accompany him. If that wasn't bad enough, they would be doing so in their Sunday best. So there would be two fewer Zeroes doing battle with the Heroes online that day, and Max was not looking forward to the ear-bashing he knew was in store for him at Ash's house. Max sat up in bed and looked in disgust at the dark suit, white shirt and tie his mother had placed on the armchair in his room. He sighed and climbed out of bed.

Ash lived three streets away, and Max was there in two shakes of a Zero's tail. He parked his bike in the open garage and knocked at the front door. Mrs Pandian opened the door and ruffled his hair. 'The lucky winner of the very fabulous prize!' she said warmly. Mrs Pandian was a small Indian woman with a red *bindi* on her forehead. Max's eyes were now level with this dot, and he went a little cross-eyed as he addressed it. 'Thank you,' he told the dot through his dishevelled hair. 'Is Ash about?'

'Ash!' cried Mrs Pandian over her shoulder. 'Max is here.' Her gaze returned to Max, and she ruffled his hair again. 'Such a cute boy!'

'Mrs Pandian?' asked Max.

'Yes?' she grinned at him.

'Will Ash be taking a *comb* with him today?'

'Here he is now. You can ask him yourself.'

Ash came dejectedly down the stairs. He was a weedy-looking boy with thick black hair and the beginnings of a moustache. 'What happened to your hair, Max? It looks even more ridiculous than usual,' he said, as he edged past his mother and then Max.

'Bye, boys! Have a fabulous time!' Mrs Pandian called out.

'Bye, Mum! Tall order!' said Ash over his shoulder.

Max caught him up. 'Sorry about this,' he said.

'Seems to me you're always sorry about something,' replied Ash, quickening his pace. 'Of *all* the things you could have a won, it had to be a life-time's membership to a collection of wall scratchings. I mean, what a great start to the Christmas holidays!'

'*World's largest* collection of wall scratchings,' said Max.

'Not helping,' said Ash, throwing up his hands.

'I know exactly what you mean, so what's the hurry?'

'I would have thought that was *obvious*. The sooner we catch the bus, the sooner we can get there, see the dumb *wall scratchings*, and get back to being Zeroes.'

'At this rate, we're never going to be Heroes,' observed Max philosophically.

'You said it.'

Ash said very little during their bus ride over to Mansion House, and Max thought it best to leave him to his thoughts. Ash's thoughts tended to run the gamut from pessimistic, all the way through the negativity spectrum, with final destination: hopeless. The upside of this was that bad news never came as a surprise with Ash around. Max gazed out of the bus window and watched the suburban streets of South London transform into the ancient and narrow streets of the City of London.

They got off the bus at Bank Junction, an open space where nine of the oldest streets in existence converged. Mansion House rose majestically over this junction like a residence fit for a king – or, in this instance, a Lord Mayor of London. Max and Ash stood outside and gazed up its six towering columns. 'This can't *possibly* be the right place,' murmured Ash.

'I've already had this conversation. It *is* the right place,' said Max, reaching into his inside pocket and pulling out the roll of parchment. The main entrance was on the first floor, and you had to climb one of the two staircases that converged outside it. 'After you,' said Ash, motioning to the stone steps.

The door at the top of the steps was the biggest door either of them had ever stood in front of. 'Looks like the entrance to a dragon's lair,' said Ash, running a nervous hand through his jet-black hair. Max stepped forwards and rapped hard on the door with his knuckles. As he winced and shook his hand, Ash rolled his eyes and pointed to an intercom to the right of the door. Max straightened his tie and reached for its button.

'Yes? Can I help you?' enquired a female voice.

'I have an invitation to come here today,' said Max, holding the parchment up to the CCTV camera above the intercom. The enormous door opened, and they stepped into a small but grand foyer with a very high ceiling. They approached a lady sitting behind a desk, who forced a smile and held out a hand for the parchment. She turned it over, looked at Max and said, 'Is this some kind of a joke?'

Ash nodded.

'No joke,' said Max. 'We've been invited to see the wall scratchings.'

The lady cast a nervous glance at the security guard who'd opened the door. 'To see the *what*?' she said.

'The *wall scratchings*,' repeated Max, a little louder, as though the woman must be hard of hearing.

'Invited by whom?'

'By the Ancient Order of Wall Scratchings, obviously. Who else?'

'I can assure you there's no such Ancient Order in the city of London, young man.'

Max shook his head. 'Their address is on the invitation,' he said, pointing over the desk at the parchment in her hands.

'Where?' exclaimed the woman, holding up the parchment. 'It's blank!'

'No, it isn't,' said Max impatiently, taking it from her. Max and Ash gazed incredulously at the parchment. It was indeed blank. 'There were words here ... large words, written in fancy letters! Tell her, Ash!'

Ash felt the presence of two security guards looming behind them. 'I'm too weedy to go to prison,' he said, in a small voice.

'Show these pranksters out,' said the lady curtly.

The pranksters heard the heavy door close behind them. Ash glanced at Max, who was examining the parchment. 'The words are gone, but ...' whispered Max.

'What *now*?' said Ash.

Max swallowed hard. 'They're coming back.'

Ash took a step away from him. '*Back*? How do you mean, back?'

'Back as in *back*. Only ...'

'Only what?' said Ash, taking another step away.

'They're not the same words.'

'Do I want to know what they say?' asked Ash, now three paces away.

Max held up the parchment, on which two words were now spelled out

14

in big letters: *Max Hastings*?

'That's you,' said Ash unnecessarily, pointing at his friend.

The name *Max Hastings* rubbed itself out before the boys' astonished eyes, and was replaced by *Ashokkumar Pandian*? The boys stared at each other. 'What should we do?' they chorused. By way of a reply, the following words appeared on the parchment: *Try not to panic.*

'That's easy for you to say!' said Max.

'He's right. You're a sheet of paper!' said Ash.

Parchment, the parchment corrected him. That word was quickly replaced. *You've come to the wrong entrance.*

'What?' said Max.

The wrong entrance. The entrance you want is directly below you. The door at street level.

'You could have put that on the invitation,' said Max. He looked at Ash. 'What are you shaking your head at me like that for?'

'Oh, I don't know. Could it be because you're having a conversation with a sheet of paper?'

'Parchment!' corrected Max, pointing out the single word *parchment!* now on the parchment. He turned and began to descend the stone steps.

'Where are you going?' asked Ash.

'Where do you think?'

'To get us rooms in the nearest loony bin?'

'Yes, obviously, but *first* I'm going to see if the parchment is telling us the truth.'

'Us?' repeated Ash, rooted to the spot.

'Come on. You must admit this just got a whole lot more interesting.'

Ash glanced fearfully behind him. 'Creepy, you mean.'

'Come on! We're already late.'

They soon stood outside an ordinary wooden door at street level. 'Is this the door?' Max asked the parchment. *Yes, it is. Stick me to it,* it read.

'How do I do that?' asked Max, glancing at Ash, who was shaking his head in disbelief again. 'What's the matter now?'

'You might wanna keep your voice down when you're talking to your new *friend*. There are people around,' said Ash, grinning at a party of Japanese visitors walking past.

Max lowered his voice and addressed the parchment in his hands again. 'Stick you to the door with what?'

Hold me against it and I'll do the rest. As it turned out, the parchment didn't just stick to the door, it was absorbed into it, and the door began to creak open.

Max and Ash gazed into the darkness beyond. This was no ordinary darkness; it was akin to a black void, like looking into a cosmos without any stars.

Max and Ash stumbled as the ground they were standing on moved towards it.

Ash yelled incoherently into Max's face.

Max yelled incoherently into Ash's face.

They spun about and tried to run away, but the faster they ran the quicker the ground conveyed them back towards the door and, slowly but surely, the sprinting, flailing boys were sucked inside with a *THRUUPPP!*

Four
"Breakfast"

St Bart's School for Boys, Yorkshire, 1840

Asleep on the cold, hard floor of Augustus Mann's study, Eric Kettle was roused by a finger prodding his shoulder. He woke with a start, and blinked until his eyes focused on the wall scratching he'd made in the early hours. Eric quickly rolled over and fell against the wall to hide it. In the silvery morning light from a single window, Eric met the gaze of a boy of a similar age, crouching beside him. The boy resembled a bag of bones on a collapsed pair of legs. When the bag of bones opened its mouth, it sounded sprightly enough. 'You look like you've seen a ghost, but I ain't one. Not yet, anyway.'

'Are you alright?' Eric blurted out.

'Am *I* alright? It's not me you should be worried about,' replied the boy, pointing at the gash in Eric's cheek. 'Struck you just the once, did he?' he asked, giving Eric the once-over.

Eric's hand went to his cheek, and touched a small birthmark just above the swelling. He grimaced. 'That's right. I fell to the floor.'

'Wise move. Dropping to the floor is always the best tactic during a Mann thrashing. He's so tall, and he's got a dodgy back, see? Old Mann *hates* having to lean over when he's dishing it out.'

'I'll bear that in mind,' said Eric.

'Come on, or we're going to be late,' said the boy, standing up.

Eric's stomach grumbled as he climbed unsteadily to his feet. 'I'm Eric Kettle,' he said, extending a hand.

'Don Smithy,' said the boy, shaking it and then hurrying towards the door.

'Where are we going?' asked Eric.

'Breakfast.'

'Thank goodness. I'm starved,' said Eric, patting his tummy.

'Take my advice and don't get your hopes up about food here.'

'Chance'd be a fine thing here or anywhere else,' mused Eric.

'Now look here, there's no easy way of sayin' this …' began Don, pausing at the door. 'I'm to show you to the Unwanted Table.'

'A table nobody wants?' replied Eric, grasping at straws.

Don's eyes flashed up and met his own. 'It's not the *table* that's unwanted. It's the boys who sit at it. Like I told you, best not hope for much grub,' said Don, scampering off down the corridor.

As they made their way down a winding stairwell, Eric stopped. Don continued on a little way, before realising he was alone and coming back. 'What are you *doing*? We're already late!' he said.

'I'd consider it a favour if you would show me the way out,' said Eric with as much calm dignity as he could muster.

'Out? There is no way out.'

'The front door. The one I came in last night. That leads out.'

Don folded his arms and tapped his foot impatiently. 'Oh, I get it. You mean to escape?'

Eric nodded.

'You honestly think you're the first boy to have such a notion?'

'No.'

'All the others ...' said Don quietly, avoiding Eric's gaze.

Eric gulped. 'What about the others?'

'Captured, or ...' Don ran a finger across his throat.

'*Dead*?'

Don nodded. 'Drowned in the quicksand that surrounds this school for many a mile. The graveyard over at Flushing Peak is where the lucky ones are buried.'

'The lucky ones?'

'Those they found.'

'I'll stick to the road, then,' said Eric, tapping his nose as though he had just been given a handy tip.

Don gazed at Eric's tapping finger like it was the most ridiculous thing he'd ever seen. 'You'd be captured in no time. It's twenty-odd miles to any kind of cover.'

'I could borrow Mann's carriage. Go straight back to the orphanage. I'm good with horses.'

'Now listen here: Mann's horse and carriage are locked up in a barn with padlocks this big,' said Don, bringing both his fists together. 'And they're guarded by dogs that weigh more than you and me combined. Now hurry, or you won't get even a morsel to eat all day! And neither will I.'

Eric hung his head and followed.

18

The dining room was located in what had once been a grand ballroom. It was now a shell of its former self: the once green and lush wallpaper was faded and torn, the chandeliers encased in thick dark cobwebs, and its tall windows filthy with grime. Gone was the grand table at which a hundred and fifty aristocrats had once dined, and in its place were eight cobbled-together wooden tables where the eighty pupils of the St Bart's School for Boys sat waiting for their breakfast.

When Eric entered the dining room, he felt the gaze of its eighty-three occupants burning into him: eighty boys, Augustus Mann, and, seated either side of the headmaster at the top table, two assistants who he was soon to discover were identical twins known as Mr Whip and Mr Lash. Augustus Mann sat back in his chair and sneered. 'Feast your eyes on our newest arrival, sirs!' he announced. Eric froze in his tracks as though giving them ample time to do just that. In truth, Eric's hollow legs felt suddenly numb and unresponsive. Sensing this, Don took a firm grip on his arm and led him to the Unwanted Table.

Seated at this dreaded table were three of the most desperate-looking urchins Eric had ever seen, and Eric had beheld a great many desperate-looking urchins in his time – not least the one who stared back at him every time he encountered a mirror. He sat down at the end of the table, in front of a bowl of watery gruel. The boys seated at the other tables had much larger bowls, he noticed, as well as a chunky slice of bread and a lime to prevent rickets. But even these fortunate souls salivated as a plate of steaming sausages was brought in and placed before Augustus Mann and his two assistants.

Eric looked at the other three unwanted boys seated beside him. Either his starved mind was playing tricks on him, or they looked progressively worse as they went down the table. The boy at the far end looked so broken and hungry that he might expire at any moment. *I'll be in that seat before long if I don't get out of here*, thought Eric.

'Who told you to face the front, sirs?' bellowed Augustus Mann. 'Behold Eric Kettle, the latest reprobate to join your ranks.' All the boys, impatient to begin breakfast, turned and stared daggers at Eric.

Augustus Mann rose slowly to his feet and began to slow-clap. As he clapped, he said, 'Mr Kettle has been awarded a scholarship to our fine establishment. So don't just sit there, *sirs*. Get up off your backsides and congratulate him!' The eighty pupils climbed off their benches and began clapping. Eric didn't know where to look, so he looked everywhere and nowhere. The effect of this made him dizzy. Augustus Mann stopped clapping and the room fell silent. 'Many of you have been here long enough to remember the last time a charity case was forced upon us.' The headmaster glanced down at his two assistants. 'Mr Whip and Mr Lash, remind me again, what was that fellow's name?'

Mr Whip looked across at his twin brother, who seemed to communicate the answer to him telepathically. Mr Whip nodded his pale, freakishly narrow face. 'It was Jonathan Banks, Headmaster,' he replied, revealing a mouthful of rotten teeth.

'Ah, yes, so it was,' said Augustus Mann. 'Upstanding fellow, I seem to remember. Most courteous. Remind me again what became of the upstanding Mr Banks?'

'He found himself locked out of doors on a perishing night,' said Mr Whip, shivering.

'Caught his death,' sniggered Mr Lash.

'An unfortunate accident,' added Mr Whip.

'*Most unfortunate indeed,' growled Augustus Mann. 'Sirs!' he went on. 'Feast your eyes on all the unwanted, and give thanks that your parents pay your school fees on time and in full. Be mindful that if ever this happy circumstance should change, then room can and will be found for you at their table.' Augustus Mann sank back down in his chair with satisfaction and smiled at his plate of sausages. 'You might want to remind your parents of that when you next you're allowed to write home,' he added, forking up the fattest, juiciest sausage.*

Five
The Chamber of Scratchings

The door slammed closed behind Max and Ash, and the boys found themselves in darkness. 'We're going to be murdered!' spluttered Ash.

'Try and stay calm!' urged Max, in need of his own advice.

'Why should I? I'm about to be murdered!'

Max spun about and rested his back to the door. 'A light ... I see a light!''

'What's it doing?'

'Coming this way.'

'What! Coming this way? Are you sure?'

'Yes, it's getting bigger.'

'*Bigger*? Knowing your luck, it's a train!' Ash banged on the door with both fists. 'Help!' he cried.

'It can't be a train. It's too quiet, and ...'

'And what?' sobbed Ash.

'It's swinging from side to side like ...'

'Like a train that's out of control?' whimpered Ash.

'No. More like someone coming to get us. With a lamp.'

'Ahoy there!' came the hoarse voice of a man who was clearly used to shouting a lot. 'Ahoy there?'

'It's worse than I thought,' whispered Ash, groping in the darkness for his friend's shoulder. 'We're lost at sea.'

'Ahoy!' came the voice a third time.

'Ahoy,' said Max hoarsely, much more quietly than he'd intended. He drew some air into his lungs. 'Ahoy!' he cried. 'We're over here.'

'I know where you are. Have no fear of that.'

'He knows where we are. It's game over,' breathed Ash

'He sounds friendly enough to me.'

'Serial killers always do. Don't you know anything?'

A man walked out of the darkness holding a lantern. He was a portly man of medium height wearing a splendid red and gold coat with the words *Town Crier* embossed into a lapel. The man's head was large, and so too was his grinning face, which resembled an old silver teapot. On his

21

head there rested a black tricorne hat with a plume of white feathers. 'Sorry I'm late,' he said, raising the hat and lowering it again. 'I'd have been here sooner if I'd known.'

'Known what?' murmured Ash, who was cowering behind Max.

'Known I was going to be late, of course.' The man scratched his wrinkled forehead. 'It wasn't you who won the competition, was it, young fella?' he joked. Ash shook his head.

'That's alright, then. So by a process of elimination you must be Max,' he continued, extending his bear-like hand for Max to shake.

'Yes, that's right,' said Max, shaking it.

'I'm Marlot. More pleased than you know to make your acquaintance. This must be your permitted companion,' said Marlot, narrowing his eyes at Ash.

'Yes. His name's Ashokkumar Pandian,' said Max.

'My friends call me Ash. Where are we?'

'Welcome to the Nether Void,' said Marlot, lifting his arms and gesturing about him.

'What is this place?' asked Max.

'It's nothing to worry about. Just the buffer that keeps our two worlds separate.' Marlot reached past the boys and tore the parchment from the door. 'This is yours, I believe?' he handed it to Max. 'You'd best keep it safe.'

'How do we get out?' said Ash.

'You'll be back out soon enough. Come now and follow me down the Tunnel of Sniffing Darkness. Pay no attention to the Darkness that gives it its name.'

'The *Sniffing* Darkness? What does it sniff?' said Max.

'All new arrivals. It just wants to make sure that you are who you say you are.'

'And if we aren't?' asked Ash, glancing wildly from side to side.

'Then, more likely than not, it would drag you away and you'd never be seen nor heard from again.'

'Never thought I'd be so glad to be myself,' muttered Ash.

'That makes two of us. Where are we going?' asked Max, looking into the darkness that crept close to the light, backed off, and then came close again like it was curious.

'To the Chamber of Scratchings, of course,' replied Marlot, as though it were obvious.

'Chamber of Scratchings? How is this place even *possible*?' asked Max.

'It's not for me to say. Strictly speaking, I'm only supposed to deliver you to the Chamber.'

'So, the Ancient Order of Wall Scratchings *does* exist, then? Only the lady upstairs has never heard of it,' said Max.

'Very few people from the other side of the Nether Void have.'

'So why bring *us* here?' asked Ash.

'Why? It's Max's birthright to be here, that's why,' said Marlot, shooting a glance at the small, squiggly birthmark high up on Max's left cheekbone.

'It's my *what*?'

'Your birthright. What with you being Scratchling-born.'

'I'm *what*?'

'Scratchling-born,' said Ash helpfully.

Marlot scratched his head. 'Oh come now, there must have been times when you felt different from other boys, Max?'

'Different?'

'Yes, as in special,' said Marlot.

'Hardly.'

'Not true,' said Ash. 'You must have felt special when you were put into Mrs Knot's *special* math class.'

Max gave Ash a shove. 'Are you *certain* you have the right person? If you've made a mistake, it's not too late to show us back to the door. We won't tell anyone about this place.'

'That's right,' Ash agreed eagerly. 'Your weird secrets are safe with us.'

'And it's not like anyone would believe us. They'd only think we were nuts if we did tell them.'

Marlot glanced at Max. 'Tell me this,' he said mysteriously. 'Do you consider yourself a lucky person?'

'Absolutely not,' stated Max flatly. 'I always seem to be in the wrong place at the wrong time. And I've never won *anything* until now.'

'Correction,' said Ash. 'You've still never won anything. It was a fix. You're Scratchling-born, remember?"

'So *he* says,' said Max, quietly.

'You are, lad, and it's *because* you're Scratchling-born that your luck's seemingly been deserting you all these years,' said Marlot with a twinkle in his eye.

'Oh, right. So being Scratchling-born *isn't* a good thing, then?'

Ash patted his friend reassuringly on the shoulder. 'Looks like they got the right guy after all.'

'I've said enough,' said Marlot, buttoning an imaginary button on his lips.

As they continued down the twisting tunnel, the Sniffing Darkness came so close that it all but snuffed out the light from Marlot's lamp, and then withdrew to reveal a set of towering doors dotted with metal studs. Max and Ash gaped up at the doors in wonder. 'Is there a *castle* down here?' asked Max.

'Many moons ago, yes. Bright lad,' said Marlot. 'Where we're standing I gather there used to be a moat. No need for a moat now. Not with the Sniffing Darkness on our side.' Marlot opened his heavy coat and unhooked a bell from his belt. He grasped the bell's wooden handle and shook it up and down vigorously. Max and Ash placed their hands over their ears as Marlot cried, 'Hear ye! Hear ye! I have here, by order of the Ancient Order of Wall Scratchings, Masters Hastings and Pandian! As requested!' The doors began to creak open and, as they did so, Marlot tucked the bell back inside his coat and stepped through into a vast chamber.

The chamber was circular, and it tapered upwards like the inside of a giant bell. Its walls were black as pitch, and levitating close to the walls were thousands of lit candles. Close to each floating candle a pane of glass had been attached to the wall, and below these a silver plaque glinted in the candle's flame. Marlot glanced at the boys, who were understandably transfixed by the miniature universe of candles receding up into the top of the chamber. 'Behind every pane of glass you'll find a facsimile of a scratching,' he said, puffing out his chest with immense pride.

'And what are the silver plaques below them for?' asked a breathless Max.

'That's a good question, Max. Bodes well, it does. The plaques show important information about the scratching they're under.'

'Information about what?'

Marlot folded his arms. 'Well, let's see, you'll find the date the scratching was made, where in the world the original is located, and, most importantly of all, I suppose, the name of the child who made it.'

'So Dad was right about them being scratchings made by people.'

Marlot sighed sorrowfully. 'Every scratching in this Chamber is a message from a young person in mortal peril. A terrible cry for help.'

'*All* of them?' asked Max, squinting up at the thousands of candles.

'Every last one, I'm afraid.'

Ash folded his arms. 'Like I keep telling Max, it's a cruel world we live in these days.'

Marlot shook his head. 'That may be so. If truth be told, I've never ventured forth into your time, but these messages were scratched by children throughout the ages. The earliest are facsimiles of scratchings left by children some *ten thousand years* ago in caves.'

'Oh, that's bleak,' said Max, shuddering.

'Well, maybe not as bleak as you think. The Ancient Order of Wall Scratchings exists to help these children.'

'That's nice,' murmured Ash. 'And ... ah ... what is *that?*' He stepped behind Marlot and pointed over his shoulder. In the darkened rear of the Chamber, something enormous loomed from the shadows. '*That,* young fellow, is the Tree of Scratchings,' said Marlot.

'It's got to be *three times* the size of any tree I've ever seen,' said Max, taking a step towards it. 'And it's *moving*.'

'That's right. To the return position,' said Marlot proudly.

'What's it returning?' asked Ash from behind him.

'Not so much *what* but *who*,' said Marlot.

Ash swallowed hard. 'Alright, then. *Who* is it returning?'

'You're about to find out for yourself.'

'Why's the tree so gnarled?' asked Max.

'It isn't. Those marks are facsimiles.'

'Of what?'

'Of every scratching you see here about you on these walls.'

The boys stared open-mouthed at the creeping tree as it came to a halt in the centre of the Chamber. What a sight it was, its leafless branches all wizened and contorted in a way that made them look like arms thrown about in turmoil. A third of the way up was a hollow that looked like a mouth in mid-scream. The tree made a sound like a giant's belch, and out of its 'mouth' shot a yelling blur that flew over their heads. They turned to see the blur caught in a gigantic net above the Chamber's entrance. The blur became a girl who stopped yelling, coughed and spluttered, and then dropped over the edge of the net like an acrobat and landed on her feet. She was covered from head to toe in soot, her raven-coloured hair falling wildly across her face. She looked Max up and down with piercing green eyes that provided a shocking contrast to her blackened face. This scrutiny was turned on Ash, who stepped nimbly behind Marlot. The girl's gaze settled on Marlot's face. '*That* is the last time I rescue a kid who's stuck up a chimney. I don't care if they're destined to grow up to be the Queen of Sheba!' The tree belched, and a chimney sweep's brush flew out of it and bounced off her head. The girl didn't react, not so much as a blink. She just balled up her fists after the fact and said, 'Where is he, Marlot?'

'Welcome back, Ellie. Are you talking about Caretaker Wiseman?'

Ellie placed her sooty hands on her sooty hips, cocked her sooty head, and narrowed her eyes. 'Are you trying to test my patience?'

'You know what Caretaker Wiseman always says,' said Marlot. '*Any test is a good test, so long as you can pass it.*'

'Well, when you *do* see him, you tell him from me that this is *categorically* the last time I rescue a kid from up a chimney! I mean it.'

She turned and was about to stalk off when a man's voice said, 'Of course you don't. You're just tired, Ellie.'

The boys turned to see a man walking towards them as though he'd emerged from the tree. He was quite old and quite thin, and wore quite a nice beige suit and beige tie, although his bottle-bottom spectacles indicated that he was anything but *quite* short-sighted. He pushed them nearer to his eyes to improve his view of Max as he made his way towards him.

'Just look at the state of me!' said Ellie, throwing her arms wide.

'And what of the chimney sweep?' asked Caretaker Wiseman, stopping to squint up towards one candle in particular with a smaller flame.

'As you can see, his flame has *shrunk*. He's fine,' replied Ellie, folding her arms.

'Excellent! That young man is destined to campaign – successfully, I might add – to bring an end to his brutal trade,' said Caretaker Wiseman, rubbing his hands and walking over to Max. 'It's good to finally meet you. My name's Peter Wiseman, and I'm the caretaker of this Chamber.' He leaned forward and peered at the birthmark on Max's cheek, and then shook his hand so enthusiastically that Max felt as though his arm might leave its socket.

Having observed Max's grimace, Ash was keen to avoid a similar hand-shaking fate, but a moment later he too was wincing as Max looked on, smiling. At that moment, a penny dropped in Max's mind about the shrunken candle flames that Ellie and Caretaker Wiseman had mentioned. He turned and stepped towards the wall, where he could see that there were as many small flames illuminating scratchings as there were larger ones.

Max turned to face Caretaker Wiseman. 'Why have you brought me here?' he asked flatly.

Caretaker Wiseman took off his glasses and wiped their lenses with his handkerchief. 'You're here because you're Scratchling-born,' he replied, putting his glasses back on again.

'So I've already been told. But what does it *mean*?'

'So you've already been *told*?' said Caretaker Wiseman, glancing at a sheepish-looking Marlot.

'Sorry,' said Marlot, 'but he asks so many questions, and—' Marlot had been silenced by Caretaker Wiseman's raised palm.

'Well? What does it mean?' pressed Max.

Caretaker Wiseman turned to Max. 'It means you have *the gift*,' he said reverently.

'*I* have the gift? *Me*?' said Max.

'Hold up,' said Ash. 'They haven't told you what this gift is yet.'

Caretaker Wiseman joined Max at the wall. 'Scratchling-born are the only living things in the universe capable of time travel.'

'You are joking, right?' gaped Max.

'Clearly not,' replied Caretaker Wiseman. 'How else could they rescue the children whose cries for help you see all around you in this Chamber? Ellie is Scratchling-born. She just returned from 1888.'

'1889,' corrected Ellie pedantically.

Max looked at her. 'But I'm nothing like her. I can't even help myself, let alone others.'

'It might surprise you to know that Ellie had a very similar reaction when she was first told she was Scratchling-born – and look at her now.' Both boys looked at Ellie. Caretaker Wiseman was right. Neither could believe that she hadn't taken the news of being Scratchling-born like a duck takes to water. Max turned and read a scratching behind a pane of glass on the wall: *My stepfather means to beat me until there's no breath left in me. He's only waiting on an excuse. He's locked me in the basement and means to finish me off. If there's truth to this legend, then help me!* The silver plaque below it read, *Nathan Brocklehurst. Province Island, USA. Year of our Lord 1738.*

'You're wondering why his flame still burns so brightly? Why his call is yet to be answered?' said Caretaker Wiseman.

Max nodded.

'The sad fact is, we can only help children whose scratchings become active.'

'Active?'

'Yes. When they call to a particular Scratchling. In the case of Nathan Brocklehurst, when that day comes, his voice will resonate through the ages and fill this Chamber – an echo from the past, if you like.' Max turned his head as though he'd heard something. 'What is it?' asked Caretaker Wiseman.

'That whispering.'

'Whispering?'

'Listen. You must be able to hear it.'

'No,' said Caretaker Wiseman, cocking an ear.

'Ash, you hear it, don't you?'

Ash shook his head. 'You're hearing voices, man. And that's never a good sign.'

Caretaker Wiseman placed a hand on Max's shoulder and gestured him into the Chamber. 'Seek the voice you hear,' he said quietly.

'But he *can't* seek. Not yet. He hasn't been through the Initiation Ceremony,' said Ellie.

'Hush now, Ellie, and let's take Max at his word.'

Max made his way deeper into the Chamber, past the Tree of Scratchings, towards an area at the back that was shrouded in darkness but for a single burning candle. The others followed in silence, which Ellie was the first to break. 'He obviously *is* hearing things.'

'Quiet now, Ellie,' said Caretaker Wiseman gravely.

'But there's only one scratching back here, and you know as well as I do that its author is beyond help. You told me so yourself.'

'Ellie!' barked Marlot. At the rear of the Chamber a single lit candle levitated above a scratching. Ellie was about to speak up again, but was silenced by a finger pressed to Caretaker Wiseman's lips. Max leaned in close to read the message and then stumbled backwards when silver light poured through the words and a voice from the dim and distant past echoed throughout the Chamber. It was the voice of Eric Kettle: 'If ever a boy was in mortal danger, it's me. Please, if anyone's there, help me!'

Six
The Unwanteds' Banquet

Eric Kettle had always liked to count his lucky stars, to see how many he needed to thank. Back at the orphanage, he'd often joked that it never took much time, so why not do it as often as possible? Tonight he thanked his lucky stars that his second night at the St Bart's School for Boys would not be spent shivering on a floor but in an actual bed. So what if his blanket was thin, moth-eaten and stank of goodness-knew-what? And so what if the bed springs felt like little razors whenever he moved? A bed was a bed, after all, and in his book any child who found himself lying in one and not on the floor was entitled to thank his lucky stars.

Eric was sharing a room with the same three boys whose table he'd shared at breakfast and supper: the Unwanted. Above their door there was even a makeshift wooden sign that said *The Unwanteds' Room*. Eric had never felt wanted, and now he thanked his lucky stars that the name of his room was so appropriate. Eric shook his head and wondered if he hadn't gone too far in being optimistic in the face of relentless adversity. By the light of a single, sputtering candle, he watched his fellow unwanted climb into bed. He'd barely exchanged a word with anyone all day, and the closest he'd got to a deep and meaningful were the rather-you-than-me looks he'd received from the other pupils.

Eric walked over to the first boy in the row of three beds. 'I don't believe we've been formally introduced. I'm Eric Kettle,' he said, doing his best to sound happy-go-lucky.

The boy reached out a shaky hand from under his bedclothes and shook Eric's hand gently. He cleared his throat and whispered, 'I'm Jack Sharpe.'

'Good to meet you, Jack Sharpe.'

Eric went to the second bed and learned that it was occupied by a boy called Henry Thomas, and the third by a lad called Ken Smith. Once all the introductions were out of the way, Eric went and sat cross-legged on the end of his own bed. 'Our stomachs are making some racket, aren't they?'

he observed, cocking an ear.

Jack sat up. 'Henry says they talk amongst themselves. Don't you, Henry?'

Henry placed his hands behind the back of his head. 'They have so much to say. So I reckon they must be.'

'Mine's been a right chatterbox since the day I got here,' said Ken.

'Did you *see* it?' said Jack, his voice filled with wonder.

''Course we saw it. We're not blind,' scoffed Henry.

'And smelt it,' said Ken dreamily.

'What are you talking about?' asked Eric.

'The pork pie that Mann, Whip and Lash were tucking into at supper.'

Eric sighed. 'I can't deny it looked delicious.'

Ken sat up too. 'Have you ever tasted a pork pie, Eric?'

'No, but there's a first time for everything,' said Eric, uncrossing his legs and placing his feet on the ground as though he intended to fetch one for himself.

'Shall we play the imagination game, then?' asked Ken, brightening up.

'Yes, let's!' whispered Jack. The three of them sat up straight and pretended to tuck napkins into their nightshirts.

'Only the best cutlery for us,' whispered Henry, raising his nose into the air and pretending to hold a knife and fork over an imaginary pork pie.

'That isn't what I meant,' said Eric. 'I think we can do better than pretending.'

'No, we can't,' said Jack, savouring a mouthful of imaginary pork pie.

Eric stood up and went to the door.

'Where do you think you're going?' asked Ken.

'That pork pie was big enough for eight people,' said Eric. 'And they only ate half of it. So the rest must be downstairs in the pantry.'

'Are you mentally disturbed?' asked Jack.

'Of course not. He's just pulling your leg,' smiled Henry.

Eric twisted the door handle and smiled when the door opened. 'It's not locked,' he said.

'Why would it be?' said Jack. 'Do you have any notion of what Mann would do to us if we were discovered out of this room at night?'

'Not to mention Mr Whip and Mr Lash.' At the mention of Mann's assistants, the three boys crossed themselves.

'You just sit tight,' said Eric. 'And don't worry. It'll be on my head.' He pulled the door open.

'But you can't! Mann will kill you,' whispered Henry.

Eric shrugged. 'He's planning on it anyway, so what have I got to lose?'

It was so dark in the corridor that Eric had to feel his way along the wall to the stairs at the end of the landing. Once he reached them, the light of the moon through a stained-glass window guided his descent. The stairs gradually wound their way down to the ground floor. The pantry was located at the farthest end of the dining room, and Eric tiptoed his way over the stone floor to its entrance and slipped inside the high-ceilinged room where he had eaten his watery gruel earlier.

Tall windows ran the length of the dining room and, although it lent the room a spooky atmosphere, Eric welcomed the moonlight that beamed through them. He made his way slowly up the length of the room, past the top table where Mr Mann had sat with Mr Whip and Mr Lash, and on towards a closed black door.

He reached out a hand and pushed the door open. It was dark inside the pantry. Eric blinked until he could make out the shape of a stool close at hand. He picked it up and wedged the door open, allowing a little moonlight to filter in. The smells that assailed his nose made his mouth water and, as he licked his lips, he caught sight of the leftover pork pie he'd come for. For once, the scope of his optimism had been found wanting: there wasn't only half a pie left, but two thirds at least. He stood over the pie and tried not to drool as the aroma of its savoury meatiness climbed his nostrils. He was about to pick up the plate, when out of the corner of his eye he caught sight of cutlery glinting on hooks. *I'll give those poor lads a proper banquet if it's the last thing I do*, thought Eric as he took three knives and three forks and placed them on the plate beside the pie. Then he opened the linen drawer and took out three white napkins and laid them atop the cutlery. He hoisted the plate off the counter and made his way back to the Unwanteds' room with the booty.

When Eric entered the dorm, the three boys sat up in bed, their eyes wide and their mouths wider still. They sniffed long and hard, and remained speechless as Eric lowered the plate onto his bed. Eric turned to face them and bowed low. 'Dinner is served, your Lordships,' he announced grandly, plucking up the napkins with a flourish. Trancelike, each boy took a napkin and stuffed it into their nightshirt. Eric cut three ample slices of pie, and placed one before each boy. 'Wait a sec ...' he said, going for the cutlery. He handed each boy a knife and fork, and then sat cross-legged on his bed watching them. 'I'll take the pie back presently,' he said. 'Who knows, perhaps they won't even notice that it's a bit smaller. Well, your Lordships? What are you waiting for? Tuck in!'

'But where's yours?' asked Henry.

Eric brushed a hand over his face. 'I only arrived yesterday. Compared to you, I'm well fed. Plump, even!' he said, puffing out his cheeks. He glanced down at the pie next to him on his bed, sighed and said, 'If I take any more they'll be more likely to suspect something.'

'Well, if you're sure,' said Ken, wiping some spittle from his lips. He didn't need to be told twice.

''Course I'm sure,' said Eric. 'Tuck in, lads!'

Eric had a smile on his face while he watched them enjoying their banquet, and such was his joy that at one point he even had to clasp his hand to his mouth to smother a fit of delighted giggles.

Once they'd finished, the boys sat with smiles on their faces and enjoyed the novel feeling of non-grumbling tummies. Eric collected their napkins and cutlery and placed them back on the plate. Picking it up, he made his way back to the door. 'I'll be back soon,' he said over his shoulder.

Henry burped contentedly. 'Eric?' he said.

'Yes?'

'Be careful.'

Eric nodded.

At the bottom of the slowly winding staircase, Eric thought he heard something in the darkness. *A footstep?* He froze, cocked his head to his left and listened. He felt suddenly lightheaded, and the plate and all its contents slid away from him towards the ground. He crouched and prevented the fall, and then, doing his best to ignore the increasing ache in his arms, stepped in the direction of the dining room.

Once again, Eric was glad of the moonlight streaming through the tall windows of the dining room. Midway through the room, he froze in his tracks. *Another footstep in front of me? And another behind me!* Eric moved as quickly as he could to the top table, knelt down, slid the plate beneath it, and crawled in beside it. He held his breath and listened ... Just as Eric was about to breathe an *I-must-be-imagining-things* sigh of relief, urgent footsteps came from *both* ends of the dining room. Eric shuffled further under the table and looked wildly left and right for signs of his pursuers. All at once, two long faces with freakishly large, close-set eyes peered in at him from either side of the table. 'What have we here?' sneered Mr Lash.

'I told you something was afoot!' cried Mr Whip, bringing his fist down on the top of the table with a triumphant crash. Panicked, Eric darted from beneath the table. A hand grabbed Eric's arm, spun him around the other way, and shoved him face down onto the table. Mr Whip leapt up onto the table and drew back his foot to kick Eric's head. Eric threw himself backwards, whereupon Mr Lash caught him, spun him about, head-butted him, and gave him a little shove. Eric stumbled back several paces before collapsing to the floor. Mr Whip crouched down under the table and slid out the plate. 'Theft. A most serious business,' he observed, sniffing the pie.

Eric groaned, and Mr Lash gave him a swift kick. 'Theft, sir! A significant breach of the law.'

'Of the very land in which we live,' concurred Mr Whip, gazing down at the savoury evidence.

'Criminals are routinely hung for less,' observed Mr Lash.

'Far less. I'll bring the pie while you escort the criminal in our midst.' Eric had imagined Mr Lash a spiteful but not a particularly strong man, but the strength required to carry a boy under one arm and to use his head as a battering ram to open doors was immense. What's more, the identical twins had identical limps that caused them to lurch forwards together in a terrifyingly robotic manner. Eric was doing his best not to think about that when his head slammed into a particularly stubborn door and he passed out.

Eric regained consciousness when a bucketful of icy water was thrown into his face. He shook the water away and leapt from the chair in Mann's office, but was forced back down into the chair by the headmaster. Mann stood over him, fisted hands on hips, his attitude that of a king woken in the dead of night to pass sentence on a wayward subject. Mann leaned down and grabbed Eric's hair. Eric grimaced, but bit his lip to stop himself giving Mann the satisfaction of crying out. In Eric's extensive experience of bullying grown-ups, the more you showed your pain, the more pain was inflicted. It was like a red rag to a bull.

Augustus Mann brought his face so close to Eric's that Eric could smell the pork pie still on his breath. 'I ought to thank you,' sneered the headmaster. 'You've given me cause to be rid of you sooner than expected. *Theft*, sir! Liked the taste of my pie, did you?'

Eric winced in pain and nodded.

'So you admit it?'

'Yes! I had my fill! You got me! Bang to rights!'

Mann released his grip on Eric's hair and stood up straight. 'A guilty plea, gentlemen. Take him down.'

'*Down*?' queried Mr Lash.

'To the dungeon kitchen, headmaster?' enquired Mr Whip.

'Yes. Chain him up without food or water, then go back and 'find' him in four days. No, wait ... He's had his fill of my pie, so make that *five* days. Tut, tut, tut! I will inform the authorities that you were told *never* to venture down into that terrible place, but that the likes of you just never listen. I gather from your notes that you like to thank your lucky stars. Well, you can thank them now that I'll need an unbeaten corpse to present to the authorities. Otherwise, sir, I would give you the thrashing you so richly deserve.'

By the light of a lantern held aloft by Mr Whip, Mr Lash manhandled Eric down some steps into the basement. At the bottom, Eric was roughly shoved along a corridor and under a number of stone archways. 'This is the oldest part of the building,' said Mr Lash. 'It dates back to 1250, when there used to be a castle here. All that remains of it now are its dungeon and kitchen.'

'And come nightfall, it's haunted by the ghost of many an angry servant,' said Mr Whip gleefully.

'So you can count your lucky stars that you won't be spending your final days alone in the dark,' sniggered Mr Lash.

Eric was pushed into what had once been the castle's medieval kitchen. From what he could make out by the swaying light of Mr Whip's lantern, it was an expansive place where dozens of servants had once toiled to prepare banquets. At its centre, hollowed out of the red brick wall, was a hearth that contained a spit large enough to roast a pig.

'They say that a meal was prepared for King Henry VIII and his entourage in this kitchen when he visited the castle in 1537,' said Mr

Whip, slamming Eric against the wall. Mr Whip slid a bracelet attached to a chain over his wrist and clicked it into a locked position. 'Never let it be said you didn't receive an education during your time here,' he spat.

'Ouch!' cried Eric, squeezing his eyes shut.

'Tight fit, is it?' smiled Mr Lash. 'That's because it was originally used to chain up a dog by its leg – a big dog, by all accounts. And savage. What do they say about that dog again, Mr Whip?'

'That its starved ghost paces this very room come midnight, in search of thieving children to devour.'

'Please! Don't do this. Don't leave me here!' Eric begged.

Mr Whip seized Eric's throat. 'Like Mr Mann told you, thank your lucky stars that the coroner must find no sign of a beating when he is called to examine your corpse. We did not earn the nicknames Mr Whip and Mr Lash for *nothing*.'

Seven
Upstairs

Caretaker Wiseman rested a hand on Max's shoulder as he hurried him towards a lift inside the Chamber of Scratchings. 'But what does all this mean? There must be some mistake,' said Max.

'How can there be?' said Caretaker Wiseman. 'Eric Kettle's scratching lit up before our very eyes.'

'And we heard his cry,' called Marlot from where they'd left him with Ellie beside Eric's scratching. The lift was a cylindrical tube, just large enough for Max, Ash and Caretaker Wiseman to squeeze into. They stood toe to toe, Caretaker Wiseman a full head taller than the boys.

'Looks like you've really gone and done it now, Max,' murmured Ash.

'Done what? What have I done?'

'You awoke *the* scratching!' Caretaker Wiseman sounded excited again.

'Is that a good thing or a bad thing?' asked Max.

'I suppose it depends on whether you can reach him in time to save him,' replied Caretaker Wiseman.

Max looked at Ash. '*What* did he just say?'

'He said it all depends on whether you can reach him in time to save him,' repeated Ash helpfully.

'Me?'

'Who else?' said Caretaker Wiseman.

'That girl Ellie, for a start! If this boy Eric is so important, won't you want your best man on the job?'

'Best *woman*,' said Ash, who was quite certain that his assistance was proving invaluable today.

'Whoever! Just not me!'

'But Eric's scratching spoke to *you*, which means you're the only one who can journey to his time period. Eric Kettle chose *you*, Max,' said Caretaker Wiseman in reverent tones.

'Is he *nuts*? Why would he choose me?'

'Because he's never met you?' suggested Ash, on a definite roll now.

'But I can't save *anybody*! I'm not ready. I don't know anything!'

Caretaker Wiseman nodded again, and Max breathed a sigh of relief. 'But on the other hand, you are *Scratchling-born.*'

Max scratched his armpit irritably. 'So?'

'So, you are more resourceful than you imagine.'

'No, I'm not.'

'Max is right,' said Ash. 'He only recently learned to tie his own shoe laces properly.' Max glanced down at his trainers, and noticed that one of his shoelaces had come undone. He was about to point out this highly relevant fact when the lift doors opened.

They stepped into a grand room with a crystal chandelier suspended at its centre. There were twenty or so men and women in the room, dressed in army uniforms from World War Two. Some were standing and surveying a map that took up the entire back wall, while others pushed objects around a table. Max glanced left and right, noting that the room adjoined similar rooms to form a seemingly endless corridor in both directions.

Caretaker Wiseman led Max and Ash through a great many of these rooms, which were all identical in activity. The only difference was that each room's occupants were dressed in clothes from different periods in history. One of the rooms they passed through contained knights from the time of the Crusades, another Quakers from the time of the founding fathers of America, and another Victorians wearing top hats and sporting handlebar moustaches. From what the boys could tell, it looked as though every period of history had its own Operations Room.

'What are all these people *doing*?' asked Max breathlessly, hurrying to keep pace with Caretaker Wiseman.

'You've heard of the concept of *good luck,* of course,' replied Caretaker Wiseman.

'Of course he's heard of it,' said Ash. 'He's just never experienced it.'

'Well, the truth of the matter is this: there is no such thing as good luck. These rooms are where what people refer to as good luck is created.'

'But why?' asked Max.

'To assist those of kind heart and noble mind.'

'Yes, but *why*?'

'So they can help maintain the balance against Those Who Leave Much to Be Desired.'

'I've never had any good luck. Does that mean I leave much to be desired?'

'Oh, come now! Of *course* not. You're Scratchling-born!' Caretaker Wiseman reminded him.

'So why does he never seem to catch a break in the luck department, then?' asked Ash.

'To throw *them* off his scent,' replied Caretaker Wiseman mysteriously.

'*Them*?' demanded Max.

'You'll find out about them presently,' said Caretaker Wiseman.

As they passed through more Operations Rooms, Max and Ash gazed at the men and women going about the business of orchestrating good luck. Then, slowly but surely, a pair of red doors loomed from the end of the corridor.

The red doors opened into a sea-blue room with a dozen windows that rose from floor to ceiling, each one providing a view of London in a different time period. A severe-looking woman was sitting behind a desk, writing urgently upon a parchment. She looked only a little older than Max's mother, but the stern expression with which she now regarded him over the rims of her spectacles surpassed anything his mother could muster. 'Can it really be true?' she said, in a voice deep enough to be a man's.

'Can what be true?' stammered Max.

The woman ignored his reply and looked at Caretaker Wiseman.

Caretaker Wiseman's voice rose to a higher pitch in his excitement. 'There can be no doubt about it! Eric Kettle's scratching ... it called to Max Hastings, a fledgling.'

The lady sat back in her chair and removed her glasses. As she studied Max through narrowed eyes, beads of sweat bubbled up on his forehead. He felt like a boy made of snow in the full glare of the midday sun. The lady somehow straightened her already straight back. 'This is hardly the time to *wilt*, Mr Hastings,' she said. 'Come closer, and let me have good look at you.' Max felt Caretaker Wiseman apply a little pressure to his shoulder, guiding him forwards. The lady stood up and came around her desk. 'My name is Mrs O, but my friends call me Mrs O.' Max could not tell whether she was joking or not, and so did not know whether to laugh. 'There's no need to look quite so confused,' Mrs O smiled. 'We've been waiting for the Scratchling-born who could activate Eric Kettle's scratching for *one hundred and seventy-five years.*'

'This really isn't helping,' muttered Max.

'Speak up, Mr Kettle. No muttering.'

'*This*. Not helping.'

'And why not?' she asked.

'It's all too much.'

'Too much what?'

Max thought hard for the right word, and blurted out, 'Responsibility!'

Mrs O looked at Caretaker Wiseman with a concerned expression. 'Has he always been this way?'

'I wouldn't know. We've only just met,' said Caretaker Wiseman.

A voice spoke up from the back of the room, '*Always.*'

Mrs O peered over Max's shoulder. 'And who have we here?'

'This is Mr Pandian. Max's permitted friend,' explained Caretaker Wiseman.

Mrs O raised her nose and looked down its impressive length at Ash. 'Has your friend always been shy of responsibility?' she asked imperiously.

'Absolutely.'

'And why do you suppose that is, Mr Pandian?'

'He's *twelve.*'

'That's right!' said Max, vindicated. 'And I won't be thirteen for another *three* months.'

'Good to hear you're still optimistic about making thirteen,' said Ash.

The doors burst open and a man rushed in. 'They know!' said the man, as he tried to catch his breath.

'Know?' said Mrs O, raising an eyebrow.

'That Eric Kettle's scratching has been activated.'

Mrs O snatched the parchment up from her desk and held it out at arm's length towards the man who'd brought the news about *them* knowing. 'Priority one!' Mrs O barked at him. 'The Tree of Scratchings must be ready to deliver Mr Hastings to the appropriate coordinates ASAP. You know as well as I do that the clock is now ticking for Mr Kettle. If he dies, all will be lost.' The messenger nodded and hurried out of the room with the parchment.

Max felt his heart pounding in his chest. 'All will be ... lost?' he mumbled.

'Yes. All,' said Mrs O. 'Now, you two follow me,' she commanded, pointing at Max and Ash.

Mrs O led them to a door at the far end of her office and up a winding stone staircase. Up and up they trod. 'Where are we going?' asked Max, the pain in his legs growing unbearable.

'To the top,' replied Mrs O.

'But why? What's up there?'

'The roof – or, to be more precise, the battlements.'

'The *battlements*?' echoed Max, glancing at Ash.

'That's right, Mr Hastings. These are desperate times, and you know what they say about desperate times, don't you?'

'They call for desperate measures?' supplied Ash.

'Precisely, and that's why I've deemed it necessary to show you something that's only shown to a *very* privileged few. It will help impress upon you the urgency of your mission.'

'I think I'm about to have a heart attack,' muttered Max, clutching his chest.

They finally emerged onto the battlements atop the Ancient Order of Wall Scratchings – an expansive area with ancient stone walls and high lookout towers. Beyond the lookout towers, the skies teemed with dark, fast-moving clouds. Two soldiers dressed in trench coats and tin helmets from the First World War saluted Mrs O, and then handed each of them a tin helmet. With their helmets on their heads, Mrs O led the boys quickly to the edge of the battlements where a trench had been crafted from sandbags. Soldiers crouched in the trench holding rifles, while others used periscopes to look out to goodness-knew-where. Max and Ash followed Mrs O into the trench, where she ordered one of the soldiers to stand aside. 'Let this boy look through your periscope,' she told him. The man nodded and moved away. Max stood on a wooden box and placed his eye against the lens.

'Well? What do you see?' asked Ash.

'You aren't going to believe this ...'

'Trust me, I will,' replied Ash, rolling his eyes and glancing around him.

'It's the top of a *massive* fortress, with battlements, and we're talking Dungeons-and-Dragons scary.'

'What you can see, Mr Hastings, is the headquarters of the League of Dark Scratchings. It is located on the site of the Bank of England, on the cusp of time. Just as our fortress is located at the same location as Mansion House.'

'What's the cusp of time?' asked Max.

'The cusp of time is where you're from. Now, tell me *who* you see?'

'No one. It's just a bunch of turrets, towers and walkways. No. Wait a minute … crossing between two turrets …'

'Well?' said Ash.

'They look like *bankers* … only bankers from the olden days when they wore bowler hats, had twirly moustaches, and carried umbrellas everywhere.'

'Like that dad dude in Mary Poppins?' asked Ash.

'Yes, exactly like that.'

'That doesn't sound so bad,' scoffed Ash.

'Look *closer*,' said Mrs O impatiently. 'What makes them different from any other *people* you've ever seen?'

Max's eyes opened wide. He pulled back from the lens and swallowed hard. Ash took a step away from him. 'What … what did you see?'

'They're all moving about in pairs,' Max said distantly, still trying to absorb what he had seen.

'In *fruit*?' said Ash.

'No, in twos, but they're not walking, they're *gliding* … like a metre off the ground, and …'

'And?' asked Ash.

'It's the creepiest thing I've ever seen.' Despite this, Max looked back through the periscope lens, while Mrs O looked approvingly on his curiosity.

'As you've doubtless already been informed,' she said, 'the Ancient Order of Wall Scratchings exists to rescue children of kind heart and noble mind – children destined to grow up and make a positive contribution to society. The League of Dark Scratchings, on the other hand, provides an identical service for children who are destined to grow into Those Who Leave Much to Be Desired. If the League of Dark Scratchings had its way, the world would be overrun by those motivated by greed at any cost, by thieves, murderers and tyrants.'

'So what's any of this got to do with me?' asked Max.

'You, Mr Hastings, are one of only *eight* Scratchling-born that can exist at any given time. You are a replacement for a Scratchling called

Edward Dawson – a fine Scratchling who had to be retired recently when he reached his seventeenth year. As all Scratchlings are. So you see, Mr Hastings, we have four Scratchling-born, and the League of Dark Scratchings has four Dark Scratchlings.'

'So what's the big deal?' shrugged Ash. 'I mean, how much difference can eight kids make in the grand scheme of things?'

Mrs O looked sharply at Ash. 'They make *all* the difference, Mr Pandian. The rescue missions that Scratchlings carry out provide the *very foundations* of everything our opposing organisations stand for.'

'How?' pressed Max.

Mrs O held her chin and tapped her nose as she thought how best to explain. 'Scales,' she said.

'*Scales*?' echoed Max.

'Think about it, Mr Hastings. When scales are finely balanced, no matter how much they hold, it requires only a *single* grain of sand to tip the balance in favour of one side or the other. The work that the Scratchling-born undertakes *is* that final grain of sand.' Mrs O beckoned Max from the box on which he stood with a crooked finger. Max stepped down as though an invisible wire connected him to this woman, and her voice reached another level of gravity when she said, 'Eric Kettle, the boy whose scratching called to you, is the long-hoped-for *Ninth* Scratchling. If we can rescue Eric Kettle, it would provide us with a clear advantage over the League of Dark Scratchings. The entire universe would become a much safer and more tolerant place.' Mrs O motioned with her chin over the top of the trench. 'This means that *they* will stop at *nothing* to make sure you fail in your mission to bring Eric Kettle back safely to us.'

Ash tore his gaze from Mrs O and looked at Max. 'My advice would be to breathe,' he said.

Eight
To Go or Not to Go?

'Of course we can't *force* you to travel back in time to rescue Mr Kettle, Mr Hastings,' Mrs O had said as she'd escorted Max and Ash back down to the Chamber of Scratchings. 'If we tried, it would make us little better than Those Who Leave Much to Be Desired. All we can do is appeal to your good nature.'

'What makes you think I'm good-natured?'

'You're Scratchling-born,' replied Mrs O simply. 'I've arranged for Ellie to have a word with you. Help you make up your mind.'

The Chamber of Scratchings was alive with activity. A dozen white-coated technicians were standing on ladders and attending to the 'mouth' of the Tree, while others gathered about its base and scribbled down calculations. Caretaker Wiseman stood at the base of the tree also, his glasses pressed to the bridge of his nose, gazing up at the work being carried out. The scene reminded Max of the launch of a space shuttle. He'd always thought how terrifying it must be to have to climb into a rocket and be jettisoned into space, and now his heart thumped at the prospect of being sent back in time.

Max and Ash were seated on a bench at side of the Chamber. Ash crossed one leg over the other. 'Have you given any thought to how Ellie is going to help you to make up your mind?' he asked.

Max shook his head. 'No, but I bet *you* have.'

'Personally, I reckon she'll threaten to break your legs if you don't go.'

'She's Scratchling-born, remember. They're supposed to be the good guys.'

'It's pretty obvious they've mixed Ellie up with one of those *Dark Scratchlings* – which means there's a nice kid over at the League of Dark Scratchlings who can't understand why he's just been told to rescue a young lad called Jack, as in the Ripper.'

Ellie was suddenly standing in front of them. Clean of soot, the boys could now see that she had a sprinkling of freckles across her pale, almost luminous face, and shoulder-length black hair. Max's gaze found the small, squiggly birthmark that was in the exact same place as his own, high up on her left cheekbone. Ash slammed his crossed leg back on the ground. 'Where'd you pop up from?' he asked.

'Would you mind?' she said, jabbing her thumb over her shoulder. 'I'd like a word with Max alone.'

'Maybe I would mind,' said Ash nervously. 'Why can't I stay?'

'You're a pessimist.'

'And?'

'And when the world's order hangs in the balance as it does now, I think you'll find there's no place for pessimism,' she replied, examining a broken nail.

'Maybe I'm a realist?' said Ash.

'Scram,' said Ellie, looking at him again.

'Only if Max wants me to.'

'It's okay,' said Max. 'Really.'

'I'll be right over here if you need me,' said Ash, getting up and giving Ellie a wide berth.

'He means well,' said Max as Ellie sat down next to him on the bench.

'I know.'

'He reckons you're going to threaten to break my legs if I don't agree to help Eric Kettle.'

'Oh, then I was wrong about him.'

'How so?'

'He's an optimist.'

Max glanced sideways at Ellie and was relieved to see she could smile after all.

His eyes focused on her birthmark. He swallowed hard. 'Snap,' he said.

'It's the Mark of the Scratchling-born. We all have one. It's a Latin word: tempus.'

'It's an actual *word*?'

'Of course it is. Haven't you ever studied it under a magnifying glass?'

'Uh, no.'

'Well. if you had, you'd have seen a *tiny* joined-up word: tempus. It means *time*. As in traveller.'

Max gulped. 'How long have you been doing this?'

'This is my second year now.'

'You must have seen some scary stuff.'

'I won't lie. There's not much about the dark side of human nature that surprises me these days.'

'Do your parents know what you do?'

'You must be kidding. They'd have kittens if they knew.'

'So where do they think you go?'

'Ballet classes. I used to want to be a ballerina.'

'But not anymore?'

Ellie bit off a broken piece of her nail. 'You think I have time to prance around in tutus these days?'

'I'd like to think I'll always have time for that,' said Max with a wistful sigh.

'A sense of humour. Good. You're going to need one working here.'

'So the missions ... they must be over pretty quickly, then? No longer than a ballet class?'

'Ah, no. Sometimes they last for days.'

'So where do you tell your parents you're going?'

'Oh, you're worried about time. Not an issue. When you enter the Nether Void, the clocks outside on the cusp of time freeze – well, as good as. So no matter how long you're here, when you step back out of that door, it's as though you've never been anywhere.'

'Handy.'

Ellie looked into Max's eyes as though searching for something. 'You *can* do this, you know,' she said.

'Why?'

'You're Scratchling-born. This is what we do. You *can* help Eric Kettle,' she asserted, with so much confidence that Max almost believed her.

'That's easy for you to say.'

'You just need to start trusting your Scratchling intuition.'

'Trust my intuition? Is that *it*?'

'You'll also have your own dedicated Operations Room upstairs. They'll be working overtime to provide you with the best luck they can. If I'm honest, I'm actually a little jealous. Do you know how *long* they've been waiting for the Scratchling who can rescue Eric Kettle, the Ninth Scratchling?'

'One hundred and seventy-five years,' murmured Max.

'Exactly! Eric is one of *us*.'

'I still think they've made a mistake about me. I'm not like you.'

'Trust me. They haven't.'

'If that's true, then why me? How did they even know where to find me?'

Ellie rolled her eyes. 'They've known you were going to be a Scratchling since before you were born. Since before your grandparents were born.'

'Okay. So why *me*? Why you? Why Eric Kettle?'

'Profound,' smiled Ellie. 'I don't think anybody here knows for sure why us. I asked Caretaker Wiseman that very question once.'

'What did he say?'

'A load of nonsense like *why does the sun set in the east?* and *why don't the stars tumble from the heavens?*'

'Doesn't gravity hold them up there?'

'Of course gravity. That's what I told him. So you see, I don't think they know *why* us. And if they do, they're staying very tight-lipped about it. Just be glad that we exist. That we're able to move through time. Do the things we can. The world would be a much darker place without us to helping maintain the balance.'

'So ... there are *four* of us good Scratchlings?'

'Yep, and there'll be five when you rescue Eric.'

'So where are the other two?'

'Out on missions. They're due back later today.'

'What are they like?'

'You'll meet them soon enough.'

'And the Dark Scratchlings?'

'The less you know about *them* right now, the better.'

'Mrs O said the League of Dark Scratchings will stop at nothing to stop me rescuing Eric.'

'Maybe so, but Eric's scratching spoke to *you*, which means you're the only one who can access his time period. He's going to starve, Max. Which is why you have *got* to get to him ASAP.' Ellie fell silent and sighed miserably.

'What is it?' asked Max.

'Eric Kettle. He's such a great kid.'

'How do you know that?'

'I've studied everything there is to know about him, and trust me, he could teach us all a thing or two about appreciating what we have. He doesn't deserve to die in that horrible way. He just *doesn't*.' Max thought he must be imagining things, but … was she welling up? Ellie stood up, looked away and said, 'I just hope you do the right thing by him. If your situations were reversed, I know he'd do the right thing by you.' As Caretaker Wiseman made his way over, Ellie headed for the lift.

'Ellie's off on an important mission of her own,' said Caretaker Wiseman. 'Now there's one more person I'd like you to meet before you make up your mind. Follow me. We must make haste. As you know, time is running out for Eric Kettle.'

Ash had been reading the messages on the base of the Tree of Scratchings. He turned and called out, 'Where are you going?'

'To meet someone *else*,' said Max.

'Can I come?'

Caretaker Wiseman shook his head. 'Max will need to concentrate. Hope you don't mind.'

'No, man. Why would I mind?' muttered Ash as Max shrugged at him and the lift doors closed.

Upstairs in the Corridor of Rooms, Caretaker Wiseman led Max towards a drawn curtain that hid an Operations Room. 'If you agree to help Eric Kettle, we'll be providing you *all* the assistance we can from here.' Caretaker Wiseman brushed through a gap in the curtain and entered the room with Max.

The room was empty but for a short, elderly man with a mop of white hair who gazed down at the table. Compared to the hustle and bustle taking place in the other Operations Rooms, Max thought his room looked decidedly under-staffed. 'This is Max Hastings,' said Caretaker Wiseman, placing his hands on Max's shoulders and easing him closer to the elderly man. The man tore his gaze from the table, stood as straight as his bent back would allow, placed a monocle in his left eye, and regarded Max.

'Max, I'd like you to meet Professor Kenneth Payne. Professor Payne is the head of our intelligence-gathering division. He's a *very* important man.'

Max glanced down at himself. 'Not much intelligence to gather here,' he murmured.

Caretaker Wiseman clasped a hand on Max's shoulder warmly. 'If Max decides to accept his mission, he must be prepped and ready to go within the hour.'

The professor's monocle popped out of his eye. 'That's not much time, is it?' he said to Max.

'You're telling me!' said Max.

'You stick with me, Mr Hastings, and you'll get through all this with flying colours,' he said, holding up his hands and smiling.

'My friends call me Max.'

'And mine call me Ken.'

'I'll leave you two to get better acquainted,' said Caretaker Wiseman. 'You have one hour, Ken.'

'So I gathered,' said Ken, turning to the table. Max walked over apprehensively and stood beside him. The table was similar in size and height to a snooker table, but that was where the similarities ended. Below the surface of this table lurked a reflection from another time, a shimmering hologram of an enormous mansion surrounded by dark brown fields. Ken placed his monocle back in his eye. 'This image reached us only moments ago. I was studying it when you arrived. It's where Eric Kettle's located.'

Max peered down at the image and, doing his best to ignore the lump in his throat, said, '*That* place is seriously scary-looking. It looks haunted.'

Ken observed him for a moment, nodded, and said, 'It's had more than its fair share of sorrowful activity, not to mention a great many injustices. You're right. It probably is haunted. If so, pay the spirits little heed. Generally speaking, spooks are our friends.'

Max looked at him like he must be crazy. 'You're actually serious. And I'm supposed to *go* there?'

'Can't be avoided. Not if you're to help poor Eric Kettle.'

'What *is* this place?'

'The St Bart's School for Boys. It's an establishment located in the north of England. Mercifully, it was closed down in 1901.' Ken motioned Max forwards for a closer look.

Max placed his elbows on the edge of the table and gazed at the sprawling mansion. It reminded him of a location in a scary video game – one of those games that was out of his age range. Way out of it. Max drew a deep breath and began to babble. 'I'm not even allowed to buy video games that take place in old mansions as scary and dangerous as *this*, and now you're telling me it's okay for me to be uploaded into a real one? This can't be right—'

'Things are rarely as bad as they seem,' interrupted Ken, smiling encouragingly to see Max nodding in agreement.

'Ash says they're often *worse* than they seem.'

Ken stopped smiling and frowned. 'It's just as well your friend Ash isn't here, then. Time to quell all this negative talk. It never helped man nor ... ah! It's arrived at last.' He pointed at another hologram that now shimmered magically into existence beside the mansion. It showed a man sitting in a tavern and drinking from a silver tankard. The first thing that struck Max was just how *big* the man was – either that, or the table he was sitting at was ridiculously small.

'He looks like a character from a Charles Dickens novel,' murmured Max. 'You know, the kind that murdered Oliver Twist.'

'Murdered Oliver Twist? If memory serves correctly, Oliver Twist lived happily ever after.'

'Only because he never met *that* guy.'

'What an excellent judge of character you are! A pre-requisite for every Scratchling throughout the ages. This man frightens you, Max?'

'Understatement.'

'On this matter, I'm afraid I can offer you little comfort. You are right to be afraid. His name is Augustus Mann. He is the headmaster of the St Bart's School for Boys,' said Ken gravely, pointing to the holographic image of the school. 'He's the brute who's prepared to let Eric Kettle starve to death, simply so he can save himself the paltry cost of looking after him. He's the man you're going to meet in that very drinking establishment in ...' Ken glanced up at the clock on the wall, 'a smidgen under an hour from now. That's right, open your eyes wide and have a good look at him. A more arrogant, pompous and vain brute you could never have the misfortune to meet.'

'His fist is as big as my head,' murmured Max.

'Which is why your best course of action would be to avoid being thumped by it.' Ken said this with a chuckle that he hoped might put Max at his ease. It didn't. 'The thing about vain brutes like Augustus Mann,' Ken went on, 'is that they're very easily flattered. So use flattery to remain in his good books. Try and see the world through his eyes, and speak only when you think he'll look favourably on what you say. I won't lie: the good books of Augustus Mann are very thin tomes. Nonetheless, tell him what he wants to hear and it will buy you some time in them. Flattery has always been the Achilles heel of vain monsters like Augustus Mann, and should you find yourself in a worst-case scenario with this fellow, then resort to the unexpected.'

'The unexpected?'

Ken began hopping in circles and clucking like chicken. He was more sprightly than he looked.

Max took a step back. 'What are you *doing*?'

'The unexpected. Now tell me it hasn't thrown you. Scrambled your train of thought?'

'Some *more*, yes.'

'Precisely! When all seems lost, it often pays to behave in a way that is *completely* unexpected. It can buy valuable thinking time.' Ken tried to catch his breath after his exertions.

Max placed his hands on the table. 'So, you're telling me to act like a complete idiot if it comes to saving my skin?'

'I suppose I am, yes.'

'Finally, something I've got covered.'

Ken placed a hand on Max's shoulder and squeezed it. 'In a little over an hour, this room will be filled with our very best people, all endeavouring to assist you in your mission. We'll provide you with all the good luck we can, so let that be a comfort.'

Two smartly dressed women rushed into the room brandishing clothes and an ironing board, arguing between themselves in French. The one with the ironing board put it down and held out a hand to the other, who handed her a white shirt. 'Hello! You must be Mr Hastings,' said the woman, taking the shirt and placing it on the ironing board. 'My name is Acel and this is Adalene, and these are your mission clothes. We must make sure you look the part.'

Adalene placed a hand on one hip and looked Max up and down. 'Caretaker Wiseman has a good eye for size. Your new suit is *perfect* for a well-to-do boy of the Victorian period, and it's going to fit you well. You have your parchment with you?'

Max stared at the woman, open-mouthed.

Ken cleared his throat, leaned down a little, and said, 'Give her your parchment.'

'Yes, of course,' murmured Max, reaching into his pocket and pulling out the paper.

Acel placed the black suit she was holding down on the table, took the parchment, raised it to his eye level and addressed it. 'You are to fit a starched collar, size ten.' The parchment transformed itself as requested, and Acel fed it into the shirt's collar, making it stiff. 'When you need it, it will be here. Just slide it out and it will transform itself back into the parchment.'

Ken folded his arms and placed a finger to his lips. 'It will direct you to Eric Kettle's *precise* location in the basement. Among other useful things.'

'You seem very sure that that I'm going to agree to go,' said Max quietly.

'I'm certain of it,' said Ken.

'But why?'

'You are Scratchling-born. It's your destiny, Max.'

Nine
The Scratchling Puddle

The last words that Ellie had said to Max had been, 'I hope you do the right thing by Eric. If your situations were reversed, I know he'd do the right thing by you.' These words had been playing on his mind as he sat staring at his mission clothes in a small changing cubicle.

When he emerged from the cubicle wearing the clothes and looking dazed, Caretaker Wiseman clapped him on the shoulder. 'You've made the right decision! I knew you would!' Caretaker Wiseman hurried Max into a cage lift, where he slid the door closed and moved a brass lever from the three o'clock position all the way over to the nine o'clock position. The lift began to move slowly up, its old ropes and pulleys groaning as it went. Max pulled uncomfortably at the starched collar that contained the hidden parchment.

'You look very smart,' observed Caretaker Wiseman.

'I feel like I'm dressed for the end-of-year school play. Oliver Twist or something,' said Max, pulling at his collar again.

'Twist was an orphan in a workhouse. He would have thought himself lucky to have such a fine suit of clothes. And there's a good reason why you must look so smart.'

'Which is?'

'Augustus Mann must see you as rich pickings.'

'And that's a good thing because …?'

'If he thinks your parents are well-to-do, and can pay good money for their son's education, he's much less likely to make an example of you. That means you'll be better placed to stay under his radar. Your mission name is Lord Cuthbert Seymour, the son of an earl.'

'*Cuthbert*? You are joking, right?'

'Not at all. I think the name suits you.'

'*Thanks,*' said Max as the lift came to a shuddering halt. Caretaker Wiseman yanked open the door and strolled out into a small copper chamber that looked like the inside of an upturned bell. It was, in fact, a miniature of the Chamber of Scratchings. *Minus the wall scratchings and the Tree*, thought Max. The only exception to the copper was a black, ink-like puddle at its centre. Ellie was standing beside the puddle dressed as a Native American: headdress, beads and holding a bow. Reaching Ellie, Caretaker Wiseman turned and beckoned Max from the lift. 'Everything's in perfect order,' he reassured him.

Ellie nodded in agreement. Max stepped cautiously into the chamber and looked at her. 'Neverland?' he murmured.

'Pardon?' she asked.

'You're supposed to be Tiger Lily?'

Ellie smiled. 'No. Tiger Lily was a *fictional* character. The places we go are only too real.'

'Ellie is off on a mission to rescue a little girl who's been imprisoned on an Indian reservation by her stepfather.'

'A man who leaves *much* to be desired,' said Ellie, feeling for the dagger in her belt.

'Maybe so, but as I've told you many times, we're not in the assassination business, Ellie.'

'More's the pity,' mumbled Ellie under her breath.

'If Ellie is successful, the little girl will grow up to do important work for the civil rights of Native Americans.'

'*If?*' said Ellie, drawing an arrow from the quiver on her back and examining its tip.

'Alright, *when,*' said Caretaker Wiseman, smiling.

Ellie placed the arrow back in the quiver and looked at Max. 'Cheer up,' she said. 'There really is nothing to it. You just step into the Scratchling Puddle and let it do the rest.'

'*Puddle?* But I thought we travelled back in time through the Tree,' said Max, sounding oddly horrified by this update.

'The Chamber of Scratchings is directly below us, Max,' said Caretaker Wiseman. 'You'll need to get up a good rate of speed, which means the drop needs to be immense, hence the illusion of the puddle. It's considerably less daunting than having to step into thin air. Right then!' He brought his large hands together in a pronounced clap, then glanced at his watch. 'The Tree will be in its launch position, its mouth waiting to receive Ellie. And then you.'

Ellie looked at Max, who was now shaking from head to toe. 'Okey dokey, I'll be off, then,' she said matter-of-factly, as though what she was about to do was the most natural thing in the world. 'Trust me, Max,' she added with a smile. 'You and Eric are going to make a capable team. I'll see you both when I get back. Good luck!' With that she dropped into the Scratchling Puddle and disappeared.

'Now!' said Caretaker Wiseman, clapping a hand onto Max's shoulder and making him jump. 'When you arrive at the inn, you'll find yourself in an upstairs bedroom.' He reached into his jacket pocket and took out an envelope, which he handed to Max. 'Inside is a letter addressed to Augustus Mann. It was penned by your 'father,' the third Earl of Seymour, and it requests your immediate enrolment in his school. You will also find an old English ten-pound note. Worth a small fortune in 1840, they were. Worth quite a bit these days, too. Ellie liberated this one from the Museum of London, but it's for a very good cause. Ten pounds is enough to cover *three terms* at his school. He'll be pleased as punch when you give it to him. The letter also says your trunk is being sent on in a couple of days, but you'll be well away from there by then, of course. As for Eric Kettle, he's chained up in the basement of the mansion. The parchment knows *precisely* where, and will direct you to him. As you know, there's no time to waste. Eric has already been without food or water for twenty-four hours. He's had a hard life, so he's a hardy fellow, but even he will be wilting by now. It's imperative that you locate him this evening, after lights out. Take him food and water if you can.'

'And then what?' asked Max.

'And then you must escape and return to the room in the inn. Scratchlings can only return from the exact location they arrived, so find your way back to the inn *as soon as possible.*'

'How?'

'Use your Scratchling initiative.'

'How?'

'Now listen here: Ellie is supposed to be the one impersonating a Native American, not you,' said Caretaker Wiseman, smiling at his terrible joke. Seeing that Max hadn't found it in the least bit funny, he added, 'Remember, Eric Kettle's a Scratchling too. That means two Scratchlings will be together in the same mission location for the first time in history! That's a great deal of Scratchling initiative, so put your heads together. The inn is only about twenty miles from the school as the crow flies.'

'Oh, is that all?' said Max weakly.

'The very best of luck,' said Caretaker Wiseman, offering Max his hand to shake. Max raised his own hand slowly, and Caretaker Wiseman grabbed and shook it as enthusiastically as he had the first time. Then he clapped him good-naturedly on the back, and Max stumbled, open-mouthed, into the Scratchling Puddle.

Dry oil! Who knew? thought Max as he plunged through it into darkness. Max screamed as he dropped through the Chamber of Scratchings and into the reclining tree's mouth. In the Chamber, Ash yelled, 'WAS THAT MAX?'

'Yes,' replied a white-coated technician absently, 'that was Mr Hastings. And here comes Marlot to show you back out to the cusp of time.'

Ten
1840

All was suddenly still and silent. Two things occurred to Max: first, that his eyes were shut, and second, that he could feel something below his feet. *The ground? You'll only know for sure if you open your eyes*, he thought. Then: *Why can't I see?* He ran his hands down his face to check his eyelids were in the correct position for open. They were. He looked down and saw the faint outlines of his shoes. Max took a step forwards and bumped his nose. 'Ouch!' *What kind of a room is this?* He crouched down and, realising he was standing inside a large fireplace, shuffled forwards into a darkened room. He cast his gaze around and saw the outlines of a double bed, a wardrobe, and a squat chest of drawers. The floorboards creaked as he made his way towards the door. He pressed his ear to it … and could hear faint voices downstairs. His throat was bone dry. He swallowed, glanced back at the fireplace, and reached for the door handle.

Beyond the door was a small landing, its walls covered in black and white prints of farm animals. A grandfather clock at the top of the stairs began to chime. *This Victorian "museum" is going to be everywhere*, he thought as he tried to ignore his heart's repeated attempts at shattering his ribs. He looked over his shoulder at the fireplace one last time, wondering if he would return safely to it, then pulled the door closed behind him. The staircase that led downstairs had a wooden banister, and Max grasped it all the way down.

At the bottom was a partially open door, the low murmur of voices coming from beyond it. Max peeked through the doorway and scanned the faces of some men sitting at a bar. All had hard, weather-beaten faces and thick beards. *They look like farmers,* thought Max as he inched forwards and cast his gaze at the alcoves in search of the big man he'd seen in the hologram. *It's like one of those films where strangers are never welcome. And the locals stop talking and stare at any stranger who enters their inn,* thought Max, bracing himself for that very reaction. It therefore came as a relief when, as he made his way around the bar in search of Augustus Mann, no one paid him the slightest attention.

There he is!

Augustus Mann looked exactly as he had in the hologram. He was sitting alone in an alcove, draining the last drops of ale from a pewter tankard. Max reached a sweaty hand into his jacket pocket and felt for the envelope that Caretaker Wiseman had given him. *This guy actually looks bigger in person*, he thought as he trod slowly forwards holding the letter. Augustus Mann placed his hands on the table and heaved himself to his feet. He noticed a deathly pale but well-dressed boy making his way over. The top of Augustus Mann's head brushed a wooden beam, and he stooped and leered at the boy now holding an envelope at arm's length in his direction. He cast his gaze behind the boy for any signs of a guardian. Seeing no one, and encouraged by the fine suit of clothes the boy was wearing, he clambered out from the booth and snatched up the proffered envelope. As he read its contents, a ten-pound note fluttered to the ground. Augustus Mann sniffed the air like a hungry bear, and then gazed down towards the money at the boy's feet. Max crouched on shaky legs, picked it up, and handed it up to the headmaster. A semblance of a smile flickered across Augustus Mann's face as he read on. *He's got to the part that says the ten pounds is his. I wish it was twenty,* thought Max.

'*Lord* Cuthbert Seymour?' slurred Mann, clearly the worse for wear.

Max shook his head, then remembered his mission name and began nodding.

Augustus Mann burped. 'Is something the matter with your head, sir?' he asked.

Max imagined he'd just called him *sir* out of respect. *He thinks I'm a lord, after all.* Max straightened his back and, with as much authority as a boy in a waking nightmare can muster, he replied, 'No, there isn't.'

Mann narrowed his bloodshot eyes. 'No, there isn't *what*, sir?'

Max scratched his temple with a shaky finger. 'No, there's nothing wrong with my head?'

Mann leaned down and brought his head close to Max's. 'You must know to whom you address your insolent manner, sir! Or you would not have handed me this letter, which is addressed to me.'

Max stared at him, open-mouthed.

'Are you simple? You will address me as sir, sir!'

'Yes, sir! Sorry, sir!' said Max, army-style. Mann stood up straight and looked at the letter. 'Reading between the lines, your parents, having heard of my fine reputation for instilling discipline into spoilt and unruly vagabonds such as yourself, are desirous of my instilling the same in the spoilt pup I see before me. I will not let them down. Now fall in and speak only when spoken to.' He zigzagged towards the door.

The first thing that struck Max when he walked outside was not Augustus Mann but the stench of horse dung. Max placed a hand over his nose and held his breath as he followed Mann to a waiting carriage. The bear-like man squeezed through the carriage door and disappeared inside. 'Fall in! Fall in now, I say, sir!' Max placed a foot on the carriage's step and stuck his head inside. The compartment within had a single, forward-facing bench, which Mann seemed to take up all by himself. Max froze and looked anxiously about for somewhere else to sit. 'Sit, sir! Sit! Woe betide any boy who makes me late for my supper. Lord or no, I'll whip you until you're scarred! Scarred for life, sir! And see if your parents don't thank me for doing it!' Mann slid fractionally to his right. The space he created was barely large enough for a six-year-old, let alone a twelve-year-old. Max wriggled into the space beside the giant. Mann knocked his cane twice against the roof of the carriage and it began to move. He looked out of his window at the flat, grey countryside passing by. 'You have grown fat, sir,' he grumbled. 'Been a glutton. Doubtless your plan is to eat me out of house and home as well. I tell you now, you shall be a glutton no more. Rest assured of that, *sir*.'

Augustus Mann snored most of the way to his school. Max remained wide awake, watching him in disbelief, his thoughts ranging from *this man has serious anger management issues* to *the man's clearly a homicidal maniac who hates children*. By the time Max reached this conclusion, his heart was thumping against his ribs as hard as the carriage's wheels over the numerous potholes.

It was dusk by the time the carriage pulled onto the school's gravelly forecourt, and Augustus Mann woke with a drunken start. He gazed down at Max with red-rimmed eyes, as though he'd no recollection of where the little tyke had sprung from. Then his whiskers twitched with the recollection of something – something important – and he tapped his breast pocket with satisfaction. 'Ten *pounds,*' he slurred. 'Quite unexpected. But most welcome.'

Max climbed out of the carriage and gazed up at the St Bart's School for boys. Two terrifying words came to mind: *Resident Hatred*. It was the game he and Ash had tried to buy, but they'd been turned away with a flea in their ear. 'If you're eighteen, then I'm twelve,' the guy in the shop had told them. *Where is that guy when you need him?* thought Max as he watched Augustus Mann climb the steps of the real-life *Resident Hatred*.

Eleven
The Dark Scratchlings

At the League of Dark Scratchings, two sixteen-year-old boys dressed in dark suits, waistcoats and bowler hats, floated silently through a grand marble entrance hall. One boy wore his bowler hat on his head, while the other clutched his to his chest. They floated through the busy space where bankers went about League of Dark Scratchings business. As the boys glided past, the bankers doffed their hats and lowered their gazes. The boys ignored them and stared ahead, unblinking, then moved silently towards a set of double doors. The doors opened as they approached, and closed again once they'd floated through into a space as black as pitch. The space they'd entered had no walls or ceiling; it was borderless, without end. The Darkness that filled it drew breath all around them, and then spoke in a voice of the deepest bass: 'I have just received word that the Ninth Scratchling's cry for help has been activated, gentlemen.'

The boy wearing his bowler hat took it off and clasped it to his chest, while the other lifted his from his chest and placed it upon his head. This exchange of hat positions was done in perfect unison, as though they were part of the same mechanism.

The Darkness drew another long breath and said, 'I'm glad you understand the seriousness of the matter. The Ancient Order of Wall Scratchings has already dispatched a Scratchling to rescue Eric Kettle – a novice called Max Hastings. Mr Hastings is the replacement for Edward Dawson, who has reached his seventeenth year.'

The Dark Scratchlings switched their bowler hats back to their original positions.

'Yes, gentlemen. A fledgling has activated Eric Kettle's scratching. They had no choice but to dispatch him immediately. How else were they to prevent Eric Kettle dying of thirst in that dungeon?'

The Dark Scratchlings switched the positions of their hats and then switched them again.

'Your concerns are unwarranted. Due to the uniqueness of this situation, the worst fears of the Ancient Order of Wall Scratchings have

61

finally been realised: for the first time since the birth of our two ancient organisations, a route has opened to the same place and time for *both* sides. A route to Eric Kettle.'

The Dark Scratchlings switched the positions of their bowler hats with lightning speed.

'Your enthusiasm is commendable. As we speak, the Tree of Mammon is being readied for your departure. I need not explain the importance of bringing Eric Kettle back where we can *persuade* him to join our ranks. The same applies to Max Hastings. As he is yet to undergo their Initiation Ceremony, he too can be *persuaded* to join our cause. Gentlemen, we stand upon the threshold of tipping the balance in our favour. The alternative? Unthinkable. Now take your leave, and show me I was correct to assign you two this most important of tasks – and not the other two.'

The Dark Scratchlings switched their bowler hats slowly and solemnly.

'You had better not, gentlemen.'

The Dark Scratchlings spun anti-clockwise and corkscrewed down into Darkness. A wisp of light mingled with Darkness and grew into a swirl that encased them as they descended.

When the Dark Scratchlings finally slowed to a stop, they were a metre above the ground in a vast chamber. The chamber was gloomily lit by the blood-red flames of thousands of candles that floated close to the walls. In the chamber's centre, a scorched and blackened tree rose up into the darkness, upon whose branches bank notes of all sizes and denominations grew, like papery leaves.

Around the outside of the chamber, close to the walls, bankers sat at desks and scribbled with quill pens onto parchments. A semi-circular desk sat at the base of the tree, and at this desk an exceptionally tall banker sat talking to another who was bent over and whispering in his ear. The seated man had freakishly narrow shoulders and he wore a tall top hat rather than a bowler. The Dark Scratchlings glided over and hovered in front of his desk under the tree's branches. The banker who was bent over and whispering stood up straight and doffed his hat to the Dark Scratchlings. 'I'll leave you to your important business,' he said gravely. The seated Caretaker nodded and the man floated away back to his desk.

The Caretaker spoke in the tones of a strict headmaster. 'I have just been informed that it is you two who will embark on this most important mission.'

A switching of hats.

'Your guess is as good as mine. I have yet to speak to the other two regarding their snubbing in favour of you two.' The Caretaker stood up and floated around his desk. He was a beanpole of a man, scarcely wider than the circumference of his top hat – a hat that rose even higher than the Dark Scratchlings. The Caretaker floated behind them and looked up into the Tree of Mammon, where several technicians were pruning money from its branches. The Dark Scratchlings swivelled to face him. Without averting his gaze from the tree's branches he said, 'I doubt they'll take the news of their snubbing particularly well, but then again, Dark Scratchlings aren't exactly known for their patience or understanding.'

Another switching of hats.

'Yes,' sighed the Caretaker. 'That would explain the incident in Whitby in 1890 – the one that started the vampire legend: deathly pale creatures with fangs and supernatural strength. Of course, that lapse in judgement was made by the other two, which explains why you two remain the most trustworthy.'

The Dark Scratchlings opened their mouths to reveal their fangs.

'Yes, of course,' said the Caretaker, glancing at them. 'You'll need a good feed before you leave to fetch Eric Kettle and Max Hastings. After all, we can't risk you snacking on them, can we? And you are categorically not to enthral and turn them to our side until you've returned with them. A ceremony is required. Is that understood?'

A solemn switching of hats.

'Good.' The Caretaker reached for a bell on his desk and gave it three sharp rings. In the rear of the chamber, behind the tree, the ground opened and a large cauldron rose up from a flame-filled kitchen below. It was accompanied by two old crones, each holding a black waterproof garment. As the Dark Scratchlings approached, the old crones held up the garments and bowed their heads. The Dark Scratchlings snatched the garments and swiftly put them on over their dark suits. They handed the crones their bowler hats and then hovered to the side of the cauldron, inside which two medium-sized crocodiles were splashing about. The Dark Scratchlings took up their positions on either side of the cauldron and bared their fangs, which grew another ten centimetres. They dipped their heads and shoulders into the cauldron and shrieked with delight as they tore into their splashing prey.

Twelve

The First Day at a New School

The sight that greeted Max when he walked through the front door of St Bart's School for Boys with Augustus Mann surprised him: eighty boys hard at work, some perched on ladders dusting the empty picture frames that rose in line with the grand staircase, while others were atop higher ladders still, cleaning the chandelier that hung from a chain secured to the ceiling six floors above. Other boys were ranged up the stairs and scrubbing the banisters. Mann filled his massive chest with air and boomed, 'You see the excellent education you can look forward to here, sir? Hands-on home economics. It instils a thorough, working knowledge of how to maintain a fine country house of repute. Mr Smithy! Where is Mr Smithy?' Mann yelled as though suddenly distracted.

'Over here, sir!' cried Don, the boy who'd shown Eric Kettle to the dining room on his first morning.

'Put that scrubbing brush down and come here, sir.' Don tossed the scrubbing brush into a metal pail and hurried over. 'This is Cuthbert Seymour. *Lord* Cuthbert Seymour, no less. You see, sirs, how my fame travels into the top echelons of society?'

All the boys nodded.

'Good. Now get back to work. No slacking, sirs.' Mann looked down at Don. 'Show him to wherever the Wanted are at this time of day.'

'Yes, sir. Right away, sir.'

'Good.' Mann lurched off towards a door on the right-hand side of the entrance hall. Max watched him go.

'Are you coming or not?' said Don, already several steps up the grand staircase.

As Max climbed the stairs, he felt the gaze of the boys burning into his back. He stopped at the landing halfway up to turn and gaze around at them. Pale and skinny with red-rimmed eyes, they were looking at Max as though he was a visitor from another planet. *Or another time*, thought Max with a shudder. 'Do they *know*?' he murmured.

'Do they know what?' asked Don.

Max gazed up at the waif.

'Why are you looking at me like *that*? 'Ave I got something on my face?' asked Don, rubbing at his nose.

'How old are you?' Max heard himself ask.

'Fourteen on my last birthday,' answered Don, a little uncertainly.

'But ...'

'But what?'

'You look about *nine*.'

'Well, we can't all come from la-de-dah aristocracy, can we? Being fed with large silver spoons.'

Max shook his head. 'I'm just a normal kid. My dad's a ... a ...'

'An earl? What's normal about that?' scoffed Don, moving away up the staircase.

Three flights up, Don left the staircase and Max followed him along a corridor with faded green wallpaper that peeled down and away from the walls as though weeping. *Welcome to the real-life Resident Hatred*, thought Max with a shudder. 'Where are we going?' he asked, trying to ignore the growing stench of damp.

'The Wanted are generally to be found in the Billiard Room at this time of day.' Don flashed Max a curious glance. 'You should know that I'm classed as Frowned Upon, which is only one step above the Unwanted. The likes of you don't talk to me unless it's to give an order. If you want to fit in, you'd better do the same.'

'Talk about grim,' said Max.

'Not to worry. You're Wanted. So your life here will be hunky-dory.'

Max stopped walking and Don turned to face him. There was something in the face of the boy, a kindness that Max felt he could trust. 'Do you know Eric Kettle?' he asked quietly.

Don took a step back, his mouth falling open. '*What* did you just ask me?'

'Eric Kettle. You *do* know him?'

'What about him?'

'Eric's a friend of mine.'

'Eric's a friend of *yours*? Eric's been an orphan his whole life. How could you know him?'

When Max's reply occurred to him, he wondered if the Scratchling ingenuity everybody kept telling him about might be real after all. 'My dad donates a lot of money to orphanages, and he takes me with him when he visits sometimes. That's how I met Eric. So how's he been getting on?'

Don shook his head gravely and opened his mouth to reply, but closed it again when a door opened and a boy with an imperious grin poked his head out. 'I thought I heard voices. Who's this, then?' asked the boy, looking Max up and down.

'Lord Cuthbert Seymour,' said Don, looking flustered. 'He's a new Wanted student.'

'Ah, a lord,' said the boy, looking Max up and down again. 'You'd better come in, Your Lordship,' he mocked as he slipped back inside the room.

Max turned to Don to ask him more about Eric, but he was already moving away on his bow legs. 'You coming in or not?' came a voice from within the room.

Inside the room two boys stood beside an old billiard table, chalking their cues. At the far end of the room, two chubby men in dark suits and bow ties were fast asleep in comfy armchairs. Max assumed they were teachers. The faded grandness of the room showed that it had clearly once been an opulent games room, but now the green felt of the billiard table was threadbare and worn. A number of rickety card tables were scattered about, and the wrought iron chandelier that hung low over the billiard table reminded Max of a giant upturned spider. Max turned his attention to the two boys. Both had jet-black hair slicked close to the sides of their heads, and superior attitudes as indicated by their noses, which appeared slightly raised at all times. *They're obviously a lot better fed than the others, and their clothes are actually clean,* thought Max.

The boy who'd poked his head into the corridor watched the other one preparing to take a shot and said, 'My name is Masters, and this is Gibbon.'

'Pleased to make your acquaintance, I'm sure,' said Gibbon, hitting the white cue ball and punching the air when a red flew into a side pocket.

'Well played!' called Masters.

'Do you play?' Gibbon asked Max.

Max shook his head.

'Fancy playing for a small wager?' continued Gibbon, smiling at him.

'Leave the lad alone. He's only just arrived,' chided Masters, winking at Max.

Max looked over Masters' head at a faded portrait of a well-dressed pair of portly gentlemen who looked exactly like ... like ... Max looked into the corner where the two teachers had been sleeping. 'Where'd they go?' he asked.

'Where'd who go?' asked Masters.

Max pointed at the faded painting over the fireplace. '*Them*. They were sitting in those chairs over there a second ago, fast asleep.'

'Glad to see you have a sense of humour,' replied Masters, lining up his next shot.

'They were part of the Rotherham clan,' chipped in Gibbon, waving a hand at the portrait of the two men on the wall. 'I gather they lived here a hundred years ago, before it was even a school.'

Masters struck the cue ball, which bounced clear of the table and landed with a crash on the bare wooden floorboards. 'Now look what you've gone and made me do,' said Masters, glaring at Max.

'But they *were* sitting there,' asserted Max, pointing at the two empty chairs.

Masters and Gibbon glanced at one another, dropped their cues down on the table, and made for the door. 'I was tired of playing anyway,' said Masters.

'Me too,' said Gibbon. 'And besides, it's almost time for supper.'

They brushed past Max, who glanced around the empty room and said, 'Wait up!'

Thirteen
The Wanted

Max followed Gibbon and Masters back to their dorm room. The room was bright and airy, with four large beds, a cheerful rug on the floor, and a fireplace. Max gazed at the unlit fireplace and rubbed his hands together for warmth.

Observing him, Masters said, 'No need to fret, Your Lordship. That scallywag Smithy will carry up fresh logs and light us a fire after supper.'

At the mention of supper, Max felt his tummy rumble. An image of poor Eric Kettle sprang to mind, chained to a wall and *literally* starving. 'What time is lights out?' he asked.

'What a strange question. Bored of our company already?' said Gibbon.

Max looked back and forth between them. 'No. It's been a long day. I did travel all the way here from London. I'm tired.'

Masters reclined on his bed, rested the back of his head in his hands and said, 'What? In one day? Fly here on a broomstick, did you?'

''Course. How'd you guess?' said Max, miming sitting astride a broomstick and swaying from side to side. The clock above the fireplace saved him further explanation when it began to chime.

'Grub's up, gentlemen!' said Masters, jumping up off the bed.

On their way down to the dining room, Max was relieved when they didn't encounter another person, alive or *dead*.

Entering the dining room, Max followed Masters and Gibbon past the boys whose bowls were receiving a single ladleful of watery gruel from a matronly-looking woman. Even amid this sorry-looking bunch, three boys stood out like sore thumbs: the Unwanted, who gazed at Max with such hollow, deathly stares that Max lost his footing and stumbled.

Max sat down beside Masters and Gibbon on the boys' top table. It was directly opposite and facing the other top table, where Augustus Mann sat with Mr Whip and Mr Lash. Max looked down at his supper. It was a deep wooden bowl filled with more lumpy porridge than he could possibly eat. By its side was a thick slice of crusty bread and an orange. Mann stood up slowly, placed his thumbs inside his thick leather belt and said, 'A new pupil has joined your ranks today, gentlemen – a boy who comes to us from a family of high standing. *Lord* Seymour has taken his rightful place at the boys' top table, and long may he remain there.' Mann paused to pat the pocket that contained his wallet. 'And now, sirs, to a less pleasant matter. Mr Kettle has been missing since yesterday. No doubt he is hiding in one of this fine establishment's *three hundred* empty rooms. He will doubtless show his face soon enough, but if any of you should see him and fail to report it ....' The headmaster glared around the room, leaving its occupants in little doubt of the punishments they could expect.

Seated on Mann's right, Mr Whip dabbed at his grinning mouth, while Mr Lash, seated on his left, looked up at his employer with admiration. Max shuddered at the sight of the terrible in-joke the three of them were sharing. Come to think of it, now he'd had a good look at them, and notwithstanding the headmaster, Mr Whip and Mr Lash were easily the most terrifying people he'd ever seen. *Like a couple of wily velociraptors disguised as human beings.*

'All rise, gentlemen,' said Mann, and the students rose obediently to their feet. Mann clasped his hands together and continued, 'For what we are about to receive, may the Lord make us truly thankful. Amen.'

Max sat down and spooned some of the porridge past his lips. Stone cold and utterly tasteless. Masters and Gibbon were tearing into their slices of crusty bread. Max gazed longingly down at his slice, and licked his lips. Then he shook his head, cast a furtive glance about him, and slid it off the table into his lap. He folded the delicious-smelling bread in two and shoved it into the side pocket of his jacket for Eric. Spurred on by his growling hunger, he spooned as much of the revoltingly lumpy porridge as he could bear into his mouth, making an effort not to grimace.

By the time Augustus Mann, Mr Whip and Mr Lash had polished off their dessert of spotted dick and custard, it was dark outside. Each table had a single lit oil lamp at its centre. The children were dismissed, and the boy at the farthest right-hand side of each table picked up the lamp and led the other boys from his table out into the hallway. Even though Max's table was the furthest from the door, all the boys at the other tables waited for them to pass and climb the stairs first. At the landing between the first and second floors, Max looked behind him and beheld a procession of lights and, between the lights, a procession of trudging boys.

When they arrived back at the Wanted dorm, Don was fanning the flames of a fire in the fireplace. Hearing them enter, he jumped up as though to attention. 'Was there anything else?' he asked, looking and sounding utterly exhausted.

'No, nothing at all. Go and get some sleep,' said Max.

Don flashed him a curious look before hurrying from the room.

Gibbon sat on the end of his bed. 'Your accent is odd, Seymour,' he said. 'What part of London are you from, anyhow?'

'All over, actually. Mum and Dad are forever moving.'

'*Mum*?' said Masters.

'And *Dad*?' chuckled Gibbon. 'Is that really what you call your mother and father?'

'Why? Don't you?' said Max, feeling like a fish out of water.

'Of course not,' said Masters, yawning.

'If I called my father *Dad*, he'd stop paying Mann his bonus each month and see me fed watery slop alongside the Unwanteds,' said Gibbon.

Masters sat down on his bed. 'My old man would take his belt to me for such insolence.'

'Anyway, I'm beat. I'm going to bed,' said Max, taking off his jacket and shoes and sliding under the blankets.

'*Beat?* You do have some peculiar expressions. Aren't you going to change into your pyjamas?' asked Gibbon.

'I can't. My stuff's being sent on. It should be here in a couple of days,' said Max, doing an exaggerated yawn.

By the time Masters and Gibbon had finally stopped jabbering and fallen asleep, the fire had all but gone out. Max gazed up at the once ornate ceiling, which was just visible in the light from its dying embers. Beneath the blanket, he felt the snuggest and safest he'd felt since arriving in 1840, and he was reluctant to go anywhere. Getting out of bed on a cold Monday morning to go to school in 2016 was bad enough, but this? *The sooner you find Eric, the sooner you can get out of here. He really needs something to eat and drink.* Max threw back the blankets, climbed out of bed, and put his jacket and shoes back on. He crept to the windowsill, where an empty bottle had been left, and filled it with water from the jug beside his bed. On a shelf by the door were a number of candles of various lengths stood on saucers. He picked one up, grabbed a box of matches, and made for the door.

Once out in the dark hallway, Max knelt and placed the bottle on the floor, then struck a match to light the candle. As the flame grew, he glanced left and right into the encroaching darkness and, with shaky hands, pulled the parchment free of his shirt's collar. As soon as it was clear of the collar, it transformed itself back into the parchment. Max unfurled it and gazed intently at it.

About time, it read. *What took you so long?*

The sheer matter-of-factness of the words was a comfort. Still crouched, Max lowered his face until the tip of his nose touched the parchment and whispered, 'It's a miracle that I've made it *this* far.'

Stop being so melodramatic. We've important work to do.

Max peered into the darkness beyond the candle's tiny flame. He swallowed hard. 'Apparently you know where Eric Kettle is.'

Yes. Move down the corridor to your left.

Max lowered the bottle into his jacket pocket, then picked up the saucer. The parchment soon rustled in Max's other hand. He held it close to the flame and read: *Your other left.*

'Sorry,' whispered Max, turning around.

Go through the door that's six doors along on the right-hand side, where you'll find the servants staircase. Go all the way down to the ground floor.

Max pushed open the door and held up the candle. 'It's just a tiny room with empty shelves.'

Then you've opened the seventh *door, into the linen cupboard.*

Max backed out and closed the door quietly. 'I can't even *count* straight, let alone think,' he whispered. He pushed open the correct door and beheld a narrow wooden staircase. By the tiny light of his candle, he made his way down one flight and turned the corner. He practically jumped out of his skin when he came face to face with a young maid with masses of red hair coming up the stairs, carrying a tray of tea things. Max opened his mouth to splutter something about a sleepwalking problem, when she passed *through* him. It was as though he wasn't there. He froze in terror and turned his head slowly, watching her disappear around the bend in the staircase. Goosebumps came up on his arms as he looked down at the parchment for some words of reassurance.

GHOST.

Max hurried down to the ground floor on wobbly legs. At the bottom of the stairs he pressed his back against the wall beside the exit and whispered, 'Why can I see those things? I don't think the other boys can.' He took a deep breath and looked down at the parchment for an answer.

Just one of the many benefits of being Scratchling-born.

Max closed his eyes and tried to quieten his breathing. 'Please … don't fill me on any of the other *benefits* right now.'

Once through the exit, Max found himself in a dingy hall lined with coat pegs. He shone his candle on the parchment.

Servants' quarters. At least, that's what they were once upon a time.

'Okay.'

Make your way to the end of the hall and go through the black door on the left-hand side.

Max followed the directions and found himself in an empty sitting room in the main house.

Go to the fireplace and pull the red cord that's hanging there. Three times, sharply.

'Are you sure? Won't it ring a bell?'

No.

Max reached up, braced himself, and yanked on the thick red cord three times. He heard the sound of stone scraping against stone, and at the edge of his vision he saw a secret door open to the right of the fireplace. He took two steps back, craned his neck, and made out a flight of stairs descending into darkness.

Fourteen
When Max Met Eric

At the bottom of the stairs behind the fireplace, Max pushed open a creaking door and stopped, holding his candle in front of him. He looked into a large room that appeared to be a medieval kitchen. On the opposite wall he could just about make out a large hearth. He glanced down at the parchment.

Eric Kettle is inside this room.

'He is?' whispered Max, poking his head inside. He stepped into the room, and just beyond the candle's glow to his right he could see a form slumped against the far wall. He walked towards it slowly, swallowed hard as the candle's flame almost sputtered out, and whispered, 'I'm not too late, am I? He's not dead, is he?'

Very much alive, read the parchment. Then the Very much faded, leaving a single word: alive.

As Max crept closer, the slumped form became a boy lying on the ground with his face buried in his outstretched arm. Attached to his wrist was a bracelet and chain that secured him to the wall. Max felt the parchment rustle in his hand.

The key to his shackle is on the shelf beside the empty jam pots. Max raised the candle and peered into the gloom. 'I see it.' As he stepped away towards the key, a weak voice behind him asked, 'Who's there?'

Max turned back and looked down into Eric Kettle's large, brown, pleading eyes. He reached into his pocket and slid out the bottle of water, knelt, and handed it to the pitiful boy who struggled gamely into a sitting position. Eric reached weakly for the bottle but drank its contents greedily. Max felt in his other pocket for the crusty piece of bread, which he drew out and presented to Eric. Eric stared at it with widening eyes, then looked at Max as though expecting him to laugh and eat it himself. Max wasn't altogether certain he could speak, but croaked urgently, 'It's for you. Eat it. Please.'

'If you're certain?' said Eric, snatching it away and biting into it. He chewed with an expression that suggested he'd died and gone to heaven.

Max glanced down and noticed a number of dusty bowls between

74

them. 'What's with the bowls?' he asked, but before he'd even finished asking the question, steaming food materialised in them, spookily transparent. Max shuffled backwards. 'What the …?'

Eric continued to chew contentedly, and motioned behind Max with his chin. Max turned his head slowly and, by the sudden light of a phantom fire that now roasted a phantom pig upon a real spit, he saw a portly woman. She was as transparent as the food in the bowls, smiling at him as she chopped vegetables with a large cleaver. Max managed a grin, and raised a shaky hand in greeting. He looked back at Eric, who was devouring the last of the bread.

'Not to worry,' said Eric through the last mouthful. 'She's a nice ghost. Did her best to feed me, but I'm no ghost.' He glanced down at the bowls of steaming spectral food as he chugged down the remainder of the water. Burping, he added, 'Ta, thanks for the grub. I'm Eric Kettle.'

'I know. I'm Max Hastings, and you have no idea how good it is to meet you.'

'Why?' asked an astonished Eric.

'Because we can get out of this place now.'

'Out?' gaped Eric.

'Yes, out,' repeated Max.

'That's what I thought you said, and if I'm honest, I got the feeling you were about to fetch the key when I spoke to you. But I put it down to wishful thinking.'

'It's not wishful thinking. I'm here to help you.' Max sprang to his feet and fetched the key.

Eric watched, agog, as Max struggled to insert the key in the lock on Eric's wrist, as though worried that if he looked away he might wake up and discover he was dreaming. 'You don't seem much surprised by the spirit cook,' he observed quietly.

'Neither do you.' replied Max, still struggling to turn the old key in the rusty lock.

'I've been seeing things like that my whole life. You're the first person I've met who can see them too – and the first I've met with a birthmark on his face that looks exactly like my own.' The key turned and the bracelet fell away from Eric's wrist.

'That's because we're both Scratchlings, apparently,' said Max, helping Eric to his feet.

'You mean we've both got nits?' said Eric, scratching at his messy brown hair. 'If I'm honest, you look too scrubbed for nits.'

Max smiled. 'That's not what I meant.'

'So, why'd you come to help me?'

'You scratched a message into a wall. You asked for help, remember?'

'You mean to say the old legend I heard back at the orphanage is real?'

'Yep. Now come on. I'll explain everything later. We need to get out of here right now.'

'And go where, exactly?' asked Eric, massaging his bruised wrist and thanking his lucky stars that the old legend was real.

'We need to get back to the Potter's Inn,' said Max.

'The one in town where Mann stopped for a drink when he brought me here?'

'That's right.'

'Have you got a horse and carriage waiting outside?' asked Eric hopefully.

'No, I haven't.'

'Then how are we supposed to get into town?'

'By using our Scratchling initiative.'

Eric scratched at his head again. 'Our what?'

Max threw his hands up. 'Apparently we need to find a way.' The parchment rustled in Max's pocket, and Eric heard it too in the cold, stony silence of the ancient kitchen.

'Pet mouse?' he asked, as Max reached into his pocket.

'More like a pet parchment,' said Max, holding the candle over it.

I'm not your pet, it read.

'Sorry. Figure of speech.'

'Spook writer?' said Eric, peering at the parchment in Max's hand. 'Only if it is, I can't see the spook who wrote it.'

'No. At least, I don't think so. It's more of a magic parchment.'

'I'm not dreaming, am I? You really are here to help me?'

Eric's heart sank when Max began to shake his head, then filled with hope again when he replied, 'From now on we need to help each other.' Max looked down again at the parchment which read: Augustus Mann's horses are in a locked barn around the back of the mansion. His carriage is in the adjacent barn.

Max looked at Eric. 'Don't suppose you know how to join horses up to a carriage, and then make them … you know … go?'

Eric nodded. ''Course, but like it says there, the barn doors are locked up tight. And guarded by dogs, I hear.'

True, read Parchment.

'Then how?' said Max.

Use your initiative, read the parchment. Max looked at the puzzled expression on Eric's face as he read it too. 'It means we're supposed to use our smarts,' he explained. 'And unfortunately it isn't joking.'

Fifteen
The Dark Scratchlings

In the fireplace at the Potter's Inn, through which Max had arrived not long before, *two* sets of black shoes hovered above the coals. The Dark Scratchlings descended a little more, until their feet almost touched them before ducking their heads under the fireplace's opening and floating out into the room. They were dressed in identical dark suits, one clutching a bowler hat to his heart, the other wearing one on his head.

Wearer opened the bedroom door into the hall, and Clutcher followed him through it. They floated down the stairs and entered the busy inn. The locals who looked blandly up from their tankards did not see two sixteen-year-old boys gliding a metre from the ground, but two smartly dressed gentlemen walking towards the exit. Wearer and Clutcher, whose names changed as quickly as the positions of their hats, floated out of the door into the street.

Once outside in the quiet, cobbled street, they glanced left and right, then floated off to the left where a fine carriage stood tethered to four black horses. The carriage's driver was waiting for his master to return from the inn, and when he spotted what appeared to be two middle-aged gentlemen he doffed his cap to them. The gentlemen did the same and then separated, Wearer gliding up one side of the horses and carriage, and Clutcher gliding up the other. At the rear of the carriage, they switched hat positions again and glided back down the carriage towards the driver. Clutcher cleared his throat and the driver looked down at him. 'Is there something I can do for you, sir?' the driver asked the 'gentleman' standing in the road. The driver felt a tap on his shoulder and gazed up, *way up*, into the dark and steely-eyes of the teenager who now floated above him on the other side of the carriage and bared his fangs.

'The devil's work!' cried the driver, as Wearer grabbed the lapels of his coat and tossed him up and over his head as though he weighed no more than a cardboard box. The large man sailed through the air and landed with a *THUD!* behind a hedgerow, unconscious. Wearer and

Clutcher switched their hats by way of congratulation, and then settled down onto the driver's seat. The newly crowned Wearer picked up the reins and brought them down with a crack upon the backs of the four horses. The horses sped off in the direction of the St Bart's School for boys.

***

Meanwhile, back at St Bart's, Max and Eric were creeping through empty room after empty room at the rear of the mansion. They were following the parchment's directions and heading for a door that led out close to the barns. The door, when they finally reached it, was secured on the inside by two dead bolts. Eric slid the bolts, and Max pulled the door open. Cold air rushed in, carrying with it the hooting of an owl. Max was just thinking how things might work for them after all when he heard the sound of heavy footfalls over the floorboards of the rooms behind him.

Eric's big brown eyes opened wide. 'It's them!' he said breathlessly.

'*Them*?' Max froze in the doorway, visualising a horde of sinister Dark Scratchlings swooping down on him.

'Whip and Lash! Run! Run for your life!' hissed Eric, grabbing Max by the shoulder and dragging him out into the cold night. Max tossed away the saucer with the candle and hurried outside.

They ran helter skelter across a moonlit lawn and towards a gap in a hedgerow. Once through the gap, they blundered headlong into another hedgerow, bounced off it like pinballs in a pinball machine, and then set off to their right down a narrow passage between the two. They ran around a corner and found themselves in yet another corridor between two hedgerows. 'This,' panted Max, glancing over his shoulder, 'is starting to look like a maze!'

'It *is* a maze!' said Eric, coming to halt at an intersection that presented them with a choice of three routes. To their left they saw a ghostly man and woman out for a stroll on a long-ago summer's day. The woman held a lacy parasol, which rested against the man's top hat. 'This way!' cried Eric, running off in the opposite direction. Around the next corner the apparition of a gardener was chopping at a hedge with a pair of shears. 'Good day to you, gentlemen,' he said, doffing his cap.

Max glanced behind him for any sign of Mr Whip and Mr Lash.

79

Nothing. 'A good day to you too! Is this the way out?' he asked, pointing the way they were headed.

'Now let me see … I'm new here. Started the day before yesterday,' said the ghostly gardener, wiping his brow.

'Come out, come out, wherever you are!' came Mr Whip's voice suddenly, from somewhere close by.

'No time!' said Max, as he and Eric ran past the gardener and around the next corner.

'Mr Kettle *and friend*? Where are you?' called Mr Lash in a jolly voice.

'They're getting closer!' whispered Max.

Eric spotted an exit that led out onto another lawn. 'There! Come on!' he urged, pointing. The boys sprinted through the opening and smacked straight into legs that shot out to block them from either side. Max and Eric tumbled painfully to the ground as Mr Whip and Mr Lash rounded on them, clapping. 'Oh, bravo!' cried Mr Whip.

'Bravo to you too!' said Mr Lash. 'Might have expected this from young *Kettle,* but who would have imagined such reckless behaviour from the new boy, Mr Whip?'

'Not all he seems, Mr Lash? An impostor in our midst, perhaps? Augustus will be *thrilled* we caught him.'

'But not thrilled to lose the money he supposed the impostor's father would have given him.'

'Only too true,' said Mr Whip, reaching down and pulling a struggling Max to his feet. Mr Lash grabbed hold of Eric and hoisted him under one arm. 'Just so long as he shoots the perpetrators and *not* the messengers.'

'Perish the thought,' said Mr Lash.

'Perhaps it would be prudent to leave Augustus sleeping, and tell him the bad news first thing in the morning?' said Mr Whip, tightening his hold on Eric.

'Yes. Once he's fully rested. That would be my thinking entirely,' said Mr Lash as he manhandled Max back towards the mansion.

***

Max and Eric were back in the ancient kitchen, sitting side by side against the wall and shackled to it by their wrists. Their only light source was provided by the bowls of glowing, ghostly food at their feet. Eric was used to being manhandled and chained up in a haunted kitchen, but this was Max's first time. Eric suspected that this was why his new friend looked so sorry for himself.

'Chin up,' said Eric cheerily, 'it could always be worse. You can thank your lucky stars for that. I've been doing it all my life.'

'And what good has it done you?' said Max in a small, scared voice.

'You're here, aren't you?'

'I repeat, what good has it done you? Lucky stars? Which reminds me: what have they been *doing* around that table?'

'What table?'

'The one back at Scratchling HQ. They were *supposed* to be helping us in the lucky star's department.' Max noticed the cook's glowing, transparent feet close to his own, and looked up.

'Sorry ... you ... got ... caught,' said the cook, enunciating clearly as though talking to a deaf person.

'Thank you,' said Max quietly. 'And I can hear you just fine, by the way.'

'You *can*?' said the cook.

'Yes!' beamed Eric. 'And it's a treat to *finally* be able to hear your voice.'

The cook gazed down at Eric like a concerned mother. 'You can hear me too?'

Eric nodded.

'I'm very pleased for that. You have *such* kind eyes, child. If there's anything I can do, just let me know. You poor abandoned spirits! I always did have the gift when it came to seeing your kind,' she sighed.

Max and Eric glanced at one another.

'I'll be over here preparing the master's supper. My kitchen staff ... they must *surely* be back anytime now.' She looked down fondly at Max and Eric. 'So just call me if you need anything.'

'Will do,' nodded Max.

'She thinks *we're* the ghosts!' whispered Eric as they watched her return to her chopping board. 'Probably best not to tell her the truth of things, not unless we really have to.'

Max nodded and pulled at the chain about his wrist. 'What do you reckon Augustus Mann is going to do with us?'

By way of reply, Eric closed his eyes and hugged his knees to his chest.

Max glanced sideways at him. 'Thanking your lucky stars?'

'Doing my best,' murmured Eric, opening his eyes.

They watched the cook slam her meat cleaver through a slab of spectral gristle. She lifted the cleaver again, then glanced over her shoulder into the hearth as if she'd heard something. She returned her attention to the meat and, as she brought her cleaver down for a second time, a dark form flew from the hearth and somersaulted through the air. It touched down with a *THUD!* with its back against the door on the other side of the kitchen.

Max and Eric glanced at one another. 'What the ...?' said Max, frantically trying to force the bracelet over his wrist.

'I get the feeling you don't know what that is?' asked Eric, doing the same.

'I've never seen anything like it!'

'It's no spook, and it's too big to be a bat!' cried Eric.

The cook looked up and shook her head sorrowfully as though she'd just seen yet *another* long-dead spirit. The hooded form jerked away from the wall and stepped towards Max and Eric, its face obscured beneath the dark folds of its hood. Max and Eric grabbed each other and were about to scream out when the thing removed its hood with a flourish.

'*Ellie?*' gaped Max.

'Of *course,* Ellie. Who were you expecting? The *tooth* fairy?' she said, veering off to her left to fetch the key to their chains.

'It's a *girl,*' said Eric.

'Less of the *it's,* moving forward, please,' said Ellie, swiping the key up off the dusty surface of the shelf.

'You *know* her, Max?'

'Yes!'

'And you're smiling, so things must be good!'

'*Good?*' said Ellie, bending over them with the key. 'Do you want the bad news or the really bad news first?' She stuck the key in the lock on Max's wrist and the bracelet fell away. As she did the same for Eric, Max said, 'We'll have the bad news first.'

They stood up and, although they were all roughly the same age, Max and Ellie stood several inches taller than Eric. 'The bad news is only *I* can return from this location, which means all three of us need to find our way back to that inn in town.' Ellie produced a water canteen from inside her robes, pulled out the stopper and handed it to Eric, who took several swigs.

'Ta, thanks.' Eric wiped his mouth and handing it to Max. 'And the really bad news?' he asked gamely, more accustomed to really bad news than Max was.

Ellie peered at him closely as though checking for damage.

'I'm Ellie Swanson,' she said, extending her hand. 'It's good to meet you at long last, Eric.'

'Likewise,' said Eric, shaking it and feeling more confused by the minute.

Max put the stopper back in the canteen and handed it to Ellie. 'So? What's the really bad news?'

'Two Dark Scratchlings are on their way here from town right now.'

'What are Dark Scratchlings?' asked Eric.

'They're like us, only darker,' said Max doing his best impersonation of an informed person.

'You mean they're from the African continent?' said Eric.

'No,' said Ellie. 'He means dark as in ...'

'Evil?' said Eric, glancing back and forth between them.

Ellie shrugged. 'As good a word as any, I suppose.'

'But you said there are *two* of them coming?' smiled Eric.

'Correct. And the reason you're smiling would be ...?'

'Well, there are *three* of us!' said Eric, slamming his tiny fist unconvincingly into his filthy palm.

'Unfortunately, it's not that simple,' said Ellie, reaching into her pocket and taking out two protein bars. She handed one to Max and removed the wrapper from the other before handing it to Eric. Max bit off a piece and chewed, so Eric did the same.

'*Blimey*!' he said. 'What *is* this?' he asked, chewing twice as fast as Max.

'Just finish it. It will give you energy,' said Ellie.

'I take it this is where we get the really, *really* bad news,' said Max, between mouthfuls.

'Afraid so. For starters, the Dark Scratchlings are older and bigger than we are — although that isn't even relevant when you consider ...' she looked at Max. 'Shaking your head isn't going to make the following any easier to hear. The truth is, they have super-human strength.'

'They have *what*?' said Max, lowering what was left of the protein bar. 'And how is that fair on us?'

'It isn't. And in the normal way of things our paths are never supposed to cross, but this is *different*. Eric is no ordinary case. He's the Ninth Scratchling, and for whatever reason, this means that the League of Dark Scratchings can access this place and time as well.'

'I'm the *Ninth* Scratchling? What does that mean?' asked Eric, pushing the last of the bar into his mouth.

Ellie watched it bulge in his cheek. 'It means that Those Who Leave Much to Be Desired would like to get their hands on you.'

'Never thought I'd be so bloomin' popular,' marvelled Eric, redoubling his chewing efforts. 'What do *they* want me for?'

'They want to brainwash you to *their* cause. Make you evil,' replied Ellie matter-of-factly.

Eric swallowed the last mouthful with a gulp. 'I'd rather be *dead* than hurt people,' he said flatly.

'I … *we* … are absolutely not going allow that to happen. Enough talk! Time to get going. The Dark Scratchlings will be here within the hour, and we need to get as far away from this place as possible.' Ellie turned away and came face-to-ample-bosom with the transparent cook.

'Is all you just said really true, lass?' asked the cook.

Ellie narrowed her eyes and nodded. 'I can *hear* you.'

'And I you, lass, although you sound further away than you are.'

Ellie spoke over her shoulder to Max and Eric. 'This is amazing. It can only be possible to hear her as well as see her because there are *three* Scratchlings together in the same mission area. And just *two* would have been a first.'

'That would explain why we could hear the gardener in the maze,' murmured Max.

'You seem like such *nice* children. My name's Mrs Booth. I always did have the gift for seeing uncommon things – spectres and the like. This is the first time I've heard any talk, though,' she said, scratching her cheek.

'That's nice. Look,' said Ellie, 'we appreciate your concern, and it's really nice to meet you, but as you overheard we really must be going.'

Mrs Booth smiled. 'Say no more. And good luck to you all!'

As they made their way to the door that led back up into the mansion,

Eric turned and said, 'Thank you, Mrs Booth, for trying to feed me. You gave me cause to thank my lucky stars.'

Mrs Booth waved him away. 'It was the least I could have done, young man.'

'Eric! Come on!' called Ellie from the foot of the staircase.

Once upstairs in the mansion, Ellie beckoned the boys past her. 'Lead the way out to the barns. We're going to borrow Augustus Mann's carriage.'

Halfway across the main entrance hall a boy appeared in the moonlight that streamed through the tall windows beside the front door. 'It's okay. It's just Don,' said Eric.

'How'd you get free, and what's this *girl* doing here?' whispered Don, looking Ellie up and down.

'This *girl* is here to rescue these *boys*,' replied Ellie testily.

'We're leaving,' said Eric. 'Thank you for the kindness you showed me when I got here. You gave me cause to—'

Ellie interrupted him with an irritable tut. 'Yes, we know, thank your lucky stars. Now come on!'

Max placed a hand on Don's shoulder. 'I hope things get better for you,' he said earnestly.

'Take me with you. Please!' pleaded Don. 'Mann won't be happy until he's starved and worked me to death.'

'Sorry, no can do,' said Ellie, brushing past him.

'No harm in asking, I suppose. It was good making your acquaintances,' said Don.

'And yours,' replied Ellie, beckoning Max and Eric to follow.

Max and Eric stayed rooted to the spot.

Ellie turned and placed her hands on her hips. 'Have you forgotten about the Dark Scratchlings? They're on their way here *now*.'

'No,' said Max, 'of course not, but—'

'But nothing! Look, I'm sorry for all the suffering in this dreadful place, I really am, but we need to look at the bigger picture here. Neither you nor Eric have undergone the Initiation Ceremony, which means if the Dark Scratchlings get their hands on you, they'll brainwash and turn you *both* to their dark ways. If that happens, the balance of good and evil in the universe will be tipped in the *wrong* direction. You think the suffering here is bad? You cannot begin to imagine the consequences of the Dark

Scratchlings capturing you both.'

'So those … *things* … are after me as well?' said Max quietly.

Ellie nodded. 'It was the last thing Mrs O told me before I left. They had no idea the League of Dark Scratchings would be able to send agents to this time and location, otherwise they would *never* have risked sending you before your Initiation Ceremony, Max.'

'What the …?' cried Don suddenly, slapping a hand against his mouth to stifle his raised voice. The eerie, transparent form of Mrs Booth had appeared in the hallway, craning her neck up the staircase. 'Where's the castle got to?' she asked, aghast.

Max turned to face her. 'This house is in the future, Mrs Booth – well, your future anyway. My past. Eric's present, and—'

'Oh, for goodness's sake!' whispered Ellie.

Max turned to Don. 'You can *see* her? You can see Mrs Booth?'

Don's open-mouthed stare left Max in little doubt about that. 'Is she a …?' croaked Don.

'A ghost? Yes. But a friendly one,' whispered Eric, his face lighting up with a smile.

'Why are you *both* smiling like simpletons?' asked Ellie.

'Don't you see?' said Max, beaming at her. 'If Don can see Mrs Booth, then it stands to reason that Augustus Mann will be able to see her too.'

Ellie sighed impatiently. 'Would you *please* get to the point.'

'Alright,' said Max. He walked over to Mrs Booth with Eric in tow. Max addressed her gravely. 'This place is a school now. The headmaster starves and beats his pupils. He's the one who had Eric locked up in your kitchen. He *wanted* him to die down there. All alone.'

'What an ogre!' spluttered Mrs Booth, her calloused hands balling into fists.

'The worst kind,' concurred Eric, 'and I've met my fair share of ogres.'

'But if you, Mrs Booth – a *ghost* – were to threaten him to change his ways …' Max fell silent and watched Mrs Booth for her reaction to hearing the news that *she* was the one in the spirit world.

The cook scratched pensively at her cheek. 'What are you saying? Are you telling me that *I'm* a ghost?'

Eric stepped towards her and nodded sympathetically. 'I'm very sorry, Mrs Booth, but it's true.'

'But I thought …' The large penny dropped, with an almost audible *clunk!,* and so too did a phantom tear from Mrs Booth's eye. 'That would explain where all my kitchen staff have got to.'

'Mrs Booth – dear, *kind,* Mrs Booth – you can help *all* the children here,' said Eric.

'How?' she asked, wiping a tear from her cheek.

'By terrifying the tyrant who runs this hellhole into changing his ways,' said Max earnestly.

Mrs Booth flattened down her apron and composed herself. 'Well, I'm no good to you standing around blubbing. Let's get on with it. I'll be back with Big Bertha presently.'

'Big Bertha?' asked Max.

'My favourite cleaver,' she replied, turning and heading back to the kitchen.

Mrs Booth returned with Big Bertha a moment later, and they all followed Don up three flights of stairs to Augustus Mann's bedroom. When they reached his room, Ellie, who had been oddly quiet for several minutes, cleared her throat and said, 'You know what's required of you, Mrs Booth?'

'I believe I do, lass, yes.'

'I hope so. Because inside this room is a man who leaves *much* to be desired. A *monster.* If Max and Eric's plan is going to work …' Ellie paused to look at them and smiled, 'it's actually a *really* good plan, by the way.'

'Thanks,' chorused Max and Eric.

'Then,' Ellie continued, looking up at Mrs Booth, 'you've got *one chance* to scare the living daylights out of him. Once we leave here, you'll never be able to talk to Augustus Mann again. He won't be able to see or hear you.'

Mrs Booth pulled a dark hood up over her head. 'Not to worry, pet. I've had plenty of dealings with the likes of *him,* and worse besides. You leave him to me and Big Bertha.' She raised the cleaver.

Ellie nodded and opened the door. As Mrs Booth walked into the bedroom, the three Scratchlings and Don huddled close to the door and listened.

Mrs Booth stood over the snoring man and cleared her throat loudly. Augustus Mann opened his eyes and blinked up into the face of a hooded,

87

glowing ghost brandishing a meat cleaver. His dark eyes widened, and so too did his mouth as he gasped at the air in readiness to cry out in terror. 'Make a sound and I'll *cleave your head in two* where you lay!' hissed Mrs Booth, with such menace that it caused the hairs on the children's necks to stand on end.

'Wh– ... wh– ... what are you?' whispered Augustus Mann hoarsely.

'A friend and protector of children! *Now mark my words,*' she said, lowering her voice and making it more menacing still, 'from this day forth you're going to treat the children in your care with nothing but kindness. You're going to feed them well – *all* of them – and show them nothing but goodwill. Do you understand me?'

'Yes!'

'I hope you do. I'll be watching you forevermore, *Headmaster,* and if I don't like what I see, then when next I return here, I'll not wake you. I'll just ...' Mrs Booth raised Big Bertha.

'You'll just *what?*' trembled Augustus Mann. Mrs Booth trembled too, but not with fear, with *rage.* By way of reply, she slammed the cleaver into the headboard above Augustus Mann's petrified face. 'Oh, dear Lord!' he cried, covering his face with his hands as splinters of wood flew into the air and landed on his bed.

Mrs Booth yanked the cleaver free. 'Let this headboard be a reminder to you. If you give me cause to return, it won't be the headboard that's cleaved in two. It will be the head that sleeps beneath it! This oath I swear to all the pupils of this school – past, present *and* future!'

Sixteen
The Escape to Town

As the children made their way back down the staircase to the ground floor with Mrs Booth, the cook asked excitedly, 'How did I do, lovelies?'

'That was brilliant! Couldn't have done it better myself. You're a real pro,' said Ellie.

'Boys?' asked Mrs Booth. 'What did you think?'

'Really terrifying. Better than I could have hoped for,' nodded Max.

'Even I believed you, Mrs Booth! Remind me never to get on your bad side,' smiled Eric.

'And me,' said Don, grinning with immense satisfaction.

They reached the bottom of the stairs. 'I very much doubt Augustus Mann will ever mistreat the boys in his care again. I reckon you put enough fear into that man to last a lifetime. Now, let's go!' said Ellie, ushering Max and Eric towards the rooms at the back of the mansion.

'Wait. What's that noise?' whispered Don. They all froze and listened.

'It sounds like a carriage,' said Eric.

Ellie ran to the windows beside the front door, and jumped up onto a ledge so she could see out. 'It's *them*. It's the Dark Scratchlings! How'd they get here so quickly?' She clambered back down. 'Change of plan.'

'Problem, lass? Something I can help you with?' asked Mrs Booth, holding up Big Bertha.

'Not this time, unfortunately. They'd laugh in your face – if they knew *how* to laugh, that is. Show us another way outside to the *front*, Don,' said Ellie, pointing to the door beyond which she imagined the Dark Scratchlings must be climbing down from the carriage.

'What? You want to go out *there*?' gasped Don.

'Yes, but obviously not through *this* door. Take us to another so we can get out the front without being seen.'

'Why?'

'We're going to escape in their carriage, that's why.'

Don nodded. 'This way!'

They'd already sprinted through half a dozen rooms when they heard the crashing and splintering of wood. The Dark Scratchlings were kicking their way through the front doors. Upstairs in his bed, Augustus Mann

89

cowered under the covers and cried, 'Leave me alone! I'm a changed man!'

Along the corridor from their employer, Mr Whip and Mr Lash leapt out of their beds, pulled on their robes and went to see what all the commotion was about.

Ellie, Max, Eric and Don had reached a side door that led out to the front of the house. Ellie turned to Don. 'Those things aren't interested in you,' she reassured him, 'but make yourself scarce all the same. They'll leave the moment they realise we've taken flight in their carriage.'

'Thanks again for all you've done,' said Eric, clapping Don on the shoulder.

'Ditto,' said Max as they slipped quickly outside into the cold night air.

'And thank you!' called Don.

As they sprinted across the forecourt towards the carriage, Mr Whip and Mr Lash were just rushing down the stairs. They were met with the impossible sight of two teenage boys dressed in dark suits and strange-looking hats, floating a metre from the ground. They glanced at one another and, for the first time in a long time, Mr Whip and Mr Lash found themselves speechless. The Dark Scratchlings flew up the stairs and were upon them in an instant, grabbing the collars of their robes and hoisting them effortlessly several metres into the air. Mr Whip and Mr Lash kicked and struggled, but it was useless. The Dark Scratchlings lowered their heads close to their captives and, without opening their mouths, shouted these words telepathically into their minds: *'WHERE IS ERIC KETTLE?'*

By way of reply, the Dark Scratchlings received an image of Eric and Max, chained up in the medieval kitchen, and a clear map of the route down there. With no further use for them, the Dark Scratchlings dropped their captives, who crashed down onto the staircase and tumbled head over heels to the bottom.

Outside, Max, Ellie and Eric sprinted across the forecourt towards the carriage and four black horses. Eric went to jump up onto the driver's seat, but Ellie grabbed his arm. 'No! You two get inside! I'll take care of this,' she commanded, climbing up into the seat. A moment later, after hearing the carriage door slam shut, she picked up the reins and cried, 'Giddy up! Go! Go!' The horses kicked up gravel and sped away.

Inside the carriage, Eric slid down his window, poked his head out, and gazed back towards the mansion. He pulled his head inside, shunted up the window, and settled back into the seat. 'The coast's clear, Max.'

'Phew! That was close.'

'I'll say. That Ellie's a bit handy, isn't she?'

'Just a bit, but girls are handy where I come from. There are tons of girl heroines in films and video games.'

'*Films and video games*?' repeated Eric uncomprehendingly.

'I get that video games are a while off yet, but you must have movies by now, surely? They used to make them in black and white.'

'No. What are they?' asked Eric, reaching up and pulling down a fancy gold mirror on a hinge.

'Well, you know what a photograph is?' asked Max.

Eric nodded at his own reflection. 'I saw one once,' he said proudly. 'Boy, did I thank my lucky stars that day.'

'O-*kay*,' said Max. 'Well, a film is a just a load of photographs shown quickly one after another. It makes it look as though people are moving around and doing stuff. Usually blowing stuff up or trying to kill each other.'

Eric looked at him.

'They're actually a lot of fun. No, really.'

Eric's face lit up. 'I've heard about something similar. You have to put a penny in an *incredible* machine and turn its handle. Inside the picture *moves*,' he said almost disbelievingly. 'Never seen one myself, but back in the orphanage, Derek Stacy said his mother had actually *been* in one. It's what led to her downfall, apparently.' Eric pulled the mirror as close to his face as it would reach on its hinged arm, and studied his reflection. 'Are you *sure* you've rescued the right person? I don't look like much. Just skin and bone.'

'You're half-starved. You need burgers, fries, and pizza – all you can eat – and *gallons* of fizzy drinks. You'll start growing again in no time, trust me. I know what you mean, though. I couldn't believe it either when they told me I'm Scratchling-born.'

'Why ever not?'

'You're kidding, right? My friend Ash summed me up perfectly once: he called me an *amiable loser*.'

'What's that?'

Max shuffled in his seat and thought for a moment. 'A waste of space who's okay to have around.'

'No idea what you just said.'

'Maybe that's because I'm from the future.'

Eric pushed the mirror away and drew breath to ask what seemed to him a *very* important question. 'So what *year* do you come from, Max?'

'Two thousand and sixteen.'

'Noooo!'

'Yes,' replied Max.

'*Two* thousand and six*teen*? Noooo!'

'Yes!'

'Blimey!' said Eric, falling silent for half a minute. 'And that's where you're taking me?'

'That's the plan.'

'Blimey!'

'I know.'

'So what's it like there?'

Max slid to the window, pulled it down and poked his head outside, meeting with nothing but cold air and darkness. He slid the window up and sat back down beside Eric. 'For starters, the teachers are more likely to get beaten up by their pupils, rather than the other way around.'

'Noooo!'

Max nodded. 'You wait and see. We've got this whole political correctness thing going on.'

'Po-lit-i-cal corr-ect-ness? What does *that* mean?'

'No idea, but if a teacher so much as *looks* at a kid funny, he can get into serious trouble.'

'So Augustus Mann wouldn't be able to run a school in *two* thousand and six*teen*?'

Max shook his head seriously. 'They'd lock him up and throw away the key.'

'In clink?'

'Clink?' said Max.

'Prison.'

'Yep. Or a secure hospital for nut jobs.'

'And Ellie?'

'I get the impression she's allowed to walk the streets freely.'

'That's not what I meant. How long have you known her?'

'About five minutes longer than you have. I literally met her, like, the day before yesterday. She's been doing this Scratchling thing and rescuing kids for a while now.'

'That explains why she's so good at it.'

'Exactly.'

'And we're going to be like her?'

'Yeah, only without the bad attitude. Hopefully.'

With so much new information to absorb, Eric fell silent. A minute later, Max glanced at him and smiled. 'Don't tell me, you're thanking your lucky stars.'

'Never had so many,' said Eric, falling silent again.

Forty minutes later, the carriage slowed to a stop and they heard Ellie climb down. The carriage door opened. 'Come on!' she urged. 'We'll run the rest of the way. The main street and the Potter's Inn are just around this corner.'

The boys climbed out. 'Why not take us all the way there?' asked Max, glancing up the road behind them.

'The Dark Scratchlings probably stole this carriage,' replied Ellie. 'And the last thing we need right now is to be caught with it. They'd lock us up.'

They ran around the bend and into the deserted high street. Although the pub was closed for the night, a faint glow came from the bar downstairs, where the landlord was counting the day's takings. Ellie led them down a narrow passageway leading between the inn and the tobacconist shop next door. She stopped at a drainpipe and gazed up at the window beside it. '*That's* the room we need to get into. Give me a leg up, Max.'

Max clasped his palms together and Ellie stepped into them. She shimmied up the drainpipe, and once she reached the window she withdrew what looked like a divider attached to a plunger from her pocket. She pressed the plunger against the window and cut a circle out of the glass. She reached inside gingerly and pulled up the latch. 'We're in!' she whispered, sliding the window up.

'Here,' said Max, cupping his palms again for Eric.

'Much obliged,' said Eric, stepping into them. He took hold of the drainpipe, looked down at Max and asked, 'What's up here that's so important anyhow?'

'A portal that leads back to 2016.'

'What's a portal?'

'A magic door.'

'A magic door? Why didn't you just say so?' said Eric, shimmying slowly up the drainpipe. Ellie reached down and dragged him over the window frame and inside the room. Ellie's head popped back out of the window and she beckoned to Max. 'Come on!' she whispered urgently. 'The Dark Scratchlings won't be far behind.'

Max climbed up the drainpipe, expecting Ellie to appear and give him a hand inside. She didn't, but Eric did. 'Thanks,' said Max, tumbling through the window.

Inside the darkened room, Ellie was crouched in front of the fireplace. As Max and Eric stepped towards her, she held out a flat palm and hissed, 'Stay back!'

'What is it?' asked Max.

'The fireplace. It's been booby-trapped.'

'*Booby-trapped*?' echoed Max, stepping towards her.

Ellie got to her feet, placed a hand on Max's chest, and pushed him back. 'You want the bad news or the really bad news?'

'The bad news, obviously,' said Max, backing up into the bed.

'Well, the bad news is there's no way we can return the way you came now.'

'Why? What would happen?' asked Max, looking into the fireplace, which looked no different than it had before.

Ellie drew a deep breath. 'We'd be delivered somewhere we *really* don't want to be. They've rigged it in case we got back here first.'

'How do you know that?'

'Trust me. When a Scratchling hunch is *this strong*, it pays to listen.'

'Where would it deliver us?' asked Eric, mystified.

Ellie looked at him. 'The League of Dark Scratchings, would be my guess.'

'So what's the really bad news?' asked Eric.

'The really bad news is that our only option now is to find our way back to Mansion House in this time period.'

'What? London must be miles away!' said Max.

Ellie nodded grimly and moved swiftly towards the window. 'Two hundred miles, to be exact, so we'd best get going.'

94

At that very moment, Augustus Mann's carriage came to a thundering halt beside the carriage that Max, Ellie, and Eric had just abandoned. The Dark Scratchlings floated down from the driver's seat and sniffed the abandoned carriage like a couple of bloodhounds. They didn't even bother looking inside, just floated off around the bend and into the high street.

Ellie slid down the drainpipe first; next came Eric, followed by Max, who lost his grip on the icy pipe and fell most of the way.

'This way,' whispered Ellie, rolling her eyes.

'But the carriage is *that* way,' said Max, climbing to his feet with a wince.

'It's too late to go back there now,' said Ellie, sprinting down the passage away from the high street. Max and Eric followed, and the moment they'd disappeared around the corner, the Dark Scratchlings entered the alley from the other end. They floated to the drainpipe, reversed the positions of their bowler hats, levitated up and climbed through the open window. They landed silently on the carpet before the fireplace and, believing that Ellie, Max, and Eric had fallen foul of their trap, climbed inside and disappeared.

Five minutes later, they returned and flew to the window.

Max, Ellie and Eric were several hundred metres away at the other end of the village. They were crouched in a ditch, looking out into the darkness beyond its southern border. 'Unless I'm very much mistaken, *that* is the Yorkshire Moors,' said Max.

Ellie squinted into the darkness. 'That's the Yorkshire Moors alright.'

'So what do we do now? They brought us up here on a school trip once. The Yorkshire Moors go on for*ever*. The Dark Scratchlings will easily catch us on foot.'

'True,' ceded Ellie. 'But we *have* to cross them. It's the only way we can get to York and catch a train to London.'

'And how far is York?' asked Max.

'About fifty miles as the crow flies,' said Eric.

'Which means we could really use some *luck* about now,' said Ellie, raising her voice as though hoping to be overheard.

'Luck? A miracle, more like,' said Max.

'You hear that?' said Eric, looking back into town.

'Yes, it's a carriage,' said Ellie. 'I have a Scratchling hunch. Follow me!'

'Wait!' protested Max. 'What if it's the Dark Scratchlings?'

'We'll stay well hidden,' said Ellie.

A minute later, they were crouched in a muddy alleyway between two stone cottages. Across the cobbled street, two men were unloading sacks from the back of a red carriage. 'It's the posties,' said Eric. 'They're delivering the post to the post office.'

Max opened his mouth to speak, but Ellie silenced him with a finger to her lips. 'Just stick close to me,' she said, darting across the road.

The men had just entered the post office with a couple of bags, and they'd left the carriage doors open. Ellie peered inside. 'It's all unloaded! Quick!' she whispered, clambering inside. At the far end was a heap of empty mail sacks, which Ellie quickly set about covering Max and Eric with. Once they were hidden, she lay down and covered herself as best she could. 'Nobody speak. Don't make a sound,' she whispered. Eric felt himself begin to cough from the dust in the sacks, and clamped a hand to his mouth. The postmen returned and hurled three sacks of post into the back of the carriage, in front of the hidden children. A third man came out of the post office and said, 'So what time to you call this, then? You were due here hours ago.'

'Tell us 'bout it,' said one of the postmen. 'You wouldn't believe the luck we've had this evening. Anything that could have gone wrong did. For starters, the front left wheel bolt came loose, and the wheel darned near fell off!'

'And when we went to change it,' said the second postman, 'most of the tools we needed were missing. The last crew took 'em in for repairs and forgot to replace 'em. And that was just the start of our bad luck today.'

'Be that as it may, you're already three hours late, so I suggest you stop yer jabbering and be on your way to York,' said the man who ran the post office.

'Right you are,' said the postman, slamming the carriage doors and locking the padlock on the outside.

'That's the thing with arranging good luck for us,' whispered Ellie as the carriage moved off. 'It sometimes involves others having a bit of what they might think of as bad luck. But without that bad luck, this carriage would have been long gone when we needed it. But you know what they say?'

'No,' said Eric. 'What do they say?'

'That you can't make an omelette without breaking some eggs.'

Back in the village, the Dark Scratchlings came around a bend in the road just in time to see dust kicked up at the southern end of town. They sniffed at the air, switched their bowler hats, and glided back for the carriage their prey had abandoned.

Seventeen
Invisible in Plain Sight

Max and Eric were lulled into a deep sleep by the gentle rocking of the carriage. Not so Ellie. She sat cross-legged with her back to the wall, some empty sacks covering her legs for warmth. They were making good speed, so she felt confident of making it into York ahead of their pursuers, but she also knew that the League of Dark Scratchings had agents everywhere – and that the Dark Scratchlings would be able to summon them telepathically. *They'll have raided minds back at the school,* thought Ellie, *so they'll know what Max and Eric look like. And if they know, so will their agents in York. They also know we have to get back to Mansion House to find sanctuary, which means they'll have people at the railway stations looking out for us – not to mention the stage coach depots and canals.*

Ellie looked down fondly at the two fledgling Scratchlings. 'My only hope of getting these two on a train back to London is to make them invisible somehow,' she murmured. *Then there's that* other *tiny problem of it being 1840.*

Ellie heard a rustling from under the sacks. *I'd recognise that sound anywhere; it's Parchment,* she thought. She lifted up the sacks and saw it lying on the ground close to Max, where it had fallen out of his pocket. 'Fledglings can be so careless. I forgot Max had you,' she whispered, picking it up.

Hello, Ellie. It's been a while.

'I'll say. The last time we spoke, *I* was a fledgling.'

How's the mission going?

Ellie smiled. 'I've missed your sense of humour.'

In a bit of a pickle?

'A world of pickle.'

How so?

'We're headed for York station, where we need to catch a train to London.'

Oh dear.

'Oh dear is right. There *was* no train service between York and London in 1840.'

They haven't even laid the tracks yet.

'No need to rub it in.' Ellie fell silent.

What is it? asked the parchment.

'As they've rustled up this late post carriage for us back at HQ, then knowing the problem we face, maybe they've sent us what we need,' said Ellie, casting her gaze upon the three mail sacks. She drew a deep breath. 'Please be on top of your game, Professor Payne,' she murmured as she made her way on all fours towards the three bulging sacks.

She squeezed and felt all around the first sack for the cylindrical, baseball-sized object she was hoping to find. *Nothing in here but letters and parcels,* she thought, turning her attention to the second sack. Ellie had a good rummage around the outside of the second sack … and her heart sank as she cast her gaze upon the third and final sack: their last chance. Ellie crouched over it and blew on her hands. *If it's here, then it would certainly be lucky if it was at the bottom of the sack,* she thought, sliding a hand beneath it. A smile spread across her face, and she breathed a sigh of relief as she grasped a round object at the bottom of the sack. She took a penknife from a pocket, opened the blade, and cut into the sack. A moment later, a golden orb the size of a baseball dropped out onto the floor. Ellie scooped it up, gave it a kiss, and shoved it into a pocket. She produced a small sewing kit from another pocket, and removed a needle and thread from it. Once she'd sewn up the hole in the mail sack, she picked up the parchment. 'We've got a Century Orb!' she enthused. 'Which, as you know, means we can now leap forwards in time as much as one hundred years.'

Don't forget that the League of Dark Scratchings will have taken the possibility of your having a Century Orb into account.

Ellie tutted. 'As if I would. But their agents will be stretched pretty thinly over the coming century.'

Any idea which year you'll leap to?

'Nope. Just as long as there's a train at York station waiting to take us back to London, I'm not fussy. Now, any idea how I can make these two invisible for the journey?'

I'm about facts. Ingenuity is Scratchling territory.

'How did I know you were going to say that?'

I have told you before now.

'*Countless* times. I'd better get back to trying to come up with a solution,' said Ellie, folding the parchment and shoving it into a pocket.

An hour later, Ellie's eyes fluttered open. *It might just work at that,* she thought, reaching out and shaking the boys awake. 'Wake up! We've arrived in York.'

Max and Eric sat up sleepily and watched Ellie shuffle to the doors and peer out of a slat. She couldn't see much, just the occasional flickering lamp in shop fronts and passing carriages. Max and Eric joined her by the doors. 'We have the element of surprise,' whispered Ellie, 'so when the doors open, we're going to use it to maximum advantage.'

'How?' said Max.

'By leaping out together and screaming like banshees.'

'Act like candidates for a loony bin, you mean?'

'Exactly,' said Ellie.

Max nodded. 'The little training Ken gave me back at HQ actually covered this.'

'Trust me, you'll be a natural. It'll be more effective if we all yell the same thing. I suggest a pirate-style *ARR, ME HEARTIES!*'

'Deranged pirate stowaways it is,' said Max.

The carriage stopped and they heard footsteps. 'They're coming. Get ready,' said Ellie.

They braced themselves as they heard someone fumbling with the padlock on the door. It swung open and they sprang out at the wide-eyed postman, with flailing arms and bellowing *'ARR, ME HEARTIES!'* The man stumbled backwards and trod heavily on the foot of the second postman, who yelped and began to hop up and down. He glanced behind him at the three fleeing figures and then shoved his partner forwards. 'Check they haven't broken the seals on them three bags! And be quick about it. The little tykes are getting away!'

His partner climbed up into the back of the wagon, and moments later returned and said, 'The seals are in place. They ain't stolen nothing. Just hitched a ride.'

Ellie, Max and Eric ran to the end of a side turning, and stopped to catch their breath close to where a street gas lamp burned. 'We made it! We actually made it into York!' puffed Eric.

Max rubbed at a stitch in his side. 'Yes, but now what?'

'What would you like first?' asked Ellie, raising a concerned eyebrow at their lack of fitness.

'The good news or the *really* good news?' puffed Max. 'I think we'd like the really good news first.'

Eric nodded. 'Why not?'

'Alright, then,' said Ellie, putting her hands on her hips. 'The *really* good news is that the Dark Scratchlings will have read minds back at the school, which means they know what the pair of you look like. They will have sent your images telepathically to their agents all over England, which means they'll be on the lookout for you.'

'Even in York?' said Max.

'*Especially* in York. And even more especially at the train and coach stations.'

'Which means?' asked Eric.

'Simply stated: the only way we're going to get you safely to London on board a train is to make both of you invisible.'

'Using Scratchling magic?' beamed Eric.

Ellie shook her head and gave a slight smile. 'No. Using plain old Scratchling ingenuity.'

Max looked at Ellie. 'You're *smiling*,' he said. 'So either you've had a personality transplant in the last three seconds, or—'

'You've thought of a way to make us invisible!' said Eric.

Ellie raised her chin a little. 'See if I don't get you both back to London in one piece yet.'

'So what's the good news, then?' asked Max, bracing himself.

'I'm glad you asked that, Max. As you know, we need to catch a train from York back to the sanctuary of Mansion House in London.'

'Yeah, so?'

'So there *was* no train service between York and London in 1840.'

'So what are you smiling about?' asked Eric, his own smile departing his face.

Ellie reached into her pocket and withdrew the Century Orb. Max and Eric glanced at one another, and then gaped at the golden object in wonder.

'You may well impersonate goldfish, Scratchlings. It's called a Century Orb,' said Ellie, holding it up and admiring it in the light of the gas lamp.

'It's the most beautiful thing I've ever seen. What does it do?' asked Eric.

Ellie smiled. 'This little beaut will enable us to jump forwards in time as far as *one hundred years*, to a year when there'll be a train service between York and London.'

'Blimey. We going to use it right away?'

'No. Not right away. When we get to the station.' Ellie shoved the Century Orb back into her pocket. 'The League of Dark Scratchings will have taken into account that we might have an orb.' She sighed. 'Call it a Scratchling hunch, but in these unusual times, *something* tells me that they've been able to alert agents to be on the lookout for us at York station *every year* on this day from now until 1940. Which is why we still need to make you two invisible. Come on!'

Ellie navigated a number of back streets before heading back to the main road. It was 4am, and the usually bustling high street was deserted except for a couple of tramps sitting in the doorway of a clothes shop, smoking. 'Bingo!' said Ellie, spying the tramps.

'I hope your plan isn't to disguise us as tramps,' said Max. 'Only, Eric wouldn't look any different. No offence, Eric.'

'None taken. And this is actually my Sunday best,' said Eric, looking down at himself.

'He looks, yet he fails to see,' said Ellie to Max. 'For goodness's sake, open your eyes, Max. The *clothes* shop, not the tramps. The tramps are *ghosts*. Now pipe down, the pair of you, and follow me.'

Ellie darted across the street and down the alley opposite that ran between two shops. *Adam's the Butcher's Shop,* proclaimed one faded shop front, while the other was *Lillie's Attire for All Occasions, Weddings, Funerals and Christenings.* Ellie crouched outside the back door to Lillie's Attire, took a safety pin from her pocket, and picked the lock. She opened the door in seconds and ushered the boys inside.

Twenty minutes later …

In the shop's main fitting room, by the light of several candles, what appeared to be an exceptionally tall woman stood before a full-length mirror. She was completely obscured by a black, ankle-length cape and veil – the trappings of a grieving widow. She pressed a hanky to her veiled nose, and sobbed quietly into it. She glanced to her right and said sternly, 'You look fine. Now come *here.*'

A similarly dressed grieving child, a girl with blonde hair that cascaded from under a dark veil, shook its head. 'Is this really necessary? It docsn't feel at all right, and this wig itches something rotten,' complained the girl.

'I'm reassured to hear it doesn't feel right, man,' came Max's voice from somewhere in the woman's midsection. The widow appeared to wilt sideways suddenly. 'You're making me *slouch*,' she said. 'Make sure you hold me up *properly*, Max. For goodness's *sake*, Erica! Come here this instant!'

"Erica" took a fraction of a second to thank her lucky stars, and then stood beside her grieving "mother." They looked at their image in the mirror. 'Go on, Max,' said Ellie.

'Go on what?' came Max's muffled voice.

'You know what. Hold your daughter's hand.'

The grieving woman jiggled what looked to be her chest.

'If only you could have seen that,' said Ellie.

'Seen what?'

'What you did just then. Stationary women *never* jiggle their chests about like that.'

'It's not possible,' agreed Erica.

'Whose side arc you on?' asked Max.

'Just *hold her hand!*' snarled Ellic.

'Why don't *you* hold her ... *his* hand?' Max protested.

'Because *I* need both of mine to hold onto your shoulders and remain upright.'

Max sighed and lifted his hand towards Eric, who took it very reluctantly.

'Excellent!' said Ellie. 'See how it adds a whole new level to the disguise?'

'I can't see *anything,* which is a big plus right now. But how am I supposed to walk around like this? I really can't see a thing. Ouch. And ouch! What are you doing?'

'A tug on your left ear means go left, a tug on the right ear means go right, and when I hold your lobes down together like *this,* it means walk in a straight line.'

'*OUCH!* How am I supposed to walk straight when I can't see?'

'We're a grieving widow, and it's common for grieving widows to have a little too much to drink.'

'If you're going to act half-rats then you should probably slur your words,' said Erica.

'Scratchling ingenuity. That's what I like to hear! We'll make a first-class Scratchling of you yet, Erica.'

At 7.30am, townspeople hurrying by paid scant notice to the tall, grieving widow standing outside the entrance to York station, in full mourning regalia. She was holding the hand of her similarly attired daughter. The widow fumbled in her pocket and the next moment a golden orb dropped to the ground at her feet. It vanished instantly, engulfing the widow and her daughter in a puff of orange smoke. 'Welcome to the year nineteen hundred and fifteen, Scratchlings,' murmured the widow once the smoke had cleared.

'1915? *Really*? Are you certain?' asked her daughter, glancing about through her veil.

'I am. Look over there to your right, Erica. Have you ever seen a soldier dressed like that?'

Erica watched an injured First World War soldier limp out of the station's exit on crutches. The soldier was followed by a group of well-dressed ladies, chatting amiably. 'Well, I never.' muttered Erica. 'You're right, I never have seen a coat like that. *Or* ladies dressed like that.'

'The man is wearing a trench coat, standard issue for the poor soldiers of this terrible period, and the art nouveau dresses the ladies are wearing are typical of the time. Now come on, we have a train to catch.' A twin tug on two ear lobes caused the human structure to lurch forwards awkwardly. Ellie tugged on a left lobe and then mumbled, 'No. The *other* left,' under her veil as the wobbly "widow" starting moving to the right. The pair walked very cautiously towards the ticket booth, and the man inside it thought it very odd when she bumped right into it.

'You all right?' asked the man, scratching his head.

Ellie raised the pitch of her voice an octave and did an impersonation of a maiden aunt. 'Yes, I'm quite alright, thank you, young man. As alright as a woman in the depths of despair may ever be.'

'I'm very sorry for your loss,' said the man in the booth automatically.

'Thank you, young man. Now, two tickets to London, please. First class,' she said, flicking Max's nose. This was the pre-agreed signal to hand over the money. Max let go of Erica's hand to reach into his pocket, and withdrew the gold sovereign that Ellie took on all missions for emergencies. He slammed the coin against the window to the left of the transaction hole. Ellie tugged frantically on Max's right lobe, and he slammed the coin against the window to the right of the hole. The man inside the booth peered down at Erica with a sympathetic expression.

'*Left* a bit,' said the grieving woman under her breath.

'In the gin bottle? I somehow doubt that,' murmured the man under his. The gold sovereign finally landed with a *chink!* in his tray. The man gazed down at it, clearly thinking that some people had more money than sense.

'Now, tell me, my good man. Does the train have any private compartments?' asked the widow.

The man nodded, reached for his pencil, licked its nib, and began to write on two tickets. 'A first-class private cabin for madam and her daughter. Your train will depart from platform four at eight o'clock.' He handed the tickets through the hole. The widow plucked at the air to the left of the tickets, and then plucked at the air to their right, before her daughter stood on tiptoes and snatched them up. Her daughter then scooped up their change, which consisted of several large bank notes. 'You hold onto the change for now, Erica,' the widow instructed her daughter.

'Blimey, I'm temporarily rich,' murmured her daughter, folding and pocketing the notes.

They were making good progress across the concourse towards platform four when Ellie whispered, 'There's trouble at twelve o'clock.'

'What? You're a fortune teller now?' said Max.

'No,' said Ellie through gritted teeth. 'I meant twelve o'clock as in directly in front of us.'

'I think I see them,' murmured Erica from under her veil.

'See what?' asked Max.

'A couple of bankers,' said Erica.

'How can you be so sure they're bankers?' asked Max.

'Well,' said Erica, 'they've got bowler hats on their heads, newspapers under their arms, and they're swinging umbrellas with every long stride.'

'Excellent, Erica,' said Ellie. 'Those bankers are agents, all right, and what's more, they're heading straight for us. Fortunately, they imagine there's only a tiny chance of our having jumped to *this* particular year to catch our train.'

'All the same, why no tugging on a lobe so we can get out of sight?'

whispered Max.

'For this very important reason: there is no better place to hide than in *plain sight.*'

'Have you lost your mind?' said Max.

'Watch and learn, fledglings. Watch and learn.'

The agents were striding purposefully, swinging their umbrellas and casting furtive glances about as they scanned the station for Max and Eric. They paid little heed to the grieving widow and her daughter as they approached, and even less when the pair lurched towards them, forcing them to step aside and let them pass. Max felt a rapid tug on his left ear and veered towards platform four. 'What just happened? Are we being followed?'

'Not a bit of it,' said Erica. 'And we would have bumped right into them if they hadn't made way for us.'

'A valuable lesson,' said Ellie. 'When you behave in a way that's the complete *opposite* to what's expected, you blend in with your surroundings.' A scruffy-looking porter approached them and enquired after their baggage. 'We carry only the baggage of grief, young man,' replied the widow haughtily.

'I only wish I could help you carry that burden, madam.'

'Yes, well, that's all well and good,' replied the widow, 'but you'll earn yourself a sixpence if you show us safely to our private compartment.'

The man's dirty round face lit up. 'Can I see your tickets please, madam?'

'Yes, here they are.' The widow held up their tickets at an awkward angle, and the porter leaned across to take them.

'All the first-class compartments are at the front of the train. Follow me along the platform, and I'll have you there in three shakes of a skunk's tail,' he said. They walked alongside the steam train, its black and silver metal work polished and gleaming, and on towards the front of the train where steam from its funnel rose languidly into the cold morning air.

Once they reached the carriage where the first-class compartments were, the porter took the sixpence, thanked them kindly, and watched the odd pair climb the steps onto the train. *Saints preserve us*, he thought, grimacing. *She's leaning way too far forward for my liking.*

Eighteen
London-bound

Inside their private compartment on the eight o'clock train to London, "Erica" slid the bolt on the door into the locked position, while the "widow" collapsed onto a plush row of seats. In Max's voice she cried, 'Get off me already!'

A minute later, Eric and Ellie were sitting opposite one other by the window. Max was standing at its centre, between the seats, rubbing his lower back.

'I take my hat off to you both,' said Eric. 'You got us to York *and* on board a train in one piece.'

'True. But we're not home and dry yet,' sighed Ellie.

The train pulled out of the station with a hoot from its whistle, and Eric nestled back contentedly into his seat. 'Eric Kettle,' he said, 'on a train to London, in a first-class carriage no less. The lads back at the orphanage would *never* believe it – not if I told them till I was blue in the face. And if I did go blue in the face, they'd just think I'd got pneumonia again.'

Ellie gazed out of the window. 'Where we're going, you'll never get pneumonia.'

Max sat down next to Eric, stretched his legs out and placed his hands behind his head. 'Not unless you jump up and down on a frozen pond like Ed Peters did in Year One for a bet. He completely disappeared for, like, half a minute. *And* he had to give Roger Clement his pocket money for a whole month.'

'Sounds like a real genius,' said Ellie, gazing into the distance.

'You both got families where we're going?' asked Eric.

'Yes,' said Ellie.

'I thought so. They must worry about you a lot.'

'They would if they knew what we were up to,' said Ellie.

'They don't *know*?'

'They can't. The work we do is top secret.'

Max cleared his throat nervously. 'And while we're here, time pretty much stands still back home. Ellie told me so herself.'

'Relax,' nodded Ellie. 'When we get back, only moments will have passed since we left.'

'Glad to hear it. Now when do we eat?' asked Max, looking at Eric.

'Soon,' said Ellie. 'I saw a notice out in the hallway that said food is served in the buffet car thirty minutes after the train leaves the station.'

Max felt his stomach grumble. 'Tell me we don't need our disguises while we're on the train?'

'Of course we need them,' said Ellie.

'Do you think there'll be agents on the train?' asked Eric.

Ellie nodded. 'Put it this way: I'd be very surprised if there weren't.'

'How am I going to eat, then?' asked Max.

'I'll ask a for doggie bag.'

'Well, tell them I'm a Great Dane, then. I'm starving.'

Eric stared out of the window, but his pensive expression suggested that far from seeing anything, he was deep in thought.

'Something on your mind?' asked Ellie.

Eric placed his left ankle on his right knee. 'If we do make it all the way back to *two* thousand and six*teen*, will I be put in an orphanage?'

Max shook his head. 'No way!' he said, looking at Ellie for confirmation. 'He won't be put in an orphanage, will he?'

Ellie smiled. 'Of course not.'

'Then where will I live?'

'The Ancient Order is loaded. They'll sort something out,' said Ellie.

'Might they have me adopted?'

'Would you *like* to be adopted?'

'Of *course!*' nodded Eric emphatically. 'It's all we dreamed about at the orphanage.'

'So what happened to your mum and dad?' asked Max.

Eric fidgeted uncomfortably and looked down at his hands.

'No need to talk about it,' said Ellie, 'not if you don't want to.'

'Don't mind talking about it. Truth is, there's not much to say about it. They up and left, is all.'

'*Both* of them?' asked Max incredulously.

'Yes, when I was a baby. Father went to seek his fortune and Mother went looking for him.'

'At least, that's what you've always been told,' Ellie murmured under her breath.

Max looked at Ellie. 'Do you think the boffins at Scratchling HQ will be able to find out what happened to them?'

Ellie shrugged and stared out of the window at the dark fields receding into the distance.

'*Might* they be able to find out what became of Mother and Father?' asked Eric, brightening a little.

'Maybe,' said Ellie quietly.

The three children jumped at a loud *RAP! RAP! RAP!* on the door. Max and Eric looked wide-eyed at Ellie, whose own eyes had narrowed to slits. 'Attendant to check your tickets,' came a friendly voice from outside the door.

Ellie reached for the veil at her side. 'Just a moment!' she called out, sliding it over her head.

The short grieving widow in a veil and too-long black cloak climbed onto Max's back, where she grew magically in stature until she was an exceptionally tall grieving widow who fit it perfectly. She slid the bolt and opened the door a couple of inches.

'Here are our tickets, good man,' she said, as Max's hands held up their tickets. The attendant, who was short and stout and wearing a black suit with gold braid, took the tickets and punched holes in them. The "widow" stifled a sob and asked, 'Is breakfast being served yet? I find grief makes me terribly hungry.' The attendant handed back the tickets and said he was sorry for her loss, and that the buffet car would open in ten minutes' time.

Ten minutes later, the widow-and-daughter illusion was reassembled by the compartment's door. 'Let's do this,' said Ellie.

They were the first to arrive in the buffet car. The "widow" sat down at a table, *very* carefully, and her "daughter" sat opposite her. The waiter was thin and moustached, and he placed a gold-trimmed menu on the table. The daughter picked it up and nodded wholeheartedly at everything on it. 'Might I *actually* have a steak?' asked the grieving child from beyond her veil. 'I bet they don't serve up no bow-wow mutton here.'

The widow looked up at the open-mouthed waiter. 'She always has had an unusual way with words.'

'I quite understand, madam.'

'Good. Now be off and bring us three of the biggest steaks you have.'

'*Three*, madam?'

'Yes, that's right. We're absolutely famished.'

'Very good, madam. And potatoes?'

'Yes.'

'For three?'

The widow nodded.

The waiter picked up the menu and sauntered off down the carriage towards the kitchen.

Several other diners had entered the car by the time they began tucking into their meal, and the gasps of delight coming from beneath the veil of the widow's daughter as she chewed her steak caused many a raised eyebrow. Ellie had just wrapped Max's steak in a napkin when the train jerked and screeched to a halt, throwing all the passengers violently forwards and back. 'What's going on out there?' whispered Max.

'I don't know, but I don't like it,' Ellie whispered back.

'We're in our disguises, so whatever it is we should be okay,' said Eric, wondering how anything could possibly go wrong when your belly was filled with steak.

'Time to go, Max! Get up! Come on, Eric, we're leaving,' said Ellie.

The widow got up *very* gingerly, and passed back through the door into the corridor with her daughter. Once through the door, Ellie looked back through its window into the dining car. 'Put me down, Max!' she said, struggling to climb down off his back.

'But what about our disguise?' came Max's voice.

'Our disguise is *useless* against the Dark Scratchlings ... and they've just entered the dining car!'

Max released Ellie's legs. She slid off his shoulders and onto the ground, pulling off her veil. Eric removed his veil too, and peered through the window into the dining car. 'They're gliding this way!'

'Of course they are. They'll search the train from top to bottom. Come on!' said Ellie, darting several metres down the corridor to a window. She slid it up, stuck her head out and looked up towards the roof of the train. 'Follow me!' she cried, reaching up and grabbing a brass rail that ran down the side of the train. She clambered up onto the train's roof, turned and called down, 'Eric next!'

'Hurry, Eric!' urged Max, glancing to his right and seeing the Dark Scratchlings making their way up the dining car. Eric climbed out of the window and reached up for the brass rail, beyond which Ellie's outstretched hand beckoned. Max supported Eric's legs until they disappeared above the window frame. He placed a knee on the window ledge and, glancing fearfully into the dining car one last time, saw the Dark Scratchlings being confronted by two men. *The train driver and the guard*, thought Max, hoping for the best. His hope was crushed, however, when the Dark Scratchlings tossed the men aside like rag dolls.

'Max!' came Ellie's voice from outside. Max climbed out of the window and, with Ellie's help, pulled himself up onto the roof of the now stationary train. They found themselves close to the front of the train, and Ellie beckoned them to follow her as she took off at full tilt towards its rear.

'Where are we going?' asked Max breathlessly, catching her up and glancing left and right at the rolling landscape that appeared to go on forever on either side of the train.

'For starters, we're going to put as much space between us and the Dark Scratchlings as possible. No. Wait!' she said, stopping in her tracks. She looked behind her and then ahead of her again. 'You reckon we're roughly in the train's middle?'

'Yeah, I guess. So?'

'Get down and lay flat on your stomachs. Now!' commanded Ellie. 'You two face the front of the train. I'll watch the rear, and with any *luck* ...' She kneeled down and gazed up at the cloudless sky.

'And with any luck *what*?' pressed Max.

'They'll search the train and then leave.'

'And what if they decide to check the roof?' asked Eric nervously.

'Then we'll just have to wing it.'

'Wing it *how*?' asked Max.

'By rolling with the punches.'

'Get *pummelled*, you mean. It's alright for you. How are my parents supposed to *wing it* if their son is brainwashed and turned to the dark side?'

'You're starting to babble, Hastings. Pull yourself together!' barked Ellie, checking along the roof of the train, forwards and back. 'And while we're on the subject,' she went on, 'as I'm the only one who's undergone the Scratchling Initiation Ceremony, those evil Scratchlings will tear me limb from limb. So spare a thought for *my* poor mum and dad. I'd forever be a missing person.'

'Never thought I'd have an opportunity to thank my lucky stars that

I'm an orphan,' said Eric.

'Well done, Eric,' said Ellie. 'An excellent example of positive thinking under pressure. Chin up. They'll be working overtime back at Scratchling HQ to bring us some good luck about now.'

'They're obviously not working hard *enough*,' said Max, pointing towards the front of the train.

Ellie shot a look over her shoulder, and saw the Dark Scratchlings float up in their eerily menacing way above the dining car some fifty metres away. 'It's time to roll with those punches!' said Ellie, scrambling to her feet. The boys did the same and, reverting to the previous plan to put as much distance between them and the Dark Scratchlings as possible, they sprinted towards the rear of the train.

The driver blew the train's whistle, and great clouds of smoke billowed from its funnel as it began a slow chug along the tracks. As the train picked up speed and the winds increased, the Dark Scratchlings were forced to settle on its roof and use their legs.

Max looked back over his shoulder, trying to keep his balance on the moving train. 'They're gaining on us!' he shrieked.

The distance between the escapees and the end of the train was running out ominously, as was the distance between them and their pursuers. Ten metres from the end of the train, Ellie stopped so suddenly in her tracks that the boys were forced to swerve dangerously close to the edges of the carriage to go around her. They spun about and looked at her. 'Why are you stopping?'

'Tell me you see what I see,' said Ellie, pointing behind them to the rear of the train. The boys turned and beheld the outline of a transparent steam train racing up alongside their own on the parallel track, going in the opposite direction.

'Is that a *ghost* train?' said Eric, his jaw dropping open.

'No,' said Ellie. 'Unless I'm very much mistaken, it's *the* Ghost Train.' She cast a glance back at the Dark Scratchlings, who were now only thirty metres away and running hard.

'We're going to have to jump onto it!'

'Jump?' said Max, aghast. 'We can't! It's *transparent*; we'll fall right through it onto the tracks!'

Ellie took a step back and prepared to make a leap of faith. 'Take my hands!' she instructed, holding them out to the boys who were standing either side of her.

'Are you nuts?' yelled Max.

'Call it a Scratchling hunch! Take my hands. Now! We must jump *together.*' The boys took hold of her hands. The Dark Scratchlings were nearly upon them. 'On three. One ... two ... three!'

They ran forwards and jumped the metre gap onto the transparent train, which became solid under their feet the moment they landed. They turned just in time to see the Dark Scratchlings leap across the divide after them and descend upon them with flailing arms. Ellie stepped protectively in front of Max and Eric, lashing out as the Dark Scratchlings plummeted through the train and fell onto the tracks.

Ellie, Max and Eric looked at one another in shock for a moment, before breaking into whoops and cheers. They ran to the end of the train and showed the Dark Scratchlings some very specific hand gestures as they receded into the distance.

Max looked down at the train under his feet. 'What just happened?' he asked breathlessly.

'We've been rescued ... by a ghost train,' said Eric. 'Talk about lucky stars!'

'Like I said, not *a* ghost train. *The* Ghost Train,' said Ellie. 'The one that made it into popular culture and became a ride at every fun fair.'

'You've heard of this actual train?' said Max, pointing down at the train.

Ellie looked around her on the train's roof, and was relieved to see a ladder leading down to a platform at the rear of the train. 'I'll say. This train is the stuff of legend in Scratchling circles.'

'You're smiling. So I take it it's all good?' said Max hopefully.

Ellie's smile vanished. 'Like most legends, the finer points are shrouded in mystery. All I've heard – all *anybody* in the Scratchling community has heard – is that the Ghost Train is manned by the ghosts of children who were rescued by Scratchlings. Children who were able to grow up and fulfil their destinies because of our efforts,' explained Ellie, climbing onto the ladder. 'Come on. It would be rude to keep our hosts waiting, and I can't wait to see if the stories I've heard about this train are true.'

Ellie climbed off the ladder at the bottom, and stood before a red door with a large brass knocker. She waited for Max and Eric to join her and then reached for it.

'Are you *sure* that whoever's inside is going to be friendly?' asked Max doubtfully.

'Do you really imagine they'd have gone to all this trouble to save us from the Dark Scratchlings if they wanted to harm us?' scoffed Ellie, taking a deep breath and banging the knocker three times.

The door opened, and they looked into an elegant red carriage that resembled a long hallway. Standing to attention down both sides was a welcoming committee of apparently flesh-and-blood children who regarded them with awe. Each child stood beneath an oil painting of an old man or woman. As Ellie, Max and Eric stepped into the carriage, these children began to applaud uproariously. Max glanced at Ellie and saw that she was blushing. He nudged Eric mischievously. 'Look, she's human after all,' he whispered.

Ellie was too distracted to overhear, and walked slowly towards a little girl standing alone at the furthest end of the carriage. Max and Eric followed her. 'It *can't* be,' murmured Ellie as she drew near. As they walked through the carriage, the children's applause was accompanied by whistles and cheers. The children seemed to look upon their visitors as celebrities, and Max imagined he must be blushing too now as he gazed up at the paintings above each child to avoid eye-contact. As he looked from one painting to the next, he began to discern a resemblance between the old person in each portrait and the child standing below it. 'Are they their *parents,* Ellie?' shouted Max above the applause.

Ellie smiled at him over her shoulder. 'It's *them*, Max. It's the old person they became, thanks to a Scratchling answering their call for help.'

'OK, but who's she?' Eric asked, gesturing at the stern little girl at the end of the carriage beneath a portrait of a *very* old lady.

'She's the first person I ever rescued,' said Ellie as the little girl broke into a smile and ran towards her, her white dress billowing as though caught in a gale. The little girl jumped up and threw her arms around Ellie's neck. 'Florence!' cried Ellie joyfully. 'Is it really you?' The little girl nodded into her neck as Ellie swung her around. Max swallowed the lump in his throat.

Ellie put the little girl down. 'Max and Eric, may I present Florence Nightingale?'

'The famous *nurse*?' gaped Max.

114

Ellie smiled down at Florence and nodded. 'Florence here was such an inquisitive child that she climbed down a disused well on her uncle's estate and couldn't get back out.'

'If Ellie hadn't rescued me, I expect I'd still be there to this day,' smiled Florence, who sounded considerably older and wiser than the eight-year-old child she appeared to be. 'I hope you're pleased with your welcome,' continued Florence, flinging an arm around to include all the silent and beaming children. 'They – *we* – owe you everything.'

'And we you,' said Ellie. 'How did you know to help us?'

'We didn't, not really, but we received word that those *things* – the Dark Scratchlings – were here and pursuing *something*. It's most unlike Dark Scratchlings to be in pursuit of anything. In the usual way, they swoop in, rescue a child who's destined to grow into Someone Who Leaves Much to Be Desired, and then swoop out again. The children *they* rescue are the polar opposites of the team that mans the Ghost Train today.' Florence looked proudly around the carriage. 'Please allow me to introduce you to some of them.' She walked over to a boy dressed in the black and white tunic of a young sailor from the time of the Napoleonic wars. 'This is Jimmy Blake. Jimmy used to fetch the cannon balls during battles, which was a *very* dangerous occupation. He was blown across the deck and knocked unconscious by an explosion, then left for dead in the morgue below decks.'

'If a Scratchling hadn't answered my call, I'd have died in that terrible place,' said Jimmy, reaching out to shake Max, Eric and Ellie by the hand.

Florence looked up at the portrait of Jimmy as the old man he became. 'Jimmy's name is just one of the *many* that sadly have been lost to history. But Jimmy's contribution to humanity has been immeasurable. His tireless research paved the way for the development of medicines that would ease the suffering of millions. And over here,' continued Florence, crossing the carriage and stopping before a little boy dressed in top hat and tails. 'This is Richard Martin, whose nickname is Humanity Dick. Richard was a founder member of the Royal Society for the Prevention of Cruelty to Animals. The RSPCA.'

'I fell out of a tree,' said Richard, 'and cut my arm wide open. The wound turned septic, and it would have killed me had not a Scratchling travelled back in time and given me a phial of miraculous pills.'

'Those pills were antibiotics,' explained Florence. 'They were delivered to Humanity Dick a hundred years before they were invented. And over here,' she crossed the carriage yet again to stand before a little black girl. 'This is Rosa Parks. Rosa was the first person to refuse to give up her seat to a white person on a bus just because she was black. That single, brave action sparked the civil rights movement that led to the equal treatment of all, regardless of colour, in the United States of America.'

'It's an absolute honour to meet you, Miss Parks,' said Ellie fervently, shaking the girl's hand with both hands.

'Please. Call me Rosa,' said Rosa. 'And the honour is all mine. I never thought I'd meet another Scratchling, and now three stand before me.'

'I'm sure we're all wondering about the presence of *three* Scratchlings …?' said Florence.

Max cleared his throat. 'I was the only person who could be sent to rescue Eric here,' he said, patting Eric on the shoulder.

'And when we were captured, Ellie came and rescued us both,' added Eric.

'Which explains why there are three of us here,' said Ellie.

'And where are you all going?' enquired Florence.

'London. To Mansion House,' replied Ellie. 'Max and Eric are yet to undergo the Scratchling Initiation Ceremony, so it's imperative they're kept beyond the reach of the Dark Scratchlings. Mansion House is the only place we can find sanctuary and a portal back to the safety of the cusp of time. The train's heading to London?'

Florence nodded. 'We are now.'

Ellie looked relieved. 'Sorry to be so much trouble. I've heard tales about the Ghost Train, but …' She cast her gaze around her.

'But what?' asked Florence.

'Nobody knows what you *do,* exactly.'

'Well, having been so fortunate ourselves,' said Florence, 'we feel it's our duty to give something back.'

'By riding around on a train and spooking people?' said Max.

'Max!' admonished Ellie.

Florence smoothed down her dress with flat palms. 'The truth is,' she said, 'those of us who volunteer to work on the train spend most of our time *off* it. We visit towns and villages the length and breadth of the country, whispering words of advice and encouragement into the minds of children of kind heart and noble mind. All of us have a *lifetime's* worth of experience to share.' She fell silent and looked as though she was remembering something troubling.

'What is it?' asked Ellie with concern.

Florence raised a bare arm and examined the fine hairs on it, which were standing on end. It felt suddenly icy cold in the carriage.

'What's happening? What's going on?' asked Max.

'It's the *other* one,' murmured Florence with frightened eyes.

'The other *what*?' urged Ellie.

Florence shuddered. 'Unless I'm very much mistaken, the other *train*.' She clapped her hands quickly, twice. 'Chop! Chop! Prepare for the transformation! You three follow me.' She made her way briskly down the carriage to the front of the train. Ellie, Max and Eric glanced nervously at one another and followed.

The next carriage contained a row of roll-top desks down each side, each with a single chair in front of it. As they hurried down the centre of the carriage, Ellie asked, 'What's going on, Florence? What other train are you talking about?'

'The other ghost train,' said Florence. 'It's manned by children that were rescued by the Dark Scratchlings. They travel the world, just as we do, only *they* whisper advice to children who are destined to grow up to become Those Who Leave Much to Be Desired. Adults who will do more harm than good.'

'Are they going to attack us?' gulped Max.

Florence shrugged her little shoulders. 'Our trains have only crossed paths a handful of times over the centuries. On those rare occasions, no more than warning shots were exchanged, but your presence on board cannot be a coincidence. This time it may be different.'

'Warning shots from *trains*?' said Max.

Ellie sounded excited. 'You mentioned something about a transformation just now?'

'That's right. No time to explain,' said Florence as she hurried into the train's centremost carriage, and reached for a golden lever on the wall. 'You're about to *see* it with your own eyes.' Florence pulled the lever, prompting their surroundings to bend and distort in all directions around them and giving the impression that the train was turning inside out. Although the ground on which they stood remained flat and solid, Ellie, Max and Eric stumbled about trying to keep their balance. 'The

117

transformation is almost complete,' said Florence, who remained rooted to the spot with her eyes closed. Moments later, they became aware that they were standing on the deck of a ship.

Ellie looked up at the vast sail that billowed above her, astonished. 'It's the *Haunted Galleon!*' she whispered in awe. 'I thought this ship *was* just a legend.'

'As you can see, she's very real,' said Florence. The ship's deck was swarming with children hurrying to their positions. 'You all know the drill! We've practised it many times in case of an event like this. Battle stations, everybody!' She rushed to the side of the ship, whereupon a boy hurried over and handed her a brass telescope.

Ellie, Max and Eric joined her and gazed with bewilderment over the ship's rail. Although they couldn't tell how high they were exactly, they were obviously flying thousands of feet from the ground – and it was definitely ground, not sea, that they could see rushing by below. Just below them on the quarterdeck, they could see the business ends of thirty cannon jutting out. 'Look! There! At ten o'clock,' said Florence, pointing over the side of the galleon, her eye pressed to the telescope. Ellie, Max and Eric followed her finger, and as they squinted into the blue-grey gloom a ship began to take shape: a vast pirate ship with a black sail and fifty tightly-packed cannon down its side. The ship drew closer, as though about to ram them, and there were sighs of relief from all around when instead it pulled up alongside their own. The faces of at least a hundred children regarded them over the rail of the ship's main deck, and an angrier, leerier collection of malcontents Max, Eric and Ellie hoped never to see again.

The sound of raised voices floated across the gloom, and Max, Eric and Ellie could just about make out a commotion in the centre of the deck. The children there scattered, and a platform was moved into place against the side of the ship. A boy of about ten climbed this platform, dressed in white robes with a curved dagger tucked into a wide silver belt. The boy stood straight-backed with his thumbs pressed down into his belt. He looked at Florence across the misty void and called challengingly, 'You know who I am, Nightingale?'

'I do,' said Florence, trying to disguise the fear in her voice with a superior tone.

'Then you will know that you are no match for me in battle.'

'You forget, Mr Khan. I have been in the midst of battle many times.'

Genghis Khan chuckled dismissively. 'Yes, but as a *healer*. I have led great armies into battle, slaughtered *millions*, and conquered a quarter of the known world.'

'You're such a hero, Mr Khan,' said Florence sarcastically. 'What is it you want?'

Genghis lifted his arm and pointed first at Eric and then Max.

'Over my dead body!' shouted Ellie.

'That too is part of our plan. Hand them over now or suffer the consequences, Nightingale.'

'You bluff,' said Florence. 'Those Who Leave Much to Be Desired are no longer a threat to us. We're already *dead*.'

'My orders are clear. I am not to allow these *Scratchlings* to return to their sanctuary at Mansion House.'

'Yet that sanctuary is *precisely* where we are taking them,' said Florence defiantly.

'We cannot allow it,' said Genghis. 'Either you hand them over, or we'll blast your ship from beneath you and they will *fall* to their deaths!'

'Hand them over? Never! Prepare to taste the fury of our plasma cannon, Mr Khan!' Florence turned and ran up a short flight of steps to where a small boy stood before a large wheel. Ellie, Max and Eric followed her. 'This is Edward Smith,' said Florence by way of introduction to the little boy at the ship's wheel. 'Edward, meet Ellie, Max and Eric – a genuine trinity of Scratchlings in our care.'

Edward saluted them. 'It's an honour,' he said.

'I am soon to give the order to open fire. So prepare for battle, Edward.'

Edward grabbed the wheel and spun it away from the other ship, whereupon Florence turned her gaze upon the Scratchlings. 'Rest assured,' she said, 'we're in the very best of hands with Edward at the helm. He was the captain of the *Titanic*, you know.'

'The *Titanic*? That sounds very impressive,' said Eric admiringly.

Max, who had turned suddenly rather pale, looked at Eric as though he'd squandered all his marbles. 'But the *Titanic sank*.' He looked at Florence. 'You do know the *Titanic* sank, right?'

'It was a little after my time, but of *course* I do. It wasn't Edward's fault that it struck that iceberg.'

Edward hung his head. 'No, I must shoulder the lion's share of the blame, Florence,' he said.

'Nonsense. The people to blame were the ones who cut corners and didn't provide enough lifeboats for everyone on board – people who undoubtedly leave much to be desired and are more likely to be on board the *other* ship.' Florence picked up a receiver close to the wheel and bellowed, 'Gun deck!' down it.

'Lifeboats,' murmured Ellie.

'What about them?' asked Florence as she waited to be connected to the gun deck.

'Do you have any?'

Florence shook her head. 'What use have the dead for lifeboats?'

'That's where you're wrong. We do have a lifeboat,' interjected Edward sheepishly.

Florence raised an eyebrow at him.

Edward shrugged his tiny shoulders. 'I installed one myself at the aft of the ship, just below the gun deck.'

Florence lowered the eyebrow. 'But why, Edward?'

'For old times' sake, I suppose,' said Edward. 'It felt like something I should do.'

'That's lucky,' said Ellie, looking up above the sail and smiling. '*Please* tell me the lifeboat will float? I mean, *fly*?'

'Of course it will,' said Edward proudly.

Florence's eyes widened. 'You mean to escape in it?' she said.

Ellie nodded. They heard a shrill sound like a build-up of energy and the darkness beyond the ship was lit up by a green spectral glow.

'Everyone hit the deck!' cried Edward, dropping to his knees as a broadside of plasma blasts from the other ship's cannon struck the *Haunted Galleon*. The deck shuddered violently.

From her crouched position on the deck, Florence bellowed, 'Return fire!' into the receiver that she still clutched in her hand. After another shrill build-up of energy, their surroundings were lit by a spectral blue as their own plasma cannon returned fire.

Ellie jumped up and looked over the rail at their target. 'A direct hit!' she cried triumphantly. Florence remained crouched and talking to Edward Smith in hushed tones, while Max and Eric joined Ellie and peered over the rail. The other ship had a metre-high slice erased from its centre.

Florence got up to join them. 'An excellent volley of shots, but I fear the damage we sustained will have been greater still. We must get you off this ship immediately. Edward will lead you to the lifeboat. He's volunteered to accompany you and see you safely back to London.'

'It's the least I can do,' called Edward as the air turned green again. 'Hit the deck!' he cried. They threw themselves onto the deck as the ship shuddered and lurched to one side.

'When we're gone, will you be okay?' Eric asked Florence, crouching amid the chaos.

'Yes. Their plasma cannon can't hurt us, only our vehicle. Now go with Edward,' she commanded, jumping to her feet.

Ellie jumped up and threw her arms around the little girl. 'Thank you, Florence!'

'Nonsense. It means the absolute world that I had this opportunity to return your kindness. Now GO!'

Nineteen
The Flying Lifeboat

Edward crouch-walked across the deck towards the ship's stern and, once there, he looked over his shoulder and watched Ellie, Max and Eric follow in his footsteps. Once they were alongside him, he whispered, 'The lifeboat is lashed to the stern just below us over this rail. It will suit our purposes if the strongest out of the three of you climbs down into the lifeboat first. You'll be able to help the other two get safely into the boat.'

Ellie and Max stepped up to the rope that would take them down into the lifeboat. They bumped shoulders, looked at each other for half a second, and then Max shrugged and took half a step back. Ellie climbed onto the rail and looked over its edge: the lifeboat was suspended by ropes some five metres below. She took hold of the rope, gave it several firm tugs to check it was secure, and then began to climb down.

Next to descend the rope was Max. He stepped gingerly over the rail, grabbed onto the rope as though his life depended on it, then stopped. With wide, pleading eyes, he looked at Edward. 'A strapping lad like you should be just fine,' said Edward.

'Strapping? *Really*? That's a first,' said Max, looking pale and not in the least bit reassured.

'Strapping by the standards of this time,' clarified Edward, who glanced at Eric's skinny form by way of comparison. Just at that moment, the ship took another volley of plasma blasts and shuddered so violently it seemed as though it might break in two. With his heart still pounding against his ribs, Max loosened his grip on the rope and slid quickly down.

Eric stepped forward. 'No offence, lad,' said Edward, placing a hand on Eric's chest, 'but you're nought but skin and bone. I'd best give you a piggy-back down.'

Eric raised an eyebrow. 'No offence to you,' he replied, 'but you look about *six* yourself.'

'Actually, I was *seven* when I was rescued by a Scratchling. Appearances are mighty deceptive here, lad. You'll do well to remember where you are and *what* I am,' said Edward, climbing over the rail. 'Come on now, son, and climb on my back.'

With no further argument, Eric did just that and, once they were safely aboard the lifeboat, Edward untied the ropes that lashed it to the side. He sat down on the centremost of the lifeboat's three benches, picked up the oars and began to row. The lifeboat sailed quickly away from the ships into darkness, as though shooting down rapids. Ellie, Max and Eric squinted above them at the warring galleons, which were both illuminated in the phantasmal green and blues that preceded their plasma cannon blasts. The wind picked up to gale force as Edward rowed faster, and the three Scratchlings clung to the sides of the little wooden boat that soared through the air.

'Fear not!' cried Edward above the roar of the wind, 'for barring icebergs, which are unknown at ten thousand feet, I'll have you out of harm's way in no time.'

Before very long, all that was left of the two galleons could be blocked out behind the tip of Ellie's thumb and, shortly after that, even the lightshow of blues and greens was devoured completely by the darkness of the night.

Ellie slumped against the side of the boat and looked at Edward, whose glowing form was now their only source of light. 'Thank you, Captain,' she said. 'You're a star.'

Edward looked away, uncomfortable with the praise. 'There was a time when they called me the star of White Star Line, but that was before I lost their flagship on its maiden voyage. Fifteen hundred souls drowned that day aboard the *Titanic*.'

'That iceberg *really* wasn't your fault, I know. I've seen the movie *twice*,' said Max.

'That's what those poor souls have told me every year since then at our annual meeting. It doesn't make it any easier, though.' Edward looked thoroughly downcast.

'Did you die that day?' Eric asked him.

Edward nodded proudly.

'He chose to go down with his ship,' said Max. 'Stayed right at the wheel. Trust me, I know. I've seen the film—'

'*Twice*,' said Ellie.

'Look!' cried Eric, pointing over the side at something down below on the land. Ellie and Max peered over the side.

'London,' said Ellie.

'There!' cried Eric excitedly. 'The dome of St Paul's Cathedral!'

Ellie, Max and Eric gazed hungrily down at the city. Its ancient streets were illuminated by street lamps and by the moon, which had just emerged from behind a cloud.

Max tried to gauge how far above the city they were. 'Never have been one for heights,' he said queasily, trying to ignore the lurching feeling in his stomach. 'But still, it's really good to see home, even if it is ninety-nine years in the past.'

'My orphanage was down there. I wonder if it still is,' said Eric, leaning a little too far over the side for Ellie's liking.

Max moved to the front of the lifeboat. 'My sense of direction was never the best but ... if that's St Paul's Cathedral directly ahead, and we're heading *east*, then Mansion House can't be more than a kilometre away.'

'Correct,' said Ellie, who felt her ears pop as the lifeboat descended towards the sleeping Edwardian city.

The boat flew so low over the dome of St Paul's Cathedral that they could almost have reached down and touched it, then on it sailed over the streets and rooftops towards Mansion House.

As Edward set the boat down on Mansion House's flat roof, the Scratchlings braced themselves, fully expecting the V-bottomed boat to topple over onto its side. Edward released the oars and smiled for the first time. 'She's floating a smidgen above the roof,' he explained when it didn't topple over.

Ellie stood up and climbed out of the boat. 'Come on, Scratchlings,' she said purposefully, looking into the night's sky in the direction from which they'd come. 'We don't know for certain that no one's followed us.' As Max and Eric climbed out of the boat, Ellie reached a hand across to Edward. 'Thank you for getting us here in one piece, Edward,' she added, shaking his tiny hand.

'It's been a privilege helping you all return safely to your sanctuary.'

Ellie looked at Max and Eric. 'We haven't found sanctuary *quite* yet. There's still one small problem we need to address.'

'Problem? What problem now?' asked Max.

'A problem arising from the fact that we're currently in 1915.'

'So?'

'So the entrance to the Ancient Order of Wall Scratchings can only be accessed on the cusp of time in 2016.'

'What are you saying?' asked Max.

'That we need to activate Protocol 101, which means breaking into Mansion House and waking up the incumbent Lord Mayor of London.'

'Doing *what*?'

'You heard,' murmured Ellie. She closed her eyes, and her lips moved as she went through the list of Lord Mayors in her head. With her eyes still closed, she concluded, 'They've been electing a new Lord Mayor of London every year since 1189.'

'That's a *lot* of Lord Mayors,' remarked Eric.

'Don't I know it. And in 1915 they elected one Sir Charles Wakefield. Mr Wakefield is the man we need to talk to.'

'About what?' asked Eric.

Ellie opened her eyes. 'About Protocol 101, of course.'

'And he'll know about it?' asked Max hopefully.

Ellie tapped her chin thoughtfully. 'As far as I'm *aware,* they will have told him about Protocol 101 when they swore him in. Then they'd have sworn him to secrecy about it.'

'As far as you're *aware*,' said Max.

Ellie nodded and made her way to a door that looked like an entrance to a small cabin at the centre of the roof. Max and Eric smiled at Edward, raised a hand in parting, and followed her. 'I'll leave the boat where it is,' called Edward.

'Meaning?' queried Ellie over her shoulder.

'Meaning it will still be here when you get back to the cusp of time – invisible to everyone but you three. Only you three will be able to touch or interact with it.'

Ellie, Max and Eric turned and faced him. 'Will it still *fly*?' asked Ellie.

'Of course,' confirmed Edward.

'Thank you!' they chorused.

'Think nothing of it. Hope it comes in handy.'

'But how will *you* get home then, Mr Smith?' asked a concerned Eric.

In reply, Edward morphed before their eyes into the fully grown and bearded Captain Edward Smith he was to become. The captain of *RMS Titanic* straightened his back, saluted, smiled a reassuring smile, and then dissolved into thin air. Max and Eric turned away to see Ellie picking the lock on the door. She was muttering something about the lock being state-of-the-art for the time period, and that that was why it was taking her so long to … then *click!* She pulled open the door to reveal a flight of stairs. 'Stick close and don't make a sound,' she whispered as she set foot on the top step.

The stairs led down into the attic rooms where the Lord Mayor's servants slept. Ellie, Eric and Max crept along a narrow corridor past a dozen closed doors, behind which the occasional snore or yawn could be heard. 'I take it you know where you're going?' whispered Max. 'I still have the parchment if you don't. It's pretty handy with this stuff.'

'No need to bother the parchment. I've memorised the floor plan of all six floors. It's part of the training, and you'll discover that *I* have the parchment now anyway, if you check your pockets.'

'But how …?' whispered Max, doing just that.

Ellie rolled her eyes.

At the far end of the corridor they descended the servants' stairs into Mansion House proper, and crept along a palatial landing illuminated by lamps. The carpet was emerald green and thick enough to bury your toes in – a point not lost on Eric, who took off his shoes and cooed as he scrunched his toes around in the soft fibres. As he walk-scrunched, he gazed about in awe at the fine antiques. 'I imagine Buckingham Palace must be just like this. It's quite something; makes me feel like a prince in a one of those fairy tales.'

'You're starting to *babble,* Eric,' whispered Ellie.

'Don't take it personally, Eric,' said Max. 'Ellie hates it when people babble and she *especially* hates it when I babble. I think it's because—'

Ellie wheeled around, fixing him with a headmistress glare. Max closed his mouth, whereupon Ellie turned and made her way to a flight of stairs.

At the bottom of the stairs, Ellie led them to a set of double doors at the far end of a wide corridor. 'This is the Lord Mayor's bedroom,' announced Ellie in a whisper, pulling open the doors and stepping inside. They crept towards a four-poster bed that stood opposite a lit fireplace. Seeing only one person in the bed, asleep on his back, Ellie breathed a sigh of relief.

With Max and Eric standing anxiously behind her, Ellie reached out a hand and gently shook the sleeping figure by the shoulder. 'Mr Wakefield?' she whispered. The Lord Mayor grunted in his sleep and mumbled something about his robes needing more starch. 'It simply isn't good enough, you know,' he grumbled.

'Mr Wakefield!' said Ellie loudly, losing patience and pinching his arm. 'Wake up! This is important!'

The Lord Mayor sat up suddenly and peered myopically at her. 'Is that you, Miss Treestock? Has something happened?'

He's obviously as blind as a bat, thought Ellie as she scanned his bedside table for a pair of glasses. *Bingo*, she thought, picking up a gold-rimmed pair. 'I suggest you put these on,' she said, handing them to him. The Lord Mayor took the glasses and slid them on. He looked at Ellie, did a double-take at Max and Eric, then opened his mouth in readiness to call for help. Only the following words could have prevented him: 'Scratchling Protocol 101,' pronounced Ellie in her most no-nonsense tone.

'*What* did you just say?' asked the Lord Mayor in amazement.

'Scratchling Protocol 101,' she repeated in the same flat tone. 'We need you to activate it. *Now.*'

The Lord Mayor raised his hands to his fat and ruddy cheeks, and his mouth dropped open.

Ellie softened her tone somewhat. 'We are Scratchlings, and we really need your help, Mr Wakefield.'

'What, *all* of you?'

'Yes, all of us.'

'But … but … but I was given to understand that Scratchlings are so very *rare*. Like *mythical* creatures. Since 1189 when this office was created, only *one* has ever been seen!'

Ellie smiled. 'Calm down, Mr Wakefield. You're quite right. Dick Whittington encountered a Scratchling called Richard Durrent in 1397. He got into a spot of bother and needed help, just as we do now. It's nice to know they keep the Lord Mayors so well informed.'

The Mayor wiped the sleeve of his nightshirt across his brow. 'Scratchling Protocol 101. Oh, dear me!' he exclaimed, pushing back his sheets and climbing out of bed. He glanced towards the doors to his bedroom. 'Then you must be in grave and present danger?'

'We need to return to the cusp of time with some urgency, yes,' Ellie confirmed.

'And where is the cusp of time currently located?' he asked, reaching for his dressing gown.

'*Two* thousand and six*teen*, Your Lordship,' stated Eric from the shadows.

'Nooo, surely not!'

'Yes,' said Eric, 'and they're going to take me there, Your Lordship.'

'I can scarce believe it.'

'That makes two of us, Your Lordship.'

'If I remember correctly, I'll need my official baton of office,' said the Lord Mayor, glancing about as though it could be relied upon to be within arm's reach.

Ellie nodded. 'It's the only thing that can transform what's behind the door at street level.'

'Yes, yes, that's right. So it will open onto another realm, the one where the Ancient Order of Wall Scratchings is located,' said the Lord Mayor, growing increasingly excited about the duty that only one other Lord Mayor before him had ever had to perform – and *he* had been Dick Whittington, the most famous Lord Mayor of them all. He was determined to rise to the occasion.

The children followed the Lord Mayor out of his room, down a flight of stairs, across a corridor, and into the Lord Mayor's official robing room. Lit with electric lamps turned down low, the room was spacious and rectangular, with tall windows that let in the moonlight. At the far end of the room was the biggest mirror Ellie, Max and Eric had ever seen. In front of the mirror stood a tailor's dummy dressed in the official robes of the Lord Mayor of London. Upon its folded arms rested the official baton of office that would grant the Scratchlings access to the spectral realm beyond the outside door. The Lord Mayor hurried over and snatched it up rather unceremoniously. The Mayor was a heavy-set man and already out of breath when he spun about with the baton and ambled (with as much speed as he could muster) back towards the other end of the room without saying a word. Ellie, Max and Eric watched him. 'Either he's forgotten we're with him or he's lost his marbles,' murmured Max out of the corner of his mouth.

'I fail to see the difference,' whispered Ellie.

Max and Eric looked at her.

'Well, if he's forgotten we're with him, it could only mean he's lost his marbles.'

Max and Eric nodded in agreement. They watched the Lord Mayor huff and puff his way to the end of the expansive room. 'Come on,' said Ellie. 'That's a man on a mission if ever I've seen one.' They ran after him and emerged from the dressing room to see him hurrying as best he could towards a staircase. 'He's not in the best of shape. Maybe he thinks if he stops moving he won't be able to start again,' suggested Ellie as Wakefield descended the stairs and disappeared from view. They hurried down the stairs after the Lord Mayor, who was making an ungainly bee-line for the main entrance, where a security guard was stationed just inside the enormous doors. 'Who goes there?' demanded the guard.

'Never … never mind all that!' snapped the Lord Mayor, puffing and putting a hand to his chest. 'Just get these doors open. What's the *matter,* man? Close your mouth and open these doors this instant!'

'Yes, yes of course, My Lord Mayor.' He lifted a large bunch of keys from where it hung on his belt and singled out a key.

The guard opened the huge doors that led out to the grand frontage of Mansion House and stepped back to allow the Lord Mayor's passage. Only then did he notice the three children. 'And who might you be?' he asked.

'Never mind who *they* are,' growled the Lord Mayor. 'In fact, I order you to forget that you ever saw them! Do you understand me?' The guard nodded and stepped back into the shadows. 'You'd better have. Don't close this door; I'll be back presently.' The Lord Mayor hurried outside.

Ellie, Max and Eric huddled around him at the door at ground level. The Lord Mayor of London was still in his dressing gown and slippers, and clutched his baton feverishly. He wiped the sweat from his brow with his sleeve and racked his brain for the emergency words he'd been told to learn by heart. He cleared his throat nervously and glanced down at Ellie, who was standing on his left.

'Perhaps you'd like me to remind you of the words?' offered Ellie.

The Lord Mayor looked at her pleadingly. 'If you wouldn't mind. You see, in all the excitement …'

'Of course I wouldn't,' said Ellie, reaching up and patting him on the shoulder. 'Ready?'

The Lord Mayor wiped his brow again. 'As I'll ever be.'

Ellie spoke the following slowly and clearly: 'By the power vested in me as the incumbent Lord Mayor of London, I hereby sanction the use of Scratching Protocol 101 for the express and sole purpose of helping Scratchlings in peril.' His memory suitably refreshed, the Lord Mayor repeated these exact words. Then, at Ellie's direction, he knocked the tip of his baton against the old wooden door three times. The door began to glow a familiar ghostly green, at which point the Lord Mayor remembered a *very* important detail about the ground conveying those standing directly outside the door into another realm. Wide-eyed, he stumbled to its side.

'Thank you for your help,' said Ellie as the ground beneath her feet began to inch towards the glowing door.

'Yes, cheers, man!' said Max, stepping onto the conveyor belt.

'Thank you, Your Lordship!' said Eric, giving a little bow. The Mayor's mouth fell open, and whatever he wanted to say seemed to get stuck in his throat as Ellie, Max and Eric vanished through the door.

Twenty
The Return

On the other side of the door, the children found themselves pitched into darkness. 'Blimey. Have I gone blind?' Eric's voice exclaimed.

'Relax,' said Max, from somewhere near him. 'It's *supposed* to be dark here.'

Eric audibly swallowed the lump in his throat. 'Then how are we supposed to see in *two* thousand and six*teen*?'

'You're not *in* 2016 yet, Eric,' came Ellie's reassuring voice in the darkness. 'What you *can't* see is the path that leads to the Ancient Order of Wall Scratchings. A chap with a lamp and a bell called Marlot is supposed to come and meet us, but our movements must have been difficult to track of late.' Ellie fell silent. 'Did anyone else hear that?' she asked.

'It sounded like someone muttering in their sleep,' said Max.

'It came from over there to our left,' said Eric.

'You two wait here,' said Ellie. She walked with arms outstretched in the darkness, zombie-fashion, towards the source of the noise, until she bumped into someone lying on the ground. The someone woke up with a start and began to scrabble around for something. A moment later, a lamp glowed into life and Marlot blinked up at her. 'Saints preserve us! Is it really you, Ellie?' he said, scrambling to his feet.

'How's it going?' smiled Ellie.

'How's it going, she asks. Have you any idea how worried everyone's been?' said Marlot, picking up the lamp and holding it aloft to illuminate Max and Eric standing by the door.

Ellie turned towards her two companions. 'I have a fair idea, yes. You've already met Max,' she said, 'but allow me to introduce *Eric Kettle*.'

'I can scarce believe it!' cried Marlot, walking over and taking in every inch of the Victorian urchin.

Eric glanced down at himself. 'I'm not much to write home about, I know.'

'That's not it at *all,* dear lad!' laughed Marlot. 'I never imagined we'd meet. As I live and breathe, the Ninth Scratchling!'

'And as I live and breathe, London's town crier. Never thought to meet so many important people,' said Eric, visibly notching up another lucky star.

'It's kind of you to say so,' said Marlot. 'Although it's been many a long century since I performed that duty beyond this door. Come on now and follow me! Poor Caretaker Wiseman has hardly slept a wink since you left. The cusp of time may have been standing still, but it's dragged very slowly here. Do you know, Caretaker Wiseman has hardly left the Chamber of Scratchings in *days*. I expect we'll find him in there now, catching forty winks on his makeshift bed. He's been worrying himself sick about you.'

When they entered the Chamber of Scratchings, they discovered Caretaker Wiseman lying asleep on the small bunk bed below the Tree of Scratchings.

'This place ... it's *incredible*,' said Eric, not knowing where to look first: the humongous and enchanted-looking tree, or the countless burning candles hovering around the walls of the vast Chamber.

'Welcome home, Eric,' said Ellie loudly, in hopes of waking the sleeping man.

Caretaker Wiseman roused slowly, sat up, and pushed his thick glasses close to his eyes. 'Can it be *true*?' he said, climbing off the bunk.

'What? You doubted us that much?' joked Ellie, placing a hand on Eric's shoulder. 'May I introduce Eric Kettle?'

'The *Ninth Scratchling,* in person!' said Caretaker Wiseman, approaching the party with an outstretched hand. Max assumed the next victim of Caretaker Wiseman's over-enthusiastic handshake was to be Eric, but in truth he didn't mind at all when Caretaker Wiseman grabbed his hand first. 'Very well done, Max!'

'Really? But I ended up needing a rescue myself.'

'Never mind that!' said Caretaker Wiseman. 'You're a *fledgling!* Considering the danger you've faced, it's a *miracle* you played the part you did! Isn't it, Ellie?'

To Max's surprise, Ellie nudged him affectionately and said, 'Absolutely. A first-rate effort, considering. Just don't let it go to your head, Hastings.'

Caretaker Wiseman turned to Eric now. 'If only you knew how long I've waited to meet you, old man,' he said, looking emotional.

'Old man?' said Eric, glancing at Max and swallowing hard.

'Don't worry,' said Max. '*Old man* is a term of endearment. You haven't aged a hundred and seventy-five years or anything.'

'Well, of *course* it's a term of endearment,' said Caretaker Wiseman, extending his hand.

'Only wish I'd known about all this good will when I didn't seem to have any,' sighed Eric, taking Caretaker Wiseman's hand. Max was relieved to see Eric giving as good as he got during the hand-shaking assault.

'You're a good deal stronger than you look,' said Caretaker Wiseman, letting go of Eric's hand. 'And now we must get you upstairs, where the head of our esteemed organisation will be absolutely *thrilled* to meet you.' Caretaker Wiseman turned to Ellie. 'Mrs O will be keen to speak with you, too. She'll be expecting a *thorough* debriefing, Ellie.'

'What, *now*?' said Ellie. 'Can't it wait until tomorrow? That is standard procedure, after all.'

'Maybe, but there's been nothing standard about this mission, and the outcome is monumental: we finally have the edge on Those Who Leave Much to Be Desired! Exciting times. Exciting times indeed.' Caretaker Wiseman placed his arms about Ellie and Eric's shoulders and ushering them towards the lift. 'Max, Marlot will take you to your clothes, then I insist you go home and have a well-deserved rest. But we'll expect you back *first thing* tomorrow. Rest assured that it's still Saturday morning on the cusp of time.' He stopped to check his watch. '10.37am, to be precise.'

Eric stepped away from Caretaker Wiseman and walked back to Max. 'Thank you for coming to rescue me. And to think you didn't really know what you were doing! I would never have guessed.'

Max glanced at Ellie. 'You'd have done the same for me,' he said shyly.

Eric's big brown eyes lit up with excitement. 'Are you going to see your mother and father now?'

'Yes,' said Max, feeling a little guilty for having a family when Eric had none.

'I'm happy for you,' said Eric sincerely.

'Come on, Eric,' said Caretaker Wiseman quietly. 'Max is coming back tomorrow.'

'The Christmas holidays have just started, Eric, so I expect you'll be seeing a lot of me over the next couple of weeks.'

Twenty-one
Mrs O Will See You Now

Ellie, Eric and Caretaker Wiseman had been sitting and waiting outside Mrs O's office for several minutes when her secretary came out. 'Mrs O would like a word with you first, Caretaker Wiseman,' she said. 'Alone.'

'I won't be long,' said Caretaker Wiseman, standing up and following the secretary into Mrs O's office.

I bet you won't. It's not you she's champing at the bit to see, thought Ellie.

Eric took in the palatial surroundings of the ante-room they were in, and shifted nervously in his seat as he gazed into the busy Operations Rooms that joined it, and that telescoped as far as the eye could see into the distance. 'Mrs O must be *very* busy if she's in charge of all this, Ellie,' he murmured.

'Maybe, but you're the Ninth Scratchling. You're a bona fide celebrity around here, Eric. Mrs O will act like she's not impressed, like it's no big deal you're here, but it's an act. She just likes everyone to know she's the boss.'

'Blimey,' gulped Eric.

Ellie had been right, for no sooner had Caretaker Wiseman gone into Mrs O's office and the door closed, than it opened again and Caretaker Wiseman was being shown back out. 'Mrs O will see you now,' the secretary said to Eric. Eric looked at Ellie for some final words of advice.

'Just be yourself. She can hardly find fault.'

'Mrs O *is* waiting,' said the secretary curtly.

The secretary showed Eric into Mrs O's office and pulled the double doors closed behind him. Mrs O was reclining in her chair as though she hadn't a care in the world, reading a sheet of parchment in her hand. Eric trod slowly across her office towards her. When he reached the chair opposite her desk, Mrs O cleared her throat and said, without looking up from her parchment, 'My name is Mrs O. Please take a seat, Mr Kettle. I'll be with you in a moment.'

'Right you are, Mrs O. No hurry,' said Eric, lowering himself into the seat. He gazed in wonder out of the windows at the views of London from various times in history. When Eric's gaze found the view that showed the present day, his mouth fell open. 'What are *those*?' he marvelled, pointing at the cars whizzing along Westminster Bridge towards the Houses of Parliament.

Mrs O had no need to look behind her to see what he was gawping at. 'Those are motorcars, Mr Kettle,' she said, trying not to smile.

'Mo-tow-cars. Are they like moon rockets?'

'No. They're nothing like *moon rockets*. Please sit down, Mr Kettle. There'll be plenty of time to see motorcars later.'

'Sorry,' said Eric, who hadn't realised he'd stood up. He sat quickly back down.

Mrs O put the parchment down on the desk and sat up straight in her chair. She steepled the tips of her fingers against her chin and observed Eric intently. Eric didn't know where to look, and when his gaze found the motorcars again, Mrs O said, 'Look at me, please, Mr Kettle.'

Eric took a deep breath and looked across the desk at Mrs O. 'I know I'm supposed to be someone special, but in truth I've always been a bit of a disappointment.' He was surprised to see Mrs O shaking her head.

'You may be frail due to mistreatment at the hands of Those Who Leave Much to Be Desired, but I strongly suspect you have the heart and courage of a lion, Mr Kettle.'

'I don't know about *that*. But I do try and thank my lucky stars as often as I can.'

'I don't doubt it for a moment,' said Mrs O. 'Just as we here at the Ancient Order of Wall Scratchings are thanking our lucky stars that we were able to rescue you.'

'Where am I going to live, Mrs O?' said Eric quickly, asking the question that had occupied his mind the most.

Mrs O looked a little taken aback. 'You'll live here for the time being.'

'I'm not to be sent to live in an orphanage, then?'

'Rest assured, Mr Kettle, that your days of living in an orphanage are far behind you.'

'That's music to my ears. I know it's asking an awful lot, but … might you find me a foster family?'

'Is that what you'd like?'

'More than anything, but not if it's at the expense of some other boy or girl getting a family. I wouldn't want any special treatment, but if there's a list … I'm just saying I'd like to be on it.'

Twenty-two
Truth

During his bus ride home, Max had struggled to keep his eyes open. *It's been an eventful few days,* he thought as he shook himself awake for the third time.

Max forced himself to look out of the window. *Hope Eric's talk with Mrs O is going okay*, he thought. Max tried to put himself in Eric's shoes, arriving in a place and time where everyone you'd ever known died long ago. *Well, he knows Ellie and me. At least that's something. And to say he had a lousy life where he came from would be something of an understatement.*

'Something of an understatement,' muttered Max. It was a phrase he'd heard his father use many times. As in, "To say the youth of today is going to the dogs is something of an understatement." *I can't believe I just used a phrase,* any phrase, *my old man would use. I hope this extra responsibility isn't going to make me more mature*, thought Max.

Just as Ellie had said, time had indeed stood still while he had adventured back in time. Max arrived home ninety minutes after he'd left, and nothing had changed except him. The first thing he saw when he opened the front door was his mother decorating the Christmas tree in the living room.

'Oh, look what the cat's dragged in,' said Mrs Hastings, rummaging through a box of shiny decorations. 'I didn't expect to see you back so soon.'

Max slumped down into an armchair, formulating an excuse about not seeing the scratchings after all. But curiously, Mrs Hastings said nothing about it. Instead, she looked up from the box of decorations and gave him the once-over. 'What's the matter?' she asked.

Max shook his head unconvincingly, and then blinked away the moisture in his eyes.

'Max? Whatever's wrong?'

'Nothing,' said Max.

'Well, something's obviously upset you. Have you had a row with Ash?'

Max shook his head, then brightened a little. 'No. Which reminds me. There's this kid that Ash and I met recently, and ...'

'And what?' pressed Mrs Hastings.

'He's an orphan, Mum.'

'This is the first I've heard of him. What's his name?'

'Eric,' said Max, looking at his mother. 'He's a really great kid who ...'

'Who what?'

'Has no family of his own.'

'That's generally the case with orphans,' pointed out Mrs Hastings. 'So docs Eric live with a foster family?'

'No. He's between foster families, and ... and I was wondering if he might be able to come and stay with us over Christmas?'

'With *us*?'

'Yes, I don't think he's ever spent a single Christmas with a family or even had turkey or any presents. Not ever.'

'Oh, come now, Max. You make him sound like an urchin from a Charles Dickens novel.'

If only you knew.

Mrs Hastings sat cross-legged on the ground and rested her chin in her palms. 'Can this boy be trusted? Has he ever been in any trouble with the law?'

'No. Like I said, he's a great kid.'

'Well, but there must be procedures with these things, surely? It's not as though you can just *adopt* a boy for Christmas.'

'How about if I get the number of the orphanage and you ask their permission?'

'Orphanage? I don't think they're called that anymore, Max, but I tell you what: I'll have a word with your father and, if he agrees, I'll speak to the *orphanage*, okay? I can see you really care about this boy.'

'Thanks, Mum.'

'You're over-tired. Why don't you go and have a lie-down? I'll call you when your lunch is ready.'

'Thanks, Mum,' repeated Max, getting wearily out of the armchair.

'In the meantime, why don't you invite Eric over so we can meet him?'
'Alright. I know you'll like him.'

***

Back at the Ancient Order of Wall Scratchings, Ellie had been sitting outside Mrs O's office with Caretaker Wiseman, waiting for Eric to come out. Caretaker Wiseman had been talking nineteen to the dozen for the last couple of minutes about the mission they'd just returned from. Ellie had nodded from time to time, but she hadn't really been listening. She was mulling over a suspicion she'd had for some time about the true fate of Eric's parents, and now was the time to broach the subject. Ellie leaned forwards and looked up into Caretaker Wiseman's excited, chattering face.

'And to think you can verify the existence of a *Dark* Ghost Train and Galleon, and what's more ...' Caretaker Wiseman noticed the expression on Ellie's face and fell silent. 'Is there something on your mind, Ellie?'

Ellie nodded. 'Actually there is. It's about Eric's parents.' Ellie observed Caretaker Wiseman shifting nervously in his seat. 'What about Mr and Mrs Kettle?' he asked, raising an eyebrow.

'Well, it seems to me that they *didn't* just up and leave as Eric has always been told.'

Caretaker Wiseman cleared his throat. 'What on earth makes you say so?'

Ellie rolled her eyes. 'Because given all that's gone on, and knowing the League of Dark Scratchings as I do, the whole abandonment by his parents thing stinks to high heaven.'

'So what are you trying to say?'

'I'm not *trying* to say anything. I'm making a statement of fact: the League of Dark Scratchings *kidnapped* Mr and Mrs Kettle.'

'Ellie Swanson!'

'I'm right, then!'

Caretaker Wiseman shook his head. 'How on earth have you jumped to that conclusion?'

'You wouldn't have just *Ellie Swansoned* me otherwise.'

Caretaker Wiseman crossed one leg over the other and clasped his hands together on his knee. 'On no account are you to bring this up with Mrs O,' he said firmly.

No can do, I'm afraid.

At that moment, the door to Mrs O's office opened and Eric trotted out looking dazed. They had just enough time to exchange a glance before Mrs O stuck her head out of the door and said, 'Come in, Ellie.'

'Congratulations are in order,' said Mrs O as they sat down either side of her desk.

Ellie folded her arms. 'Just doing my job, Mrs O.'

'All the same, to find yourself in the same time frame as two Dark Scratchlings must have been ... challenging, to say the least.'

'I was more frightened for my wards than for myself. In a strange way, it's always helped to have others to worry about.'

'Spoken like a true Scratchling. You were in a unique position to observe your wards in the field. What did you make of them? Mr Hastings first.'

'Max ... well, let's just say he's a lot braver – not to mention cleverer – than he looks and acts. Although, given the way he looks and acts that wouldn't be difficult. I'm not saying there weren't times when he wasn't scared, but he actually dealt with it pretty well. Using humour, mostly.'

'You believe he'll make a good Scratchling, then?'

'Raw as he is, he's already a good Scratchling. Could be that being so raw worked in his favour.'

'How so?'

'It gave his Scratchling instincts a chance to develop in the field.'

'And Mr Kettle?'

'Eric? What can I say?' sighed Ellie. 'He's a lovely kid who always tries to see the best in people. His glass isn't so much half full as overflowing, despite what an awful life he's had.'

'A coping mechanism, you think?'

'He's not simple, Mrs O, so I don't see what else it could be.'

Mrs O nodded. 'How mentally strong would you say he is?'

'As strong as any of us.'

'And how did he and Max get on?'

Ellie smiled. 'I got the impression they bonded from the off. Eric's so frail that Max took him under his wing and, even though they're the same age, he looked after him like a younger brother. And as for Eric, he must have been thanking his lucky stars that he'd met someone who genuinely cared about what happens to him. I'd say they bring out the best in each another.'

'Excellent. Now, I believe you have interesting news regarding the Ghost Train?'

Ellie's gaze fell to the desk and she looked thoughtful.

'Well?' pushed Mrs O, struggling to hide the excitement in her voice. 'There has only ever been a handful of confirmed sightings, but you had far more than that. You actually went *on board*?'

'Yes. And I'll tell you all about it in my report. There's something else I wanted to ask you about,' said Ellie, still looking down at the desk.

Mrs O folded her arms, mirroring Ellie's body language. 'What is it you want to know, Miss Swanson?'

Ellie's gaze moved across the desk and rose to fix on Mrs O's face. 'It's about what really happened to Eric's parents.' The moment the question was voiced, Mrs O darted a glance at a painting on the wall over Ellie's right shoulder. Trying not to smile, Ellie thought, *So behind that painting is where your safe is hidden, and unless my Scratchling intuition is very much mistaken, it's where I'll discover the truth about what really happened to Mr and Mrs Kettle.*

'Regarding Mr and Mrs Kettle, you know as much as I do, Miss Swanson,' said Mrs O dismissively.

'Oh, yeah. That his father went off to seek his "fortune"? And then his mother went off to seek *him*?'

'A sad tale, but a true one.'

'Really? So it's just a coincidence that their son's the Ninth Scratchling, then?'

Mrs O shook her head seriously. 'I'd like you to drop this subject right away, Miss Swanson.'

'I can't. My Scratchling intuition's been on overdrive about it *for days*, and …'

Mrs O narrowed her eyes. 'And what, Miss Swanson?'

Ellie placed her arms onto the arm rests of her chair, and met Mrs O's steely gaze with her own. 'And the League of Dark Scratchings found a way to kidnap Mr and Mrs Kettle, didn't they?'

Mrs O rolled her eyes. 'Why would they want to kidnap Eric's parents?'

'So they could use them to blackmail Eric if they'd caught us, perhaps?'

'You must drop this immediately, Miss Swanson,' said Mrs O, tapping her foot impatiently.

Ellie leaned forward in her chair, undeterred. 'But what I can't understand is this: if they *were* able to send Dark Scratchlings back to *that* place and time, why settle for kidnapping Eric's parents? Why not take baby Eric?'

Mrs O stood up, turned her back on Ellie, folded her arms and looked out of the window. 'You always did remind me of a bloodhound, once you get a whiff of something.' She sighed ruefully. 'I suppose it's part of what makes you such a good Scratchling. The truth of the matter is, they *weren't* able to send Dark Scratchlings. As you're well aware, that would be impossible without a scratching becoming active, and opening a route to that place and time. But they *were* able to send a Black Puddle.'

Ellie jumped up. 'Of *course*,' she murmured.

Mrs O nodded and turned back to face her. 'They materialised one outside the Kettles' front door. Mr Kettle stepped, or rather *fell*, into it and "disappeared." Later that day, Mrs Kettle followed in his footsteps. Literally. The League of Dark Scratchings doubtless hoped that one of them would be holding baby Eric when they did so. We can thank our lucky stars that neither of them were.'

'So where are Eric's parents now?'

'Now *that* information *is* classified, Miss Swanson,' said Mrs O, darting another look at the painting. 'And you're not to breathe a word of this to anyone. Do you understand me? No good can come from Mr Kettle knowing what really happened to his parents. To the contrary, it would only serve to make things personal and cloud his judgment.'

Twenty-three
Initiation

The following morning, a famished Max shovelled cereal into his mouth as though he expected someone to snatch the bowl away. Mr Hastings regarded him over the top of his newspaper. 'Anybody would think our son only gets fed once a week,' he observed wryly.

Mrs Hastings picked up her mug of tea and took a thoughtful sip. 'He's had a *serious* appetite since he came home yesterday.'

Mr Hastings returned his attention to his newspaper. 'I gather we're to meet a new friend of yours, Max,' he said, scanning the page and finding nothing of interest.

'Yes, that's right. His name's Eric.' Max poured more cereal into his bowl.

Mr Hastings folded his newspaper and placed it on the table. 'I'm not so sure about him staying with us over Christmas. You can't know much about this boy, and don't forget we have your baby sister to consider. I doubt Maxine would like to have a stranger around on her first Christmas.' At the mention of her name, Maxine threw her Snow White spoon in the general direction of Mr Hastings as if to say "I'd rather you didn't speak for me, thank you very much!"

Max stopped eating, put down his spoon and looked suddenly deflated.

'I don't think we should make up our minds until we've met the boy,' said Mrs Hastings.

'Thanks, Mum,' said Max, standing up. 'I know Maxine will like him.'

'What makes you think that?' said Mr Hastings, reaching down to pick up the blue and white spoon.

Max lifted his puffer jacket off the back of the chair and slid into it. 'She's a good judge of character, Dad.'

'So where are you off to now?' asked Mrs Hastings.

'Nowhere much. In fact, I'll be back before you know it.'

On his way to the bus stop that would take him back to Mansion House, Max knocked on Ash's door, assuming his friend would be curious about how the mission went. Max realised this was something of an understatement when the door opened and Ash jumped out, then pulled it closed behind him. 'You're alive!' he said, looking him up and down. 'When did you get back?'

'Yesterday.'

'Yesterday! You're kidding. Why didn't you stop by on your way home?'

'I was beat. Never been so tired in my life.'

'So? What happened?'

'Take a walk with me to the bus stop and I'll tell you all about it.'

'So? Did you save that Eric Kettle kid?' asked Ash as they set off.

'Yes.'

'How?'

'For starters, you wouldn't *believe* what the school was like. We're talking *Resident Hatred* here.'

Ash looked suitably impressed. 'We couldn't even *buy* that game.'

'Tell me about it, and I was inside a place just like it trying to rescue Eric.'

'So where'd you find him?'

'Chained to a wall in a haunted kitchen.'

'*Haunted*? Really?' Ash sounded doubtful.

'Yes. By the ghost of a cook. On Maxine's life. She had this massive meat cleaver called Big Bertha.'

'She tried to chop you up with it?'

'No. She helped us out with it.'

'You and Eric?'

'And Ellie.'

Ash stopped walking. 'I think I know what's coming next.'

Max shrugged, then pulled his friend back into step. 'There were these two psychos called Mr Whip and Mr Lash. They captured Eric and me in this haunted maze, and chained us *both* up in the haunted kitchen. If the Ancient Order of Wall Scratchings hadn't found a way to send Ellie to help us out, we'd have been caught by the dark side and brainwashed to join them.'

'How come?'

'The bad guys sent a couple *Dark* Scratchlings to get us. You should have seen them, Ash.'

'Scary?'

'*Resident Hatred* scary.'

'Hope I never do see them, then.'

'It's unlikely. I don't think they're able to access the here and now. Anyway, thanks to Ellie we escaped to York.'

'And?'

'And from there we travelled back to London with the Dark Scratchlings after us. Not just them. The League of Dark Scratchings had agents all over.'

'So how'd you get away?'

'We disguised ourselves and caught a train.'

'What were you disguised as?'

'A grieving widow and her daughter.'

Ash stopped walking again and looked at Max. 'Which one were you?'

'I was half of the grieving widow.'

'Which half?'

'Bottom.'

Ash nodded as though all this now made perfect sense, and then walked on. 'So, what's Eric like?'

'He's like the complete opposite to you. A really nice kid.'

'Thanks.'

'You know what I mean.'

'Actually, I don't.'

'He's incredibly optimistic. I mean, he thanks his lucky stars all the time. Even when things look completely desperate.'

'He's a bit simple, then?'

'Not at all. He's had such a hard time. He would probably have given up long ago it if he didn't at least *imagine* things were better than they were. I've asked Mum and Dad if he can come and stay with us over Christmas.'

'And they were okay with that?'

'They want to meet him first, but Eric's the kind of kid people really like.'

'The opposite to me, then.'

'Yep,' said Max, smiling fondly at his friend.

'So you're headed back to Mansion House now?'

'Affirmative. I think they just want to talk to me about what happened during the mission,' said Max as they reached the bus stop and his bus pulled up.

'Good to have you back,' said Ash as Max climbed on board.

'It's good to be back,' smiled Max as he disappeared inside.

***

When Max approached the street-level door at Mansion House, the ground started to shudder and the invisible conveyor belt moved him towards it without him having to do a thing.

On the other side of the door, Max came face to face with Marlot, his big round craggy face grinning like the Cheshire Cat's. Annoyingly, despite Marlot's smile and the barely contained bounce in his usual loping stride, he remained tight-lipped about the reason for his excitement as they made their way down the tunnel towards the Chamber of Scratchings. It occurred to Max that Marlot might have been sworn to a vow of silence to prevent him giving the game away. *But what game?* thought Max.

The giant wooden doors that led through to the Chamber of Scratchings creaked open upon their approach and, as Max drew nearer, he realised the Chamber was barely recognisable: wooden stands had been erected from floor to darkened ceiling, obscuring the candles and wall scratchings completely. The stands were crammed with people in purple robes and floppy silver hats, who craned their necks for a glimpse of someone who Max presumed must be behind him. Max looked back over his shoulder to see who it could be.

'It's you they're here to see,' murmured Marlot out of the corner of his mouth.

'Me? Why?'

'I've said quite enough,' said Marlot.

Caretaker Wiseman stepped into view, his beige suit just visible beneath a black robe and his happy, round face beaming from under a floppy silver hat. He beckoned to someone on his left-hand side, and Eric trotted forward into view and stood beside him. Eric was wearing an emerald-green cloak and a floppy green hat pulled down over his right eyebrow. He looked nervous, but when he spotted Max a smile broke out on his face and he shrugged as if to say, "Just *look* at these fancy threads they've got me in, Max." Caretaker Wiseman gestured to his right and an attendant stepped into view with a green robe and hat draped over his arm.

As they entered the Chamber, the attendant unfurled the green cloak with a flourish and gestured for Max to turn so he could secure it about his neck. Max turned, and the man placed the triangular green hat on his head, pulling it down at an angle so that it rested on his right eyebrow. All this time the spectators, which must have numbered in their hundreds, had watched the proceedings raptly. Caretaker Wiseman reached out and brought Max and Eric together. He leaned forward and whispered, 'In case you haven't realised, this is your Initiation Ceremony. You're about to be formally sworn in as Scratchlings.'

Max and Eric glanced at one another, wide-eyed, as if to say "what a responsibility!" 'Does this mean the League of Dark Scratchings will no longer be able to brainwash us to their side?' asked Eric.

'Yes,' said Caretaker Wiseman. 'And what's more, you'll officially be Scratchlings – those who fight to keep the malevolent intentions of Those Who Leave Much to Be Desired in check.'

'But who are all these people?' whispered Max.

'They're employees of the Ancient Order of Wall Scratchings,' explained Caretaker Wiseman, looking about the Chamber with pride. 'Every single person in this Chamber has sworn an oath.'

'To do what?' said Eric.

'To take a stand against Those Who Leave Much to Be Desired, and above all else to assist you and your fellow Scratchlings in this goal.'

Max gazed around the Chamber in awe. His eyes soon met those of Ellie, who raised a hand in greeting and smiled sweetly.

She's up to something, thought Max.

'In case you're wondering, I'll be conducting today's ceremony, so there's nothing to worry about,' said Caretaker Wiseman. 'We've been swearing Scratchlings in since the time of King Arthur, but that's a story for another time. Follow me.' Caretaker Wiseman turned on his heels and walked towards the Tree of Scratchings in the centre of the Chamber.

As he followed on behind with Eric, Max noticed an empty space either side of Ellie. He picked up his pace, drew level with Caretaker Wiseman and asked, 'Are those empty spaces next to Ellie for the other two Scratchlings? Now that we've rescued Eric, there are *five* of us, right?'

'Yes, that's right,' said Caretaker Wiseman. 'They would have liked to be here, but they're yet to return from their missions.'

A round wooden table had been placed before the Tree of Scratchings. As Caretaker Wiseman went on ahead and made his way around to its other side, Max whispered to Eric, 'This table wasn't here before.'

'It looks so *old*,' remarked Eric.

'That's because it *is* old,' said Caretaker Wiseman, tracing a finger across its gnarled surface.

Max and Eric leaned forward to look more closely, and realised that hundreds of names had been scratched into it. 'Kids in peril?' asked Max, glancing up at Caretaker Wiseman.

Caretaker Wiseman shook his head. 'I should think we have enough of those on the walls of this Chamber. *These* scratchings,' he continued grandly, his chest inflated with pride, 'are, for want of a better word, the *autographs* of all the Scratchlings who came before you. The table once belonged to Merlin.'

Max's mouth fell open. 'The *wizard*?'

'Yes,' confirmed Caretaker Wiseman with a deep nod. 'He made it himself from wood taken from the Tree of Scratchings – a tree, I might add, that he planted himself.'

'Are you saying that this is *the* Round Table?' said a breathless Eric.

Caretaker Wiseman shook his head. 'No. That table needed to be large enough to comfortably seat *twelve* burly knights around it.'

'This one only looks big enough to seat about six,' mused Max.

'Very good, Max,' said Caretaker Wiseman. 'Our table is *exactly* half the circumference of the Round Table of legend. Merlin made it at the same time. He had what is documented as "an experiment in mind." That experiment was to become the Ancient Order of Wall Scratchings, and the work we do here.'

'That's pretty cool,' chuckled Max.

'It's a lot more than just *cold*,' said an astonished Eric. 'Back at the orphanage the story of the Knights of the Round Table was one we knew by heart. This one is *really* like its little brother?'

'Yes, Eric,' said Caretaker Wiseman, smiling at Eric's reaction.

Eric reached out a hand. 'Is it alright if I … I mean, can I touch it?'

'Of *course* it's alright. In a few moments, I shall be asking you to scratch your name into it.'

'Blimey!' said Eric.

Max opened his mouth to say "cool" again, but thought better of it. There was a small commotion to their left, and the crowd parted to let a man through. He was carrying a wooden staff, which he placed carefully on the table before backing respectfully away.

'What's *that* for?' asked Max.

'This,' said Caretaker Wiseman reverently, picking the staff up off the table, 'was Merlin's staff.' He held the gnarled and brittle-looking staff in his left hand and then very carefully pulled what looked like a large splinter out of its side with his right hand. He held the pencil-sized splinter aloft and sighed in appreciation.

Max swallowed hard. The splinter looked sharp. 'What … ah, what are you going to do with that?'

'Me? Nothing. This is the Initiation Splinter. It's what every Scratchling has used to scratch their names into our Round Table since time immemorial. And now it's your turn.' Caretaker Wiseman reached across the table and placed the Initiation Splinter down in front of Max. 'Go ahead, Max. Pick it up.'

Max glanced to his right, where Ellie smiled at him reassuringly. He picked up the Initiation Splinter carefully. 'Where should I sign?'

'In any space of your choosing.'

'Alright,' said Max, leaning over the table.

'However!' said Caretaker Wiseman suddenly, startling him.

'*Yes*?'

'Choose your spot *wisely*.'

Max took a moment to examine the different areas of the table, before drawing a deep breath and scratching his name into it. Once he'd finished, he stood up straight and surveyed his own signature, which he'd placed below and to the left of Ellie's. 'Is that okay?'

'Yes, of course,' said Caretaker Wiseman with growing excitement. 'And now it's Eric's turn.'

As Max handed Eric the Initiation Splinter, he noticed that Ellie was gone. Max's instincts told him not to look around or draw any attention to this fact. 'Anywhere I like?' asked Eric. Caretaker Wiseman nodded, and Eric scratched his name below and to the right of Ellie's, creating a triangle of their names.

Once he'd finished, Mrs O stepped silently up behind them and looked over their shoulders, murmuring this question under her breath, '*The Scratchling Trinity?*' No sooner had Mrs O made her observation than a gust of wind whipped up inside the Chamber, a swirling breeze that carried on it the whispered cries for help on the walls about them. Max and Eric looked up at Caretaker Wiseman, whose broad grin put them instantly at ease. Caretaker Wiseman motioned down to the table where the signatures of past Scratchling-born seeped a green mist that swirled clockwise around the table before disappearing inside the names that Max and Eric had just carved. The audience rose swiftly to their feet and clapped thunderously as Max and Eric marshalled their courage and gazed around the Chamber.

***

Upstairs, Ellie was sprinting through room after empty Operations Room towards Mrs O's office. When she reached the doors, she turned the handle and shouldered her way inside. She approached the painting she suspected hid the safe she wanted to crack. It was a copy of *The Laughing Cavalier* by Frans Hals. Ellie stood on tiptoes and ran her hands down behind its sides. Midway down, she felt a catch on its left-hand side. She released the catch and the painting opened on a hinge to reveal a safe. Ellie blew nervously on her hands as she took in the safe's three dials. 'Piece of cake,' she murmured, pressing her ear to the safe's door and turning the first dial: clockwise, clockwise, anti-clockwise, clockwise, anti-clockwise ...

Ellie held her breath as she slowly gave the first dial a final clockwise turn, until she heard a *click!* She set to work on the second dial in similar fashion, and once she'd cracked all three dials she pulled the heavy metal door open. Ellie grabbed the contents, a stack of fifty or more files, and placed them on the floor, where she began scanning the titles on their covers. *Current intelligence on Dark Scratchlings* was followed by a file marked *17th century: Operations Rooms Report,* and then one marked *League of Dark Scratchings – Immediate Goals.*

'It has to be here somewhere ... bingo!' said Ellie, picking up a file marked *Kettle Family.* Ellie snapped the file open and scanned the document inside for the information she was after: *the fate,* she thought, *(and fingers and toes crossed) the current whereabouts of Eric's parents.* She scanned the first page, which gave general information about the mission to rescue Eric. 'Don't need to read this. I was *there,*' she muttered, turning the pages feverishly. When her hungry gaze at last found the information she was after, she didn't know whether to cry or punch the air with joy. *Eric's parents are alive! Imprisoned inside the League of Dark Scratchings's fortress.* Ellie twisted herself around and sat with her back to the wall. 'So near and yet so … so dangerously far,' she murmured, with her hands clutched in her hair.

***

Meanwhile, back in the Chamber of Scratchings, the Initiation Ceremony had concluded. The employees were returning upstairs to their Operations Rooms, and Marlot was seizing a rare chance to speak to Mrs O and complaining about the growing cheekiness of the Sniffing Darkness. Caretaker Wiseman was carefully placing the Initiation Splinter back inside the staff when Max sidled up to him. 'I've asked Mum if Eric can come and stay with us over Christmas,' he said.

Caretaker Wiseman looked over at Eric, who was still gazing with rapt attention at the Round Table. 'I see,' he said, 'and what did your mother say?'

'That she'd like to meet him first.'

'And what did you tell her about Eric's predicament?'

'Not much, obviously. Just that he was an orphan who's never spent a Christmas with a family.'

'And?' pressed Caretaker Wiseman.

'And that's it. What else could I tell her?'

Caretaker Wiseman cleared his throat. 'Asking your mother if Eric can stay for Christmas was a very kind gesture, Max, a very kind gesture indeed.'

Max seized the moment. 'Does that mean he can come home with me now and meet her?'

'Oh, I don't see why not. It's not as though he's a prisoner here,' said Caretaker Wiseman, throwing a glance at Mrs O, who'd just managed to escape from Marlot.

Max watched him carefully. 'Do you need to square it with Mrs O first?'

'No. I think it will do Eric the world of good to get out for a bit. And if there's a chance your parents will let him stay with you over Christmas, all the better. I'll have a word with Mrs O later. In the meantime, you will take the very best care of him, won't you, Max? After all, the 21st century is going to come as quite a shock.'

'He'll be fine. Trust me.'

'I do trust you. You're a Scratchling, after all.'

'We *both* are,' said Max, looking happily at his friend, who was now studying them both curiously. Max felt a growing excitement at the prospect of giving Eric his first taste of the modern world.

Max could see Marlot chatting to some men dismantling the stands, while at the Chamber's entrance, the glow from Marlot's lamp shone just beyond the doors. As Max took these things in, Caretaker Wiseman seemed to read his mind. 'A lamp to ward off the Sniffing Darkness appears to be ready and waiting for you and Eric. And you know what they say about the present, don't you, Max?'

'No. What do they say about it?' murmured Max absently.

'That there's no time like it, you spoon,' said Caretaker Wiseman good-naturedly.

'You don't think Marlot will mind if we borrow his lamp and make our way back to the door without him, then?'

'Not at all. He has a dozen of the things – more lamps than bells, in fact. Which is an oddity for a town crier. Go on,' said Caretaker Wiseman, 'but have Eric back here before dark.'

'Sure thing.' Max took a step towards Eric, but paused and looked up at Caretaker Wiseman.

'Something on your mind?' asked Caretaker Wiseman.

'It's about the Sniffing Darkness … what *is* it, exactly?'

'It frightens you?'

Max nodded.

Caretaker Wiseman chuckled. 'Once upon a time you would have been right to be absolutely terrified of it.'

'But not now?'

'Of course not now. The Sniffing Darkness has been on our side and very loyal, I might add, for close on five millennia.'

'It was evil once, though, wasn't it?'

'Yes, Max. Your Scratchling intuition is correct. It was originally a part of *the* Darkness.'

'*The* Darkness,' repeated Max with a shudder.

'There's no need to get into all that now. All you need to know is that a falling-out occurred between, for want of a better word, the Sniffing Darkness and its father, and so destructive was their argument that it did the one thing it knew would punish its father the most: it switched allegiance to us.'

'But how can the Ancient Order trust it?'

'The records strongly suggest they didn't think they could.'

'So what made them change their minds?'

'Such was the Sniffing Darkness's grievance against its father that it agreed to have its memory and motivations wiped clean, and new ones inserted. In short, it agreed to be reborn as part of the Ancient Order of Wall Scratchings. It's been a loyal servant ever since. Now go on, borrow Marlot's lamp and take Eric home to meet your family.' Satisfied, Max nodded and approached his friend.

'Is everything alright?' asked Eric, searching Max's face for clues.

'Better than alright. Now come on! Before Caretaker Wiseman changes his mind.'

'About what?' asked Eric, hurrying after Max towards the Chamber's exit.

'About your visiting the cusp of time *right now*.'

'You mean I'm actually going to visit *two* thousand and six*teen!*'

'No. You're going to visit 2016. No need for emphasis on the *two* or the *teen*. People will think you're weird if you keep saying it like that, and if there's one thing you need to know about 2016, it's that everybody likes to be just like everybody else.'

Eric stayed close to Max as they made to their way through the tunnel, the light from Marlot's lamp in a constant battle to keep the Sniffing Darkness at bay. 'It's alive, isn't it?' said Eric uneasily.

'Your guess is as good as mine. Just try and ignore it.'

'It's so … *curious,*' observed Eric.

'That's its job. If we weren't supposed to be in here, it would drag us away, apparently.'

'And do what to us?'

'Kill us, apparently.'

When they reached the door that led back out to the cusp of time, Max put down the lamp. He looked at Eric and then down at himself. 'We need to ditch the initiation robes,' he frowned, taking off his own and placing them on the ground beside the door. Eric did the same, revealing the clothes the Order had given him: a pair of black jeans and a chunky black sweater. 'Nice threads,' said Max.

'Thanks. They've been so generous to me, Max.'

'You are the Ninth Scratchling. Now brace yourself.'

'What for?'

'Two thousand and sixteen,' said Max, reaching for the door's handle.

Twenty-four
Mr and Mrs Kettle

Since Ellie had discovered the whereabouts of Eric's parents, she'd been in a tailspin of fury. 'The sheer, unmitigated, downright injustice of it!' she said to herself as she placed the documents back in the safe and slammed the door. 'To take Eric's mum and dad away from him when he was just a baby!' she raged, spinning the dials and slamming the picture closed. *To think they're imprisoned just a few hundred metres from here! Locked up in some stinking dungeon, wondering what's become of their son,* stewed Ellie as she left Mrs O's office.

In the distance, people were spilling out of stairwells on their way back to work. 'Oh, fiddlesticks,' murmured Ellie, darting to her left and flattening herself against the wall. She drew a deep breath, resolving to hide in plain sight. *If anyone dares to ask me what I'm doing up here, I'll just tell them I need to discuss something important with Mrs O,* she thought, just as Mrs O walked into view and spotted her.

'Miss Swanson?' she said, looking past Ellie at her closed office doors. 'What are you doing up here?'

Ellie folded her arms. 'I was looking for you. What else would I be doing up here?'

'I don't appreciate your tone, young lady.'

'I'm still furious.'

'Yes, I can see that. But furious about what?'

'About what happened to Eric's parents.'

'An unfortunate business, but one we are powerless to do anything about.'

'Really? Isn't it in our remit to put unfortunate business right?'

Mrs O brushed lint off her wide lapel, avoiding Ellie's eyes. 'It's too late to right *that* wrong. What's done is done, and we don't even know where they're holding Mr and Mrs Kettle.'

Liar, thought Ellie bitterly.

'And anyway,' Mrs O went on, 'even if we did know, any rescue attempt would be much too risky.'

Ellie raised an eyebrow.

'As you are fully aware, we aren't equipped to go up against the League of Dark Scratchings directly – which is exactly why we fight them *indirectly*. Don't look at me like that, Miss Swanson. After your recent encounter with Dark Scratchlings, you of all people should be aware that it's in our best interests to avoid them at all costs.'

'Well,' said Ellie, who was keen to get away now. 'If that's absolutely your final word on the matter, then I won't take up any more of your valuable time.'

Ellie went to walk past Mrs O, who grasped her shoulder. 'I sincerely hope you're not thinking of doing anything stupid regarding Mr Kettle's parents.'

'How could I? I don't even know where they are.' Ellie and Mrs O exchanged a raised eyebrow, and then parted.

Ellie wasted no time, making a beeline for Professor Kenneth Payne's study. She knocked on the door and entered the cosy little room without waiting for a reply. One large window looked out on a live view of Tower Bridge in April 1942, the height of the Second World War, which was Professor Payne's particular passion. His office was decorated with memorabilia from the period: gas masks, tin helmets and a wind-up gramophone were amongst the rare and valuable artefacts. Professor Payne was hunched over his desk, engrossed in a file, but he closed it quickly when he saw his visitor. 'Come in and sit down, Ellie,' he said, waving a hand at the chair on the other side of the desk.

'You were reading about the mission I just came back from?'

'That's right, I was. And what an *extraordinary* mission! Max did remarkably well considering. Do you know we had less than an hour together?'

'He certainly surprised me, that's for sure.'

Professor Payne leaned back in his chair and steepled his fingers. 'Well, he did get caught.'

'I should think so too, after an hour's training and prep. The important thing is that he and Eric are good listeners, and keep a clear head under pressure.'

'Excellent news! And thoroughly fleshed out in your report,' said Professor Payne, drumming his fingers on it for emphasis.

Ellie changed the subject to the reason she was there. 'Eric Kettle's parents ...' she began, sitting back in her chair and observing Professor

Payne's initial reaction. But Professor Payne gave no reaction. He didn't even blink. *Oh, he's good*, thought Ellie. *But I suppose he did teach me almost everything I know.*

The Professor folded his arms and smiled as he turned the tables on her. 'You know, don't you, Ellie?'

'You'll need to be more specific, Professor.'

'You know that Mr and Mrs Kettle are being held captive at the League of Dark Scratchings.'

'If I didn't, I do now.'

'You knew alright. My educated guess would be that you cracked Mrs O's safe,' he chuckled. 'The best lock-picking pupil I ever had the pleasure to teach. Now, breaking into Mrs O's safe would normally be considered a very serious breach of protocol, so if not for the fact that ...'

Ellie's heart skipped a beat. 'If not for what fact?'

'The fact that your heart was in the right place. But the fact is, you *can't* rescue Mr and Mrs Kettle, not from the League of Dark Scratchings's fortress. You of all people must know that, Ellie.'

'But you taught me yourself: there is *always* a way.'

'Their fortress is obviously the exception to that rule.'

'But *why*?'

Professor Payne's old bones creaked as he pushed himself out of his chair. He turned and closed the shutters on his window, and then went over to a framed picture hanging on the wall behind Ellie. It was a painting of Mansion House, and of the Bank of England, just across the thoroughfare. Ellie stood up and joined Professor Payne in front of it. 'Would you mind turning off the lights?' asked Professor Payne.

Ellie reached obligingly for the light switch beside the door and the room was plunged into darkness. The painting now glowed with a ghostly green hue, and it no longer depicted Mansion House and the Bank of England. It now depicted the secret establishments that were located in the same locations: the Ancient Order of Wall Scratchings and the League of Dark Scratchings. Both were revealed as vast and terrifying fortresses. The Ancient Order of Wall Scratchings was a circular fortress with a wide black moat filled with the Sniffing Darkness, while the League of Dark Scratchings looked like a fortress inhabited by vampires: semi-circular and impenetrable, its moat filled with crocodiles the size of coaches. 'The League of Dark Scratchings really *is* impregnable,' said Professor Payne, with awe in his voice.

Ellie opened her mouth to disagree, then closed it again.

Professor Payne placed a hand on his chin. 'You think I haven't thought about breaching it?' he mused. 'Gaining access to their fortress has been like a chess move I've been contemplating for over fifty years.'

'You're no slouch, Professor. So you must have thought of *something* in all that time? A first move for breaching those walls?'

'I appreciate the vote of confidence,' said Professor Payne with a smile.

'Well?'

'The walls? Never. There is only one possible first move, but even that move is impossible.'

'You might as well share it with me, then.'

Professor Payne nodded and hovered a finger over the sky above the fortress. 'The roof is the only conceivable access point, but as you know, their fortress has many turrets and all are manned twenty-four hours a day. Anyone attempting to land on the roof would be blown to bits long before they made it down. A person would need to be invisible, but not only that: they would need a silent and invisible craft capable of flight. No such craft exists.'

Ellie wasn't normally one to thank her lucky stars, but she thanked them now: *I knew there was a reason why I didn't mention that Edward Smith left us his lifeboat. Mrs O would never agree to what I have in mind,* she thought.

'And even if you could somehow arrive on the roof undetected,' Professor Payne continued in hushed and chilling tones, '*that* would only be the start of your troubles.'

'Where do you suppose they keep their prisoners?' asked Ellie, thinking aloud.

'My guess would be in the caverns under the fortress, and they are simply *enormous*.'

'They would need to be if *they're* down there somewhere,' said Ellie with a shudder. She was not referring to Mr and Mrs Kettle.

'Oh, *they're* down there, all right – *both* of them – and kept under lock and key for all our sakes. We can only hope that poor Mr and Mrs Kettle are kept well away from them,' said Professor Payne mysteriously.

When Max opened the door that led out to 2016, bright sunlight flooded through. They stepped through the door and raised a hand to shield their eyes from the sun's glare. Max squinted down at Eric, who blinked rapidly, trying to get his first glimpse of the future.

'It's so noisy, Max! Are those … mo-tow-cars?' gasped Eric, making a sudden dash for the road.

Max ran forward and grabbed his friend by the shoulders. 'Hold up! Where are you going?' Eric's feet were mere inches from the kerb.

'To get a better look at the mo-tow-cars. I saw them through the window in Mrs O's office but … just *look* at them, Max!'

'I've seen them before,' said Max, smiling at Eric's enthusiasm.

'But *look* at their colours! And see how quick they are!'

A man in a pinstriped suit had arrived on the kerb beside Eric, just in time to catch the tail-end of their conversation. He raised an eyebrow at Eric, and then looked at Max. 'He was brought up by wolves in the rainforest,' said Max, by way of a plausible explanation. The man shook his head, disbelieving, then took advantage of a break in the traffic to dart across the road.

'Where's he going?' asked Eric, watching the man disappear down the steps into Bank underground station.

'To catch a Tube,' said Max.

'A tube of *what*?'

'It's a train that runs under the ground. It's no big deal.'

'Blimey! Sounds like a very big deal. Can we catch one too?'

Max shook his head. 'We haven't got enough money for that. We'll have to make do with catching a bus.'

Eric nodded sagely. He knew all about buses. 'Horse-drawn omnibus?'

Max did a double-take. 'No. No horses. *Those* buses.' He pointed a finger at three red double-decker buses that had just turned the corner into view.

'Oh! Look at the *size* of 'em! Do they always go about in packs like that?'

'Yep. But only when they're all the same number.'

'Number … 23,' announced Eric, squinting to make out the number on the front of the first bus. 'Is that our bus?'

'Afraid not. Our bus stop is this way,' said Max, heading off along the pavement.

Once they were installed at the appropriate bus stop, their bus pulled up almost immediately. Having paid the driver, Max led Eric up the winding staircase to the top deck, where they took seats right at the front. 'You get some view of the mo-tow-cars from up here!' gushed Eric.

Max threw a glance over his shoulder at the mother and teenage daughter sitting behind them. 'They're just *cars*, man, not *mo-tow-cars*,' he whispered.

'Kaarrrs,' repeated Eric.

'*Cars*. Say the word quicker.'

'Cars.'

'There you go.'

'Cars.'

Max turned back to the mother and daughter again. 'It's okay. He's not dangerous. He just doesn't get out much.'

'This is my first time!' added Eric excitedly.

The teenage girl rolled her eyes, while her mother looked with horror at the gaunt, malnourished boy with a swelling on his cheek. As the bus pulled away with a pronounced lurch, Eric leaned forward and gripped the handrail. 'It's going so *fast!*' he said breathlessly, feeling as though he'd left his stomach back at the stop. After stopping briefly for traffic, the bus picked up speed, at which point Eric burst into a fit of giggles just as he'd done when he'd observed the Unwanted enjoying their pork pie back at St Bart's. 'Are we *flying* again, Max?' he shrieked.

Max shook his head. '*Shhh!* No, we're not, but that is,' he said, pointing up through the window at a plane leaving a vapour trail across the sky.

'Is that … the *Ghost Ship?*' whispered Eric, craning his neck for a better view.

'No. It's just a plane.'

'What's a *plane*?'

'Again. It's no big deal. It's basically a bus with wings.'

'A bus with *wings*,' murmured Eric. 'How is that *no big deal*? Where does it go?'

'Planes go everywhere. All over the world.'

The mother and daughter got up and went down the stairs. At this point it seemed to dawn on Eric that he shared the deck with other passengers. He got up, sat on the rail, and looked at the people behind them, many of whom had their heads down looking at the glowing screens of their mobile phones.

'What are you *doing*?' hissed Max.

'Me? Nothing. What are *they* doing?'

Max looked over his shoulder. 'Relax, they're just checking their phones.'

'They look hypnotised. Do their *phones* control them?'

'It's supposed to be the other way around. But you might have a point.'

'What do phones do?'

'Everything. Pretty much.'

'Why's that lady beating hers with her thumbs?'

'She's probably sending a message.'

'To who, Max?'

'To someone else with thumbs.'

Eric nodded. 'Have you got a phone?'

'No. Mum said I can have one when I'm thirteen.'

Eric sat back down. 'Blimey. What about a car?'

'What about a car?'

'Have you got one of those?'

Max shook his head.

'Why not?'

'I'm twelve. You wanna take a break with the questions already? You're starting to give me a headache,' smiled Max.

Eric sighed and then settled back in his seat to count his lucky stars.

Twenty-six
Mission Impossible

Ellie was standing in her own bedroom, looking down at the all-in-one ninja-style outfit she was wearing. She stuffed a black balaclava into a holdall that already contained a length of coiled black rope. Ellie's mother was still at work when she slung the bag over her shoulder and opened the front door.

When she reached the front gate, she turned back towards the little semi-detached house. *I know you wouldn't approve of what I'm going to do, Mum, she thought. But then again, you wouldn't approve of anything I've been doing for the last couple of years. If I didn't think I was ready for this, I wouldn't risk it. If you met Eric, I think you'd understand. If there's a chance he can be reunited with his family, then it's got to be a chance worth taking. And I'm the only one who can take it.* She squared her shoulders and walked through the gate, closing it behind her.

The phantom lifeboat that Ellie needed was on the roof of Mansion House, where they'd left it in 1840. It was invisible and untouchable to everyone but herself, Max, and Eric, so Ellie felt confident that it would have lain undisturbed for the last 101 years. And now she hoped to retrieve it from atop the battlements of the Ancient Order of Wall Scratchings in the spectral realm.

Once through the door at Mansion House, she made her way down the passageway carrying a lantern she'd hidden earlier, and then squeezed silently through the partially open doors into the Chamber of Scratchings. The Tree of Scratchings was being tended to by a dozen white-coated tree surgeons. Ellie moved silently through the Chamber towards the lift on its left-hand side. Once inside the lift, she moved a dial to the *xxx* position, and then breathed a sigh of relief as the doors hissed shut. She shouldered her holdall and grasped the handrail as the lift jerked upwards and then shot left, before finally moving up towards the circular battlements at the top of the Ancient Order of Wall Scratchings.

The lift doors opened onto a view of the trench that ran along the area of the battlements and looked across to the League of Dark Scratchings. The trench was manned by a company of soldiers, but as well as these,

Ellie had the searching gaze of thirty lookouts in thirty lookout towers to dodge. Fortunately, the soldiers were standing to attention and looking outwards from the battlements. *The lifeboat has got to still be up here*, thought Ellie as she crept out of the lift.

Ellie crouched low and surveyed the wide-open space. It was a dark night, moonless and starless, with the only light coming from torches that burned brightly around the circumference of the battlements. 'Bingo,' murmured Ellie as she squinted into the red and orange glow. The lifeboat was forty metres away, close to the edge of the roof and midway between two watchtowers. It had to be the exact location where they'd left it on the roof of Mansion House back in 1915.

Ellie pulled the black balaclava out of her bag and slid it down over her head. She slung the holdall over her shoulder, lay on her stomach, and crawled commando-style towards the lifeboat. Midway there, she paused and glanced up at the soldiers in their stone watchtowers. *Thank goodness they're all still facing the way they're supposed to be facing: outwards,* she thought as she started to crawl again.

When Ellie reached the lifeboat, she clambered up on her knees and took hold of it. It felt light as a feather as she pulled it towards her. Ellie glanced up at the two watchtowers a stone's throw away either side of her; she could just about make out the silhouettes of the tin-helmeted soldiers who were standing to attention inside them. 'It's now or never,' she murmured as she pushed the lifeboat close to the side of the battlements – a two-metre-high wall with indents like missing teeth. She lifted the lifeboat up and over the edge, then climbed up and pushed it down below the lip of the wall. She took another quick look at the men in the watchtowers, dropped down into the lifeboat, and crouched low as it bobbed up and down in mid-air.

Ellie sat on the middle seat, picked up the oars and moved the lifeboat away from the side of the fortress. With the oars in her grasp, the lifeboat seemed to read her thoughts and dip forwards, allowing her to row straight down into the darkness. Within seconds she could make out the canopy of the prehistoric forest that surrounded both fortresses. She skimmed the tops of the trees until she felt a safe distance from the prying eyes of lookouts, and then began to climb up and away from the forest into the night's sky. Up and up she rowed, until the mammoth torches on the top of the Ancient Order of Wall Scratchings looked no bigger than matches. Satisfied that she was high enough, Ellie pulled sharply on one oar and turned the boat back to face her destination: the League of Dark Scratchings.

Sitting in a boat that no one else could see, dressed from head to toe in black, Ellie was all but invisible against the starless night. 'If only Professor Payne could see me now. Just as well he can't,' she murmured as she tipped the front of the boat gently down towards the sprawling fortress that she intended to infiltrate.

Fifty metres directly above it, Ellie levelled the boat and peeked over its edge. Below her, she could make out the gliding forms of at least two dozen lookouts as they patrolled the battlements in pairs. The fortress had a gothic tower in each corner, and one that rose up from its centre. This central tower was topped with a spire. Ellie positioned the lifeboat twenty metres above the spire, opened her holdall and took out the black rope. She tied one end of the rope around the bench she'd been sitting on and tossed the rest over the side. It unfurled beautifully, coming to rest centimetres above the spire. Ellie climbed over the edge of the lifeboat, took hold of the rope and began to slide down it. The boat held miraculously fast in the air where she had left it, anchoring her descent.

She climbed off the bottom of the rope onto the spire, wrapped her legs round it, and slid smoothly down onto the tower's roof. From here she was able to climb down onto a ledge that ran around the outside of the tower, crouch down, and lower herself over the edge where, hanging by her fingertips, she swung forwards and dropped down onto the tower's uppermost lookout platform. *Unmanned. A definite oversight,* thought Ellie as she looked up at an enormous bell nestled in the rafters. 'Whatever you do, don't ring,' she muttered as she made her way to a hatch in the centre of the platform. She opened the hatch, which opened down onto a rickety wooden staircase that disappeared into darkness.

So far so good, thought Ellie as she tiptoed down the stairs. In total darkness, she placed a hand on the wooden hand rail and guided herself down to the next landing, and then the next, where her straining ears caught the faint sound of clattering coming from below. The noise grew louder and more urgent, as though the wooden steps were being hurriedly dismantled by someone or something. *Whatever it is, it's coming this way!* she thought, turning on her heels and clambering back up the stairs two at a time. She paused suddenly, puzzled by a new sensation, then felt a nuzzling all over her body, as though a pack of hungry bloodhounds was sniffing at her. Ellie's eyes opened wide and she stumbled, losing her footing and crashing down upon the stairs. She spun about onto her back, wide-eyed and panting, and stared into the darkness. 'The Sniffing Darkness? What are *you* doing here?' she hissed in a loud whisper.

'The question is,' the Darkness whispered in her ear, 'what are you doing here, *Scratchling-born*?'

Ellie gasped as something began pinching her all over, as though hundreds of clothes pegs were being attached to her body. 'You're not the same Darkness … are you?' she whispered as the staircase fell away below her.

'*How astute you are*,' replied the Darkness, holding her up and then dragging her away into the black void.

Twenty-seven
Orphan

'So this is where you live? It's a *really* nice home!' exclaimed Eric as they walked up the Hastings' driveway towards the pretty little semi-detached with a lovingly maintained lawn and window boxes.

'Thanks. Now tell me again what it is you're not to do?'

'I'm not to overreact to things.'

'What things?' pressed Max.

'Any things.'

'Correct.'

They discovered Mrs Hastings in the kitchen, unloading the dishwasher.

'Hi, Mum,' called Max, crossing his fingers behind his back. 'This is Eric, the kid I've been telling you about.'

Mrs Hastings turned around with a clean mug in each hand and gazed at Eric. 'Well, hello, young man!' she said brightly, overcompensating for the shock of seeing a twelve-year-old so small and fragile that he looked no more than nine.

'It's an honour to meet you, Mrs Hastings,' said Eric, walking over and extending a hand.

Mrs Hastings swallowed a lump in her throat and put the mugs down on the counter with a clatter. 'And you,' she said, shaking his hand gently. 'Max has told me so much about you.'

'I don't suppose that took him very long. What are you doing, Mrs Hastings?' asked Eric, peering inquisitively inside the half-full dishwasher.

'Erm ... emptying the dishwasher?' she said, scratching her temple.

Sensing Eric's next question, Max stepped forward quickly. 'It's a machine that cleans the dishes,' he said out of the corner of his mouth.

'Is it really? Oh, that's *very* clever!' said Eric, bending to look closely at the dials.

'Haven't you ever *seen* a dishwasher, Eric?' asked Mrs Hastings.

Eric glanced at Max, remembering what he was not to do. 'I suppose I must have.'

'Anyway,' said Max, hurrying to change the subject, 'we'll leave you to it and sit in the front room.'

'Alright. You're staying for lunch, I hope, Eric?' asked Mrs Hastings.

'Don't mind if I do, Mrs Hastings!'

'So what do you fancy?'

Eric shrugged and gazed around the modern kitchen.

'How about a full English?' asked Mrs Hastings, watching him carefully.

'What's in it?' asked Eric, now narrowing his eyes at the toaster.

'Sausages, eggs and bacon. How … ah, how does that sound, Eric?'

'Sausages? *Really?*' breathed Eric, remembering the ones that Augustus Mann had scoffed in front of all his pupils.

'A full English sounds great, Mum,' said Max, grabbing Eric's arm and hauling him towards the kitchen door.

The two boys sat down side by side on the sofa. Max picked up the remote, then thought better of switching on the TV and put it back down again. 'How did I do?' asked Eric, eye-balling the remote.

'Considering the obvious excitement of seeing your first dishwasher, you did okay.'

'I always have been a bit too curious for my own good. Been told as much,' mused Eric as Mrs Hastings came into the room.

'Where's Maxine?' asked Max.

'Taking a nap upstairs,' said Mrs Hastings, settling into an armchair next to Eric. 'Why don't you go upstairs and check on her, Max?'

'What, *now*?' said Max, glancing back and forth between his mother and Eric.

Mrs Hastings narrowed her eyes. 'Now seems as good a time as any, Max.'

'Alright. You'd better come and meet Maxine, Eric,' said Max, standing up and glaring at his friend.

'No. You stay *exactly* where you are, Eric. Maxine is probably fast asleep, and you look very comfortable,' said Mrs Hastings, smiling at him.

Max drew a deep breath. 'I'll be right back,' he said, heading for the hall.

'So,' said Mrs Hastings as Max's footsteps ascended the stairs, 'Max tells me you're twelve?'

'That's right.'

'And that you're an orphan?'

168

'That's also correct.'

'Don't they feed you at the home, Eric?' said Mrs Hasting, laughing nervously.

'They feed us alright.' Eric's roaming gaze fastened on the 50-inch TV. He opened his mouth to ask what it was, then closed it again.

'Have … ah, haven't you been very well?' pressed Mrs Hastings like a dog with a bone.

'Why d'you ask?' asked Eric, picking up the remote control and holding it awkwardly in his closed fist.

'Well,' said Mrs Hastings, 'you're quite pale. Don't they treat you very well at the orphanage? Has someone struck your face?'

Eric waved the remote around in front of his eyes. 'No, I fell. They treat me just fine. They even taught me how to read and write.'

'Well, *that* was very nice of them.'

Eric recognised the sarcasm in her voice and met her gaze. 'They didn't have to.'

'I suppose not. After all, that's what school's for.'

Eric shook his head. 'You could have fooled me. I've spent a few days at a school. Can't say I thought very much of it.'

'A few *days*?' said Mrs Hastings, appalled.

'What's this? The Spanish Inquisition?' said Max loudly, hurrying back into the room and sitting back down beside Eric. 'How about that full English, Mum? We're both starved. Maxine's still asleep.'

Mrs Hastings eased herself up out of the armchair. 'Did you that know Eric has only spent a few days at school, Max?'

Max nodded. 'He's on one of those rubbish government schemes for the disadvantaged.'

'What schemes?'

'The ones that Dad always moans about. Dad said the government is always cutting their funding so they can give billionaires tax cuts. That's why Eric's never been to a proper school. You must have heard Dad go on about it, Mum?'

Mrs Hastings looked down at the two expectant young faces gazing up at her. 'I suppose so,' she murmured.

'Sounds very clever, your father. Is he here?' asked Eric.

'No. He's at work,' said Max, wrestling the TV remote away from him.

'What does he do?' asked Eric, giving it up with a sigh.

'Civil servant. Works for the government at the airport. Something to do with customs.'

'What's an airport?' asked Eric.

Max looked up at his mother. 'He's joking, Mum,' he said, rolling his eyes. 'He likes to do the whole little-orphan-lost act.'

'Right, then,' said Mrs Hastings, sounding a little dazed. 'I'll go and put the sausages on.'

All in all, Max was pleased with the way lunch went. Eric made a considerable effort not to show his boundless curiosity over everyday objects and, although his mother clearly found him a little unusual, it was obvious she'd taken a shine to him. There had been *one* unfortunate incident during lunch: the baby monitor on the bureau behind Eric burst into life with Maxine's crying. Eric had leapt out of his seat and asked how Maxine had got herself stuck inside such a small box. *Apart from that, it went better than expected*, thought Max as he and Eric said their goodbyes and made their way down the drive.

'Oh, hold up!' said Max, stopping in his tracks. 'I forgot to ask Mum something. I'll be right back.' He hurried up the drive and into the house. He stuck his head inside the kitchen, where his mother was loading the dishwasher. 'So? Can he?'

'Come and stay for Christmas, you mean?'

'Yes, what else?'

'I don't see why not. He's a lovely boy. A little … unusual, perhaps, but …'

'Thanks, Mum! I'll confirm it with Caretaker Wiseman before I tell Eric the good news.'

'Caretaker Wiseman?'

'Oh … he's the guy at Eric's orphanage who makes these decisions,' said Max, thinking fast. And with that, before his mother could enquire any further, he was out of the front door.

***

Back at Mansion House, Max and Eric found the lamp still burning just inside the door where they'd left it. Caretaker Wiseman they found alone in the Chamber of Scratchings – or rather, they found his feet sticking out from under the Round Table. 'Everything okay?' asked Max, looking down at Caretaker Wiseman's brown shoes.

'I'll be with you in two shakes of a lamb's tail, Max.'

'What are you doing?' asked Eric.

'Conducting a thorough examination of the underside of the table. Considering its age, it's remarkably well preserved,' replied Caretaker Wiseman, sliding out from under it. He stood up, pressed his thick glasses closer to his eyes, glanced around the Chamber and asked, 'Is Ellie with you?'

'No, we haven't seen her since yesterday,' said Max.

'You're looking very happy with yourself, Eric! You must have enjoyed your first visit to the 21st century.'

'Yes, very much. Max took me to his house. I met his mother,' he beamed.

'Did you now?' said Caretaker Wiseman, shooting a knowing look at Max.

'Mum *really* liked him,' Max assured him.

'Did she?' said Eric in surprise.

'Yes, she did,' said Max warmly, winking at Caretaker Wiseman.

'I didn't doubt that for a moment,' said Caretaker Wiseman. 'So, Eric, how would you like to spend Christmas with the Hastings family?'

Eric looked back and forth between Caretaker Wiseman and Max, eyes glistening. 'Are you pulling my leg?'

'No, really. I asked Mum and she said you're very welcome to stay,' said Max.

A smile spread across Eric's face, and he started to tap dance in a circle.

'That's settled, then,' said Caretaker Wiseman, pushing up the knot of his brown tie decisively. 'And in the meantime, I have some good news of my own.'

'What's that?' asked Max, watching Eric doing a rather impressive soft-shoe shuffle.

'Well, I've been granted permission to venture out onto the cusp of time to give you both a guided tour.'

'Of what?' asked Eric, still dancing.

'Of one or two *very* interesting places with strong connections to the Ancient Order of Wall Scratchings,' said Caretaker Wiseman, with the kind of enthusiasm that reminded Max of Eric.

'I get the impression you don't get out much?' said Max.

'You're not wrong about that!' said Caretaker Wiseman. 'Not to the cusp of time, anyway.'

'And why's that?' asked Eric, dancing to a stop.

'Why? Because as far as people who live on the cusp of time go, the Ancient Order of Wall Scratchings is not so much a *secret* society but one that doesn't exist – which is why we like to keep a low profile.'

'Really? And what about the prize I won? Mum and Dad, *and* my teachers, have all heard of this place.'

Caretaker Wiseman took off his glasses and wiped them with his pocket handkerchief. 'And you'll find all those people will have forgotten they ever heard the name of the Ancient Order of Wall Scratchings,' he said, sliding his glasses back onto his nose.

'Even Mum and Dad?'

'*Especially* them.'

'And if I reminded them?'

'They'd think you'd jolly well lost your marbles.'

Max folded his arms. 'Hold up. What about Ash? I know for a *fact* he hasn't forgotten about this place.'

'Ash is your one permitted confidant on the outside, remember.'

'Oh, yeah, that's right.'

'Right, then!' Caretaker Wiseman clasped his hands together. 'Eric could do with some sleep now, but we'll expect you back here for our guided tour *first thing* tomorrow morning, Max.'

Twenty-eight
The Tour

It was bright and sunny the next morning when Max climbed off the bus outside Mansion House. Max was surprised to see Caretaker Wiseman already standing outside, rather conspicuously, with Eric. Even though there wasn't a cloud in the sky, Caretaker Wiseman was wearing a beige raincoat over his beige suit. He stood at the edge of the pavement with his back to the road, enthusing about some detail on the triangular pediment above Mansion House's six impressive columns. 'And here he is now!' he announced Max joined them.

'Look up there,' Caretaker Wiseman said to Max. 'Do you see that figure in the centre of the pediment?'

Max squinted up gamely, but it was really a bit too high to make out much. 'Uh-huh …'

'That's a carving of the enemies of the City of London being trampled into dust by a giant,' said Eric.

'That'll teach 'em,' said Max.

Eric nodded. 'Later on, Caretaker Wiseman is going to take us to see a couple of *real* giants – and very important giants too, by all accounts.'

'Not only important, but to this day very *dangerous*,' said Caretaker Wiseman, clapping Eric on his narrow shoulders. 'But first I thought I'd take advantage of this rare outing to visit my favourite place in the world: the Tower of London.'

'The Tower's still standing, then?' asked Eric.

'Of course it is, you daft ha'porth,' chuckled Caretaker Wiseman.

'*What* did he just call you, Eric?' said Max.

'A daft half-penny,' replied Eric.

'Oh, right. Because that makes *so* much more sense.'

Caretaker Wiseman pushed his glasses closer to his eyes, the better to see the number on the front of an approaching bus. 'The Tower of London's been standing for over a thousand years, Eric, and it will be standing for many thousands of years more. And unless I'm very much mistaken, this is our bus.'

Following an uneventful ten-minute journey, they climbed off the bus at Tower Hill. They looked across the main road towards the Tower of London: an ancient castle with its own moat and drawbridge. 'Come on,' said Caretaker Wiseman, taking advantage of a sudden break in the traffic to cross the road. 'Some of the most famous wall scratchings in history are carved into walls at the Tower. We're not talking about identical facsimiles like those in the Chamber of Scratchings,' he went on as they reached the other side of the road, 'but *original* scratchings left by prisoners for over a thousand years.'

'Which explains your fascination with the place,' said Max.

'Well, it *is* fascinating, don't you think?' said Caretaker Wiseman, his voice rising an octave in his excitement. He took off at a pace towards the ticket office beside the drawbridge.

Max and Eric hurried to keep up with him, and when they were almost level, Max observed, 'I suppose my life has got a lot more exciting now there are wall scratchings in it – and that's not something I thought I'd ever hear myself say when I won that *free membership*.'

'I didn't have much of a life at all before scratchings came along,' said Eric ruefully.

'Came *along*?' exclaimed Caretaker Wiseman over his shoulder. 'Oh, come now. They didn't *come along* in your case, Eric. You scratched your own one into a wall! A cry for help.'

'And it worked,' smiled Eric.

'So why *did* you scratch that cry for help into that wall? What made you think it might work?' Max asked.

'I'd heard about the legend at the orphanage, and it wasn't like I had anything to lose.'

'What legend?'

'The legend of the Princes in the Tower, of course,' said Eric, then he stopped suddenly in his tracks. He raised a finger and pointed towards the castle. 'Hey, isn't *this* the place where the Princes were imprisoned?'

'Finally, the penny drops!' clapped Caretaker Wiseman. 'Although, in truth, the legend had many other names before it got that one.'

'Those poor Princes,' said Eric, shaking his head sorrowfully. 'As I heard it, they were our age when their evil uncle locked them up here, Max.'

'Yes, that's right,' nodded Caretaker Wiseman. 'Their uncle Richard could only become King once his nephews were *out of the way,* if you

174

'catch my drift.'

'So are you taking us to see *their* wall scratching? Their cry for help?' asked Eric.

Caretaker Wiseman shook his head. 'Actually, no. That's the tragic thing about the Princes in the Tower.'

'What's the tragic thing?'

'Well, they never actually carved any wall scratchings. But being the most famous child captives in history, and given that they seemed to vanish off the face of the earth, an urban myth grew around them – a myth that connected them to us.'

'So what really happened to the Princes, then?'

They'd reached the ticket office, where Caretaker Wiseman shrugged and felt for his wallet inside his jacket. 'They were murdered by their evil uncle Richard, presumably.' Caretaker Wiseman pulled out his wallet, extracted a fistful of notes, and pushed them under the counter. 'Three tickets, please. One adult and two children.'

The woman in the booth stared down at the notes. 'Is this some kind of a joke? One-pound notes went out of circulation in the 1980s.'

'They *did*?'

'Yes. They *did*,' said the woman bad-temperedly, shoving them back under the window.

Caretaker Wiseman opened his wallet again. 'I take it five-pound notes are still legal tender?' he asked, pulling some out and shoving them under the counter.

'Yes, we still accept *these*,' said the woman. After she'd checked all the watermarks thoroughly, she handed Caretaker Wiseman his change and tickets.

They crossed the drawbridge and passed under a spiked and fearsome-looking portcullis. A group of tourists were congregated around a guide who was recounting the grislier details of the torture that went on inside the Bloody Tower, a high, circular turret with its own torture chamber.

'Sounds horrible,' said Max, earwigging. 'So we're going inside the Bloody Tower, I take it?'

'Not at all. We're headed straight for the Salt Tower, which, if memory serves me correctly, is just a little further along this lane on the left.'

They followed Caretaker Wiseman into the Salt Tower, and up a twisting stone staircase into a cell near its top. The cell was circular, with slits cut into its metre-thick stone walls. A few tourists were milling about in the large space, and a museum guard was sitting on a chair and scribbling in a diary.

'Weren't those slits in the walls for shooting arrows through?' mused Max.

'Yes, quite right,' replied Caretaker Wiseman, pushing his glasses close to his eyes and gazing hungrily about the cell.

'So why'd they give prisoners bows and arrows? It seems a bit lax as far as security goes.'

'As I live and breathe, another daft ha'porth!' smiled Caretaker Wiseman.

Max flushed. 'I fail to see the daft halfpenny-ness in that question. It's a cell for prisoners, with slits to shoot arrows through.'

'But it wasn't always a cell,' said Caretaker Wiseman. 'When they built it in the 13th century, it was a defensive tower at the outer ring of the castle. It only became a cell later. There it is!' He clutched Max in excitement. 'The scratching we've come to see.' He approached the wall and knelt down as though he were going to tie a shoelace. Max and Eric stood over him and looked down at the large carving he was examining. It showed a complex pattern of circles and lines. 'That's right. Come closer. It was carved by Hew Draper. Hew Draper was accused of sorcery in 1560 and locked up in here. Now, it's popularly believed to be a carving of a Zodiac wheel, and that it charts the movement of the stars, but the truth is *far* more interesting.' Caretaker Wiseman lowered his voice to a whisper. 'Hew Draper was the permitted friend of a 16th-century Scratchling called Jonathon Oak, and just as Ash was allowed to accompany you on your first visit to the Ancient Order of Wall Scratchings, Hew Draper accompanied Jonathon Oak to *his*. So you see, what we have here isn't a Zodiac chart, as many believe, but a top-down drawing of the Chamber of Scratchings. By all accounts, Hew Draper didn't heed the advice he was given about telling no one about what he'd seen – the truth is, he couldn't *stop* talking about it. That's why they imagined him involved in sorcery and locked him up in here.'

'Wow. That's pretty intense. Ash isn't going to end up here, is he?' asked Max, smiling despite himself.

'I take it you're joking,' murmured Caretaker Wiseman as he took out a magnifying glass and studied the scratching.

'I'll take that as a no, then,' sighed Max.

'So where is it?' asked Eric, kneeling down and examining the wall around Hew Draper's carving.

'Where is what?'

'Hew Draper's cry for help? If his best friend was a Scratchling, then he *must* have carved one.'

'That's the thing about Hew Draper.' Caretaker Wiseman moved his magnifying glass closer to the wall.

'What's the thing?'

'He was a bit dim. He never scratched a cry for help.'

'A *bit* dim?' marvelled Max, but he quickly forgot Hew Draper's stupidity when he noticed something moving out of the corner of his eye. He turned his head, swallowed hard, and then murmured, '*The Princes in the Tower!*'

'Yes, that's right,' said Caretaker Wiseman absently, still focused on the wall. 'The Princes didn't scratch a message for help either, but they could be excused as they lived very closeted lives. It's doubtful they ever heard about the legend.'

'Of *themselves?*' chuckled Eric, who was still crouched beside Caretaker Wiseman.

'As I said, the legend had a different name at that time.'

'Eric,' said Max, still rooted to the spot.

'Yes?' answered Eric, standing up. He turned and saw the forms of two boys. Both were dressed in fine clothes of ermine and silk, and the taller boy wore a lopsided crown upon a head of bushy golden hair. One moment the boys were solid as though present in the cell, and the next as transparent as glass. The Princes flickered from one state to the other – solid to transparent, transparent to solid – like faulty light bulbs. They were staring open-mouthed at Max and Eric, in much the same manner that Max and Eric were staring at them. Thinking how silly he must look, Max snapped his mouth closed and scanned the faces of the other people in the room, but it was obvious that none of them could see the otherworldly visitors. As though he'd read Max's mind, Eric whispered, 'Other people can only see these strange things when you, me and Ellie are together.'

'It's a good thing she didn't come along, then,' mumbled Max.

'Whatever are you two muttering about?' said Caretaker Wiseman. He stood up and turned around, whereupon he yelped, clasped a hand to his mouth and glanced at the guard on his chair. The man just looked calmly up from his diary, turned a page, and gazed back down at it again.

'I take it you're seeing what we're seeing, then?' Max murmured out of the corner of his mouth.

'Yes! And what a treat!' screeched Caretaker Wiseman excitably.

'Alright. Try and keep it down, man!' hissed Max. 'Ideally we'd like them to *close* their mouths, not open them wider.'

'Who are you and what are you doing here?' asked the older Prince suddenly.

'You can *see* us, Your Highness?' asked Caretaker Wiseman, bending forwards for a better look. If any of their fellow tourists had paid attention, they would have seen him looking from one spot where there was nothing to another spot where there was nothing.

'Of course we can see you. We're not blind. Now answer my question: who are you and what business have you here?' asked the twelve-year-old Prince again.

'*Astonishing*. My name is Peter Wiseman, and my two companions are Max Hastings and Eric Kettle. Max and Eric, allow me to introduce their Royal Highnesses, Edward the fifth of England, and his younger brother Richard of Shrewsbury.' Eric bowed and Max said, 'It's nice to meet you.' Caretaker Wiseman motioned to the wall behind him. 'We're here to see the wall scratchings, Your Highness.'

The younger Prince looked Caretaker Wiseman up and down. 'Why do you wear such strange clothes?' he enquired imperiously.

'We got them in France where they're all the fashion, Your Highness,' replied Caretaker Wiseman.

'And what news, if any, have you of our Uncle Richard? Why does he keep us locked up here? Why does he not come to visit us?' asked Prince Edward.

'He keeps you here for your own protection,' said Caretaker Wiseman, doing his best not to frighten the young Princes.

'That's not what you told us just now,' said Max unthinkingly. 'You basically said they're in terrible danger.'

Caretaker Wiseman smiled awkwardly. 'A quiet word please, Max,' he said, ushering him towards the cell's thick wooden door. At the door he whispered urgently, 'It's important that we don't tell them of their ghastly fate. It will only make their final weeks terrifying. It's quite astonishing,

Max. They're *alive,* and it's doubtless only due to the presence of you and Eric together that we're able to share the same space five hundred years apart!'

Max scratched furiously at his temple. 'Perhaps … perhaps our meeting them means they don't have to be murdered after all, then.'

Caretaker Wiseman glanced at the Princes, who had turned their backs on Eric and were watching them curiously. 'What do you mean, Max?'

'Who's being a daft ha'porth now?' smiled Max. 'If they're still alive we can help them survive, and I'm not leaving here without telling them about it.' Max looked over at Eric, who was smiling as though he'd read his mind.

'What are you going to do?' asked Caretaker Wiseman, as Max stepped towards the two Princes.

'Only what's right.' Max stood before the young royals, who clearly sensed their visitor had something important to tell them. 'The truth is,' said Max, looking down at his puffer jacket, 'these clothes aren't fashionable in France. I doubt if *these* clothes are fashionable anywhere. They only look strange to you because we're from the *future.*'

'The *future*?' said the elder Prince.

'Look,' said Max, showing the Princes his digital watch. He pressed a button on its side and *10.47* appeared in green neon.

'What kind of magic *is* this?' asked Prince Edward, curling a protective arm around his younger brother.

'It's not magic; it's just how people tell the time in the future.'

Prince Edward stared at the watch and flinched when the time changed to 10.48. 'If … if what you say is true, and you hail from the future, then you must know of our fate?'

'Absolutely. I know all about what your Uncle Richard is going to do.'

'Then tell us.'

'He plans to make you "disappear" so that he can get his grubby hands on the throne. Isn't that right, Caretaker Wiseman?'

Caretaker Wiseman nodded sadly.

Prince Edward straightened his back stoically at this news, and pulled his little brother closer to him.

'But there's a way you can both escape,' said Max hastily.

'How?' asked Prince Richard.

Max motioned to the scratchings on the wall behind them. 'By scratching a message into the wall of your cell.'

'Yes,' said Eric eagerly. 'A cry for help. I did, Your Highnesses. And Max came and rescued me.'

'Why? Are *you* a prince?' asked Prince Richard.

'Clearly not, Your Highness,' said Eric, reddening.

Prince Edward turned and stepped towards the wall. 'But what should our message say?'

'It doesn't matter, just so long as it comes from the heart, Your Highness,' said Caretaker Wiseman quietly from behind them. 'It should be your intention to do *good*, and help make the world a more tolerant or enlightened place. If not, you may find yourselves rescued by creatures who will assist you in becoming the very *worst* of people. As opposed to the very best.'

Prince Edward straightened his back. 'We will heed your warning well.'

'Yes,' agreed his younger brother. 'What did you write in your message?' he asked Eric.

'Well, Your Highness, I said I was in grave danger and that if anyone was out there could they please help me. That's all.'

'Shall we do the same this evening after lights out, big brother?' The younger Prince looked up at his older brother with hope written clearly across his pale face.

Prince Edward took his hand and smiled down at him. 'Indeed we shall, brother of mine, indeed we shall.'

Twenty-nine
Sorrow

'All's well that ends well for the Princes in the Tower, then,' said Max happily, once they were back on the bus and heading back into the City of London.

Caretaker Wiseman took off his glasses, breathed on the lenses and began to clean them with his handkerchief. 'It may be that Mrs O will take a dim view of what we just did,' he said.

'I don't see why she should!' said Max. 'According to what Ellie said, the only reason we could talk to those Princes is because Eric and I were together in the same room.'

'And if *Ellie* had been there,' Eric chipped in, 'then everyone in that cell would have seen and heard them. Just as they could see and hear good old Mrs Booth back at the school.'

Caretaker Wiseman put his glasses back on. 'It's more than that. Scratchlings have *never* been able to see spirits on the cusp of time before, let alone talk to them. That's what makes what happened so astonishing.'

'So maybe we were meant to meet the Princes today so that we could help them survive,' said Max.

'I'm inclined to agree,' said Caretaker Wiseman thoughtfully. 'Which is why I backed down when you seemed so adamant about following your Scratchling intuition.'

'Are you going back to tell Mrs O about it now?' asked Eric apprehensively.

'Not before we've popped into Guildhall. There's something I've been looking forward to seeing, and it's something *all* Scratchlings need to know about. Just in case.'

'The giants?' Eric rubbed his palms together with glee.

Caretaker Wiseman looked out of the window and nodded.

Ten minutes later they were walking across an expansive forecourt towards Guildhall, a medieval building dating back to the 13th century. 'It looks more like a fairytale palace than a hall,' said Max.

'Are the giants inside it?' asked Eric.

'Yes, in a manner of speaking they are. What's more, the forecourt that we're crossing is built on the site of the old Roman Amphitheatre. Two thousand years ago gladiators fought and died on this very spot, and there would have been stands overlooking this area where spectators would have cheered them to their deaths.'

'I thought all that went on in Rome,' said Max, puzzled.

'The Romans built amphitheatres in most of the places they conquered, to entertain the troops and remind them of home.'

Eric tugged Max's arm.

'What is it?' asked Max.

'My turn to spot a spook,' said Eric, looking to their right.

Max followed Eric's gaze and saw a ghostly gladiator practising lunges with a sword. He was thirty metres away and close to the front of a museum allowing access to Roman excavations underground. A group of businessmen walked towards and then straight through the gladiator without batting an eyelid. Max turned to Caretaker Wiseman, who was standing with his glasses pressed close to his eyes. 'Well, well. It's *certainly* not dull coming out with you two, is it? Gee whiz, as I live and breathe, a *gladiator*!'

The gladiator stopped his lunges and shook his head as yet more grey-suited businessmen strolled right through him. Once they'd gone, he began practising again. Mid-lunge, he stopped again when he noticed a man and two boys staring directly at him. The taller boy raised an uncertain hand in greeting, and smiled. The gladiator glanced behind him, saw that there was no one there, and looked back to see the younger boy waving now, while the man accompanying them pressed his glasses to his face and grinned from ear to ear. The gladiator raised an uncertain hand in greeting, and then, apparently alerted by something behind him, moved swiftly towards the museum and vanished through its wall.

'Come on, time waits for no man. Our gladiator friend is testament to that,' said Caretaker Wiseman, heading briskly off towards Guildhall.

Once inside the building, Max and Eric stared up into its cathedral-like rafters. 'It's impressive, isn't it?' enthused Caretaker Wiseman.

'It's humongous,' said Max, listening to the echo of his own voice.

'Big enough for two giants, I expect,' said Eric.

'Precisely. And here they are!' said Caretaker Wiseman, turning and pointing up above the doors. In the far-left and right corners of Guildhall, above the entrance, stood two bronze statues of bearded giants adorned with shields and spears. 'Their names are Gog and Magog ... You look disappointed, Eric,' observed Caretaker Wiseman.

Visibly crestfallen, Eric shrugged. 'I suppose with all that's been going on I imagined they might be *real* giants.'

'Of *course* they're real!' chided Caretaker Wiseman.

'Hate to burst your bubble,' said Max, 'but they're about as real as the blow-up Godzillas in my cupboard.'

'And what's more, they aren't big enough to be called giants,' added Eric, winking at Max.

'Now I know you're pulling my leg. The fact is,' continued Caretaker Wiseman, glancing over his shoulder into Guildhall, which was empty but for a solitary security guard. Max and Eric stepped closer to Caretaker Wiseman, who suddenly sounded very serious. 'What you see here are representations of the real Gog and Magog who, quite frankly, would not fit under the roof of this hall.'

Max and Eric looked up at the impossibly high ceiling, much of which was hidden in shadow. 'So, ah ... if they're real, where are they?' asked Max.

'I'll give you three guesses.'

'Middle Earth?'

'Clot!' said Caretaker Wiseman.

'Are they imprisoned somewhere?' asked Eric.

Caretaker Wiseman nodded vigorously. 'Yes! And for the safety of us all, even those who live here on the cusp of time. But where do you imagine their prison is?'

'In a dungeon beneath the Ancient Order of Wall Scratchings?' guessed Max.

'There is no dungeon beneath our own HQ.'

'The League of Dark Scratchings have them, don't they?' surmised Eric.

Caretaker Wiseman placed a hand on Eric's shoulder. 'Yes, they do.'

'But why do they have them?' asked Max.

'Long, long ago, back in the mists of time, the area we now call London was a vast forest. It was the giants' home. So fearsome were their reputations as warriors that neither man nor beast ventured into their territory – at least, until King Brutus in the 12th century BC. Brutus was the first king of England, and he had an army with a fearsome reputation.

You see, Brutus wanted to build a palace on this very spot, and so he did, but first his army needed to defeat Gog and Magog. After many hard-fought battles, his fearsome warriors, numbering in their tens of thousands, captured and imprisoned them.'

'How did they pull *that* off?' said Max.

'They built steel cages twice the size of this building. The cages were taken deep below ground and left in the vast catacombs that lay beneath where the Bank of England is now. As you know, it's the location of the League of Dark Scratchings in the spectral realm, and that is where they are to this very day. There's no need to look so worried. It's as much in the interests of Those Who Leave Much to Be Desired as it is in our own to make sure they remain locked up down there. If they were ever to get free, they'd doubtless raze the League of Dark Scratchings to the ground in a bid to escape and get back to the surface.'

'Sounds like a plan,' joked Max.

***

When they left Guildhall, the ghostly gladiator was back, only now he was sitting cross-legged on the same spot and sharpening his sword with a stone. Even from fifty metres away, it was pretty obvious that he was curious about the three people who could see him. 'I hope you realise,' cautioned Caretaker Wiseman, 'that while his weapons are quite useless against living people, they would prove fatal if used against either of you.'

'That makes a lot of sense,' said Max.

''Course it does,' said Eric. 'If we can ride in their ghostly trains and boats, it follows that their weapons would feel just as solid.'

'Quite so.' Caretaker Wiseman was about to stroll over for a chat with the gladiator when something in his pocket began to vibrate. He took a postcard-sized parchment from his pocket, brought it to the tip of his nose, and read the words now appearing on it.

'Is something wrong?' asked Max.

'I have a horrible feeling it might be, yes,' nodded Caretaker Wiseman. 'I'm to return to the Scratchings HQ without delay. The *without delay* has been underlined twice.'

'It's probably just something to do with the Tree of Scratchings,' said Max, somewhat dismissively. 'Is it okay if we go and speak to the gladiator and then make our own way back?'

'Absolutely not,' said Caretaker Wiseman gravely. 'The message is very clear: you're both to return with me. Mrs O wants to see all three of us in her office immediately.'

Twenty minutes later, they entered the lift in the Chamber of Scratchings and the doors slid closed. 'I bet Mrs O summons you to her office all the time,' said Max.

'Not at all. And our weekly meeting isn't until the day after tomorrow.'

'Maybe she's angry about me staying with Max and his family at Christmas,' worried Eric, who'd been unusually quiet.

Caretaker Wiseman shook his head. 'She thought it an excellent idea, and said that it was better for you to get acclimatised as soon as possible to the way of things on the cusp of time.' The lift doors opened onto the Corridor of Rooms, where people were busy arranging good luck for those of kind hearts and noble minds throughout the ages.

The doors into Mrs O office stood wide open. She was sitting behind her desk, straight-backed, with an aggrieved expression on her face. 'Close the doors behind you,' she said, stony-faced, as they entered. Caretaker Wiseman turned and closed the door, then sat down with Max and Eric in front of Mrs O's desk.

'What is it? Nothing too serious, I trust,' said Caretaker Wiseman.

'I'm afraid the matter is *very* serious,' replied Mrs O. She leaned forwards in her chair, looking at Max and Eric. 'What do you know of Ellie's whereabouts?'

Max and Eric glanced at one another. 'Nothing,' they chorused.

'Are you sure?'

'The last time we saw her was at our Initiation Ceremony,' said Eric.

'That's right. One minute she was there, and the next ...' remembered Max.

'And the next *what*?' asked Mrs O, leaning further forward.

Max shrugged. 'Well ... she wasn't.'

'Ellie is alright, isn't she?' asked Eric, looking decidedly pale.

'Of course she is,' said Max. 'There's nothing she can't deal with.'

Mrs O sat back in her chair and shook her head gravely.

'What *is* it?' said Caretaker Wiseman. He sounded so uncharacteristically scared that he gave Max goose bumps.

'I fear that our advantage of five Scratchlings to four has already been lost,' she replied miserably.

'*Lost*? What are you saying?'

'All we know is that *they* have her now.'

'They?' said Max looking anxiously back and forth between Mrs O and Caretaker Wiseman.

'The League of Dark Scratchings,' replied Mrs O bitterly.

'But *how*?' cried Eric.

'It appears that Ellie made an attempt to infiltrate their fortress last night. She's fallen into their clutches.'

'She did *what*?' said Caretaker Wiseman, clutching the edge of the desk.

'What do you know of a spectral craft that was left on the roof of this building?' Mrs O asked Max and Eric.

'Captain Smith,' said Eric, welling up. 'He said we could keep it.'

'A spectral craft? Is *that* how Ellie made it across to their fortress?' said Caretaker Wiseman.

'It's what our intelligence suggests,' said Mrs O.

'But why? What was she trying to do?' asked Max.

Mrs O glanced surreptitiously at Eric. 'We have no idea,' she said.

'It could only have been something she felt very strongly about,' said Caretaker Wiseman miserably, realising only too well what that something must have been.

'But you must have *some* idea why she tried to get in there!' blurted Max.

'Calm down, Mr Hastings. We don't have any idea,' Mrs O said, avoiding his gaze.

'So? What do we do now?' asked Max, looking back and forth between Caretaker Wiseman and Mrs O.

Eric wiped a tear from his cheek and answered for both of them. 'We're going to rescue Ellie, of course.'

'Quite impossible!' snapped Mrs O. 'So much for our long-awaited advantage. It lasted all of *one day*.'

'We'll get another spectral craft and follow her,' put in Eric helpfully.

'Do you imagine such crafts grow on *trees*, young man? And even if we did have one, Ellie was our best agent. Whatever trap she fell into awaits anyone who attempts to follow her. No. It would be much too risky.'

'What do you think they'll do to her?' asked Max, with a tremble in his voice.

Mrs O sighed. 'She's a prize as far they're concerned, so I think it unlikely they'll kill her – at least not right away. No. They'll try and get as much information as possible out of her first.'

'They'll torture her, you mean?' asked Max quietly.

'Not something either of you should dwell upon,' said Caretaker Wiseman.

'Caretaker Wiseman is right. We must focus our energies on helping the children that we *can* remove from harm's way.' Mrs O swivelled her chair round and looked out of the window behind her. In a softer tone she added, 'In a few days it will be Christmas. I think it's a very good thing that your mother has invited Eric to stay, Max. I suggest you use the holiday to put the strain of all this behind you. Come the first of January, you'll both begin your training in earnest.' Mrs O swivelled back around and looked at Max and Eric. 'The best thing you can do to honour Ellie's memory is to become the best Scratchlings you can. Make her proud.'

Thirty
Fledgling Intuition to the Fore

Max and Eric walked solemnly with Marlot along the path towards the cusp of time. 'I can't believe Ellie's really gone,' said Marlot, gazing at the shadows cast by his lamp. 'It seems like only yesterday when she turned up at the door. She was as green as they come, but also spirited. The first words she said to me after the door closed behind her were, ''What *exactly* is the meaning of all this? It's obviously a wind-up, and if this is one of those hidden-camera shows, then trust me, you're going to regret it.'' And then she looked me up and down and I remember thinking how fortunate I was that looks couldn't kill. Even so, she took to being a Scratchling like a duck to water. Although she hid it well, that girl had a heart the size of a mountain ...' He fell into a melancholy silence.

'*Has* a heart as big as a mountain,' said Max.

'She's not dead yet, Marlot. I *know* she isn't!' added Eric.

'Do you have any idea why she took such a massive risk, Marlot?' asked Max.

Marlot's craggy face looked sick with worry. 'It must have been something she considered important,' he said. 'Something she felt she couldn't let drop. One of the pitfalls of having a heart as big as a mountain, I suppose.'

At the door Marlot put down his lamp and shook both the boys' hands. 'A merry Christmas to you both,' he said, sounding not in the least bit merry. 'You two get plenty of rest over the festive period, you hear? I'll be here to meet you on the first of January. Which reminds me: a little bird tells me that a couple of new scratchings have appeared in the Chamber – a couple of royal Princes, no less. Don't suppose you boys know anything about that?'

'Have a word with Caretaker Wiseman. He'll tell you all about it,' said Max.

When Max and Eric walked through the door and arrived back at the cusp of time, Max shoved his hands deep into his coat pockets. 'Can you believe that?' he said. 'Even Marlot's talking about Ellie like she's already ... you know.'

'Do they think we'll just move on and forget her, Max? We owe Ellie everything! Our very lives!' They began walking, heads bowed, not knowing or caring where they were going.

'And what's more,' said Max, 'just after you signed your name on the Round Table, I heard Mrs O call us *the trinity*. As though we belonged together somehow.'

'Did she? Perhaps they think they'll call us *the pair* from now on.'

'You're not wrong, Eric. A *right* pair.' They walked in silence for a time, heads still bowed and Eric paying no attention to the wonders of the 21st century that had so enthralled him only the day before. A few minutes later they looked up and found themselves standing outside Guildhall.

'Did you bring us here on purpose, Max?'

'What? No. Why would I? I was following you.'

'But I was following *you*.'

They turned and spotted the gladiator swinging a mace and practising his aim on passing tourists.

'It's lucky for those people he's a ghost,' said Max philosophically.

'Doubt he'd be doing that if he was *actually* slaughtering them.'

'Like a video game, you mean,' sighed Max.

'I'll have to take your word on that.'

The gladiator wiped his brow and turned towards the museum behind him. This time he didn't disappear through its wall, but strolled through its open door just like a paying visitor.

'Max?'

'Yes, Eric?'

'Might your Scratchling intuition be telling you what mine's telling me?'

'Only if yours is telling you we should go and talk to that gladiator.'

'Yes. Do you reckon we *both* followed our Scratchling intuition here?' asked Eric, scratching his head.

Max shuddered and nodded.

'But why?'

'There's only one way to find out,' said Max, walking towards the Guildhall Art Gallery and London's Roman Amphitheatre. The art gallery was a palatial building of white stone that housed a collection of masterpieces above ground and the remains of the Roman Amphitheatre below.

Max bought two tickets from the booth just inside the door, and they set off down a long ramp that led deep underground. At the bottom, they entered a cavernous space lit by green neon lights. The futuristic lights illuminated the ancient ruins where gladiators had once been locked up below the amphitheatre. 'It looks like a cross between ancient Rome and a spaceship down here,' said Max.

'Never seen a spaceship, so I'll have to take your word for that. Where do you suppose he went?'

'No idea. Let's just follow our intuition again,' shrugged Max, taking a step into the ancient yet at the same time strangely futuristic-looking space.

'*There he is*,' said Eric, pointing at the two remaining walls of what was once a cell. 'He's gone behind that wall.'

They walked past several display cases containing artefacts from the Roman period: spoons, buckles, jewellery and pottery. They crossed a glass floor that looked down into an excavation showing off Roman floor tiles, before turning right and entering the remains of what, two thousand years ago, had been one of many cells in the city-like labyrinth below the amphitheatre. The gladiator was lying on a transparent bunk, his eyes closed and his equally transparent weapons around him. He had taken off his helmet and clutched it to his chest. Max and Eric stood over him. 'I pity the poor fellows who had to face him in battle. He's enormous,' whispered Eric in awe.

Max glanced at his fearsome-looking weapons. 'And he *can* kill us with those things if we wake him,' he whispered.

'If he did, it wouldn't say much for our Scratchling intuition.'

Max felt a chill. 'That's what I'm hoping, too. So, are you thinking what I'm thinking?'

'Only if you're thinking that this man might be able to help us find Ellie.'

Max examined the man's rugged yet kind face and nodded. Eric leaned over the man, close to his face. 'I'm very sorry to disturb you, sir,' he began. The seven-foot-tall gladiator leapt off his bunk, picked up his sword, and brandished it at the boys. The sword's tip was just centimetres from Eric's nose, and Eric went a little cross-eyed as he focused on it. 'S ... s ... sorry to wake you, sir,' he faltered.

'You imagine I was *sleeping,* child? I have not slept in over two thousand years.'

'We have no idea about such things,' said Max, moving beside Eric.

The gladiator regarded them in silence for a number of seconds and then said, 'So, I *wasn't* imagining things. You did wave at me earlier?'

'Yes,' said Max.

'Why is it you can see me and no one else can?'

'Because we're Scratchlings,' said Eric, as though that explained everything.

The gladiator furrowed his thick dark brows. '*Ducklings?*' he said.

'*Scratchlings*,' repeated Max.

'Apologies,' said the gladiator, remembering that he could smile. 'Your voices are the first I've heard in two millennia. Pray tell me, what *is* a Scratchling? And why can they see me?'

'They – I mean *we* – are able to travel back in time,' explained Max.

'To save children in peril,' added Eric. 'And because we can talk to ghosts like yourself, they've been known to help us out.'

The gladiator lowered his sword. 'The cause of Scratchlings sounds like a noble one.'

A couple of Japanese tourists, a man and his wife, walked up behind Max and Eric. The man had an enormous camera slung around his neck. As they began reading a plaque that explained what the little ruin of a room used to be, the gladiator shook his head and sighed. 'They think they can come into my room and make themselves at home as they please.'

Max and Eric stepped aside to allow the man to take a picture of the fake Roman bunk that was in the same place against the wall as the spectral one.

'Tell me,' asked the gladiator, pointing at the man's camera, 'what do those things *do*? People bring them in here every day and I have always wondered.'

'They take photos. Excuse me?' Max said to the Japanese man. 'Can I see your picture?' The man didn't speak English, but seemed delighted to show Max the digital image he had taken. 'And my friend would like to see it too,' Max added, motioning to Eric.

The gladiator loomed large over them all, invisible to the tourists. 'So *this* is what they've been doing when they blind me with their flashes of light!' he complained. 'During the last one hundred years, I've had to watch as these *cameras* become smaller and more commonplace.'

'You must have seen so much,' said Eric, as the Japanese man smiled and walked away to join his wife.

The gladiator sat down on the centre of his bunk. 'You're welcome to sit,' he said, gesturing to the mock-up of a Roman bunk either side of him. 'It makes a change to *welcome* visitors into my room.' Max and Eric sat down either side of him. 'My name is Marcus Octavius,' he said.

'I'm Max Hastings.'

'Eric Kettle. It's a privilege to meet a real gladiator,' said Eric earnestly.

'As it is for me to meet two Scratchlings.'

'Are you alone here?' asked Max.

'Yes, and I have no one to blame for my lonely predicament but myself,' said Marcus sorrowfully. 'I didn't follow the others towards the light, you see.'

'Why not?' asked Eric.

Marcus shrugged. 'We fought nobly, my brothers in arms and I, but were greatly outnumbered in our final battle.'

'Upstairs in the Amphitheatre?'

'Indeed,' replied Marcus.

'So why didn't you walk towards the light with your brothers?' asked Eric.

Marcus looked down at Eric with dark and piercing eyes. 'It's a question I have asked myself many times over the long centuries.'

'And?' pressed Max.

'All I can tell you is that it felt as though I had unfinished business in this realm.'

'What business?' Eric leaned closer with interest.

'That is something I'm waiting to discover, but I train daily for it. What else am I to do?'

'It's no accident that we're here, you know,' said Max.

'Max is right. Our Scratchling intuition … it *led* us to you, Mr Octavius,' said Eric mysteriously.

Marcus swung his head to his left and looked into the big brown eyes of the urchin by his side. 'Please. Call me Marcus. It's been so long since I've heard my name spoken aloud by friends.'

'Alright, Marcus,' smiled Eric.

'And why do you suppose your Scratchling intuition led you to me?'

'We don't know why, exactly,' said Eric, 'but a good friend of ours, a fellow Scratchling called Ellie, is in great danger.'

'And we've been told no one can help her, but...' Max tailed off.

'But *what,* little Scratchlings?'

'Despite our size, we don't give up easily,' said Eric with a stoicism that belied his scrawny frame.

'Ellie risked her life to save us.'

'And now Max and I are prepared to risk ours to save her,' said Eric, sounding three times his size now.

Marcus smiled down at him. 'Where is your friend now?'

Eric shuffled nervously in his seat. 'She's been captured by the League of Dark Scratchings.'

'They could be torturing her as we speak. Or worse,' added Max darkly.

Marcus leaned forwards and interlinked his fingers. 'Tell me, where is this *League of Dark Scratchings*?'

'Do you know where the Bank of England is?' asked Max.

Marcus shook his head. 'I am unable to travel beyond the perimeter of the amphitheatre above – the arena in which I died. Although, I suspect the location of which you speak is half a mile *east* of our location.'

'Yes! That's precisely where it is. How did you know?' said Max.

At that moment, a teenage girl wearing a rucksack held up her phone and took a picture of the ruin in which they were seated. The girl looked at the screen: her picture showed two boys sitting at either end of a bunk bed in the Roman cell. 'Take a picture, why don't you?' murmured Max as she walked away.

'You were about to tell us how you know where the Bank of England is,' said Eric.

'I'm well acquainted with the underground rivers that flowed below the City of Londinium when I was alive. I alone see and travel by those rivers now. They are invisible to the people who work below ground in the sewers.'

'Where do these old underground rivers go?' asked Max.

'Where *don't* they go? In my day they carried water to the north, east, south and west of here.'

'And you're still able to explore them?'

'Yes, in a small boat that I have painstakingly maintained for two millennia. But I have only dared to venture north, south and west. East?

193

Just once.'

'And that would be because …?' asked Max.

Marcus stood up, rubbed a crick in his neck, and then turned and looked down at them. 'Without a pressing reason for doing so, it is folly to follow the river east.'

'What makes you say so?' asked Eric.

'The water that flows in all other directions is emerald green and calm, while the water that flows *east* towards the Bank of England is a deep blood-red.'

'Okay. So is that all that's different about it?' asked Max.

Marcus shook his head. 'The water that flows east does so on a fast and dangerous current.'

'But that's *all* that's different, surely?' said Max.

To Max's dismay, Marcus shook his head again. 'There's *something* down there,' he replied. 'Something in the darkness, invisible, but …'

'But what?' asked Eric.

'*Alive*. On the one occasion I ventured in that direction, I barely made it back out before it caught me.'

Eric looked at Max knowingly. 'It sounds similar to our own Sniffing Darkness. Maybe that's what caught Ellie?'

'Could be,' murmured Max, looking down at his hands and frowning.

'You said it *almost* caught up with you,' said Eric.

'That's right.'

'So you outran it?'

'In a manner of speaking, and it was no easy task against the current. But in truth, I don't believe it had any real interest in me. It only wanted to see me off … to deter me from returning.'

'But wouldn't it be easier to actually outrun it in the *opposite* direction?' said Max.

'Riding the current would clearly be a good deal faster, but you would be heading straight into its lair.'

'I don't think it has a lair,' said Eric.

'That's right,' nodded Max. 'If it's anything like our own Sniffing Darkness, then it has a set area that it patrols. If we could make it past that area, then …'

'You're prepared to risk finding out for your friend?' Marcus raised an eyebrow. Max and Eric nodded wholeheartedly. Marcus ran a hand over his coarse stubble. 'Such tiny children ... *Scratchlings*. Can one of your kind really be so important?

'You ever heard the saying *the straw that broke the camel's back*?' asked Max.

'I am familiar with its meaning, yes.'

'Well, apparently we're a couple straws.' Max pointed at Eric and himself.

'We need your help, Mr Octavius – I mean, Marcus – to rescue a *third* straw.'

'And we're the good guys, by the way,' added Max for good measure.

'I do not doubt it, and if what you say about the importance of Scratchlings is true, then I've been waiting two thousand years for the opportunity to assist you.'

'Excellent,' said Max, as he and Eric stood up. Marcus looked from one to the other of his new friends. 'You mean to leave *now*? Don't you need to make plans?'

'No way. Absolutely not,' Max shook his head emphatically.

'Max is right,' agreed Eric. 'Plans involve thinking, and I for one could lose my nerve if I thought too much about what we're about to do.'

'I somehow doubt that, little Scratchling,' said Marcus with an approving smile.

'We're better off relying on our intuition, and making it up as we go along,' said Max. 'It's worked for us up till now.'

Marcus picked up a large round shield and strapped it to his back. He reached for his sword, slid it into its scabbard, and put on his helmet. 'To the boat we go, then!' he said.

Thirty-one
In Search of Ellie

Inside the museum, a cinema-sized screen along the back wall projected Roman spectators sitting in the stands of an arena. These spectators were watching Olympic-style games taking place in a small, mocked-up arena inside the museum. Marcus led Max and Eric around the side of this small arena, where life-sized figures were holding javelins, towards the left-hand side of the screen that loomed behind them. Over his shoulder Marcus said, 'Be certain that the security man we just passed isn't watching, before you follow me behind this ... whatever you call this.'

'It's called a screen,' said Max. He and Eric stopped, turned, and noticed the guard for the first time. They shoved their hands into their trouser pockets and pretended to read a plaque that explained the Roman games in the display. The guard was standing with his arms folded and looking very bored.

'He's not interested in us,' whispered Eric. 'If you ask me, he's in a world of his own.'

'His eyes do look glazed,' agreed Max. The man yawned and then turned to face a woman who'd just asked him a question.

'Time to go!' said Max.

They hurried behind the screen, where Marcus was waiting outside a door with a big entry keypad on it. He saw them coming, passed through the door, and then disappeared. Max and Eric stood outside it, looking in dismay at the keypad. To their relief, Marcus's head appeared back through the solid door above them, with a quiet *whump!* sound. '3782,' he said. 'I have observed them operating this device many times.'

'Cheers, Marcus,' said Max, quickly punching in the code.

Once through the door, they hurried down a flight of steps and entered the cluttered workshop where damaged exhibits were taken to be patched up. At the rear of the workshop, a manhole cover lay in the floor. Marcus jutted his chin at it. 'It leads into the sewers. You will find a metal tool for opening it in the bottom of that cupboard,' he said, pointing to a small cupboard in the corner. Unable to interact with it himself, Marcus watched with interest as Max and Eric struggled to lift the wrought-iron manhole cover. When they finally managed it, they peered down into the darkness that yawned away from them. Marcus floated down past them into the manhole. 'Fear not, I have a torch down here,' he said, disappearing from view.

Max and Eric looked at each other. 'Here goes,' said Eric gamely, climbing down the little ladder at the side of the hole. Max followed quickly behind. They shivered in the dank, stinking chill of the sewer as they hastened down the ladder, and were very glad of the glowing green flame of Marcus's torch when they reached the bottom. They followed him down a narrow path between steeply rising brick walls, into an open space where they no longer needed the light from Marcus's torch. Eerie dripping sounds echoed in the large space. They'd entered an underground cavern where stalagmites and stalactites were bathed in the magical glow of a unearthly green river. '*WOW!* It looks like a Christmas grotto down here,' murmured Max.

Eric's big brown eyes opened wide. 'Blimey, it's beautiful,' he smiled. A boat very much like the one they'd used to escape from the galleon bobbed gently on the surface of the water. 'Nice boat,' observed Max.

'And considering her age, very reliable,' said Marcus, putting his torch down on the ground and then climbing on board.

'Wait,' said Max. 'I reckon we'll need that.'

Marcus waved a hand towards the underground river that glowed a ghostly green. 'As you can see, the river that lies ahead is brightly lit.'

'True enough,' said Eric. 'But if that darkness comes a-sniffing, then the torch might come in handy.'

'To ward it off,' added Max.

Marcus retrieved the torch and then sat down on the boat's only bench. He handed it to Max, who'd just stepped gingerly aboard. 'Hold it while I row,' he said.

Max took the torch and made room for Eric to climb on board behind him. 'I suggest you both sit at the front of the boat,' said Marcus. The boat wobbled as they all took up their positions.

Seated at the front of the boat, Max and Eric gazed ahead as Marcus rowed deeper into what looked like the biggest ever underground Christmas grotto.

'It's a pity Santa isn't waiting to give us a present at the other end,' sighed Max.

'Well, you never know. Just *look* at this place! I'd say anything's possible down here.'

They continued in silence along the green river for several minutes before Marcus pulled sharply on an oar and the boat veered to the left and into a narrower channel. The dank smell intensified in their nostrils. The channel led to an intersection where four separate channels met, each fronted by a slimy-looking brick arch. Marcus pulled on an oar until their boat was facing one of the four arches. Max lifted an arm slowly and pointed ahead. 'That's east, I take it?' he said, in a voice so quiet that it was all but swallowed by the cavernous space. Marcus nodded.

'East doesn't look so bad,' chirped Eric optimistically.

'This is your last chance. If you wish to turn back, say so now,' said Marcus.

Eric looked at Max. 'It doesn't feel as though there *is* a back. Not without Ellie. Isn't that right?'

Max nodded. 'We *have* to go on, Marcus.'

'As you wish.' Marcus rowed beneath the brick archway.

Before very long, the glowing green water turned red, as though dead things were seeping blood below the surface, and the boat began to bounce on the surface of the increasingly faster-flowing and eddying water. It had grown much darker, too, and the ceilings were getting lower and lower over their heads. Max had to hold up the torch to see the chopping and churning blood-red water ahead. Max gulped and glanced at Eric, whose expression told him that the last thing he was doing right now was thanking his lucky stars. Max looked over his shoulder and raised his voice above the sound of the rushing water. 'Is … is the League of Dark Scratchings far?'

'We will soon be at the point where I encountered the darkness and turned back,' said Marcus, looking anxiously at the cave walls, which were closing in on either side of them. The boat lurched forwards suddenly, as though entering downhill rapids. Marcus clutched the oars with all his might as he fought to keep the boat away from the jagged stone walls. Max and Eric clung to the side of the boat, which dipped sharply and nearly threw Max out. The noise of the rushing red water had grown to a crescendo. Marcus glanced down another channel to his right and screamed, 'It's here! The darkness! It comes! Hold on!'

Max and Eric looked back and saw the ruddy glow behind them being snuffed out, as though they were being chased down a corridor by something that was turning out the lights as it went. 'Looks like Sniffing Darkness to me!' cried Max above the thunderous noise of the water.

'Crouch low!' yelled Marcus. 'If it has eyes, maybe it's best that it does not see you!'

The boys did not need to be told twice. Marcus jumped up and cast his oars aside. He tugged his shield around to the front and drew his sword. Max held the torch out towards him and yelled, 'No, Marcus! Use this!'

Marcus hurled his sword into the chasing darkness, then turned and snatched the torch from Max's hand. 'The end of this channel, the place you seek, is upon you! May the luck of the gods be with you, my friends!'

'What are you going to do?' cried Eric.

'Slow the darkness as much as I can.'

'Thank you!' the boys shouted back. Marcus nodded, turned, took two great strides and then roared as he threw himself off the back of the boat and into the pursuing darkness. Max and Eric watched helplessly as Marcus slashed wildly with his torch and, moments later, the boat shuddered violently as it crashed through some loose rocks and plummeted down ... Max and Eric yelled in panic as their little boat dropped like a stone and splashed down into the still waters of a blue lagoon.

Max and Eric raised their heads slowly above the rim of the boat, two pairs of wide eyes greedily taking in their surroundings. They saw a small body of water, the edge of which appeared to drop down into an enormous cavern. They were startled by some rocks that were still falling from the gap they'd made, and came splashing down around them. Crouching and with their hands protectively covering their heads, Max and Eric held their breaths and looked up to see if the chasing darkness would appear. They glanced fearfully at one another and began to paddle the boat back towards the wall they'd burst through.

'Do you suppose Marcus is alright?' whispered Eric, paddling frantically with his hands.

'The good news is it can't kill him.'

'I don't suppose it can lock him up, either, not like it has Ellie.'

'Also true.' It suddenly occurred to Max where they were, and he shuddered.

'I know,' said Eric. 'We actually made it into the League of Dark Scratchings's fortress.'

Max cast a glance at the rocky ceiling high above them. 'Beneath it, anyway.'

'How far beneath, do you reckon?'

'I'm thinking pretty far.' Max was strangely comforted by the thought.

'It doesn't look like the Darkness is following us. We should probably thank our lucky stars for that.'

'Yep.'

They paddled the boat to the edge of the lagoon and climbed out onto the slimy rock. Curious to see just how high up they were, they made their way carefully to its edge, gingerly stepping over fallen rocks, before lying on their stomachs and gazing out over a cavern so vast it might easily have contained a city. It appeared to be empty but for innumerable monumental pillars that rose up into darkness, and some indistinguishable shapes in the far distance. Eric peered straight down. 'It's ever such a long drop,' he murmured.

'Never have been one for heights, so I'll take your word for it,' said Max, inching back from the edge.

'You think they've imprisoned Ellie down here somewhere, Max?'

'I hope so. You know who's *definitely* down here, right?'

Eric lowered his head. 'The giants, Gog and Magog,' he whispered, as though saying their names too loudly would summon them.

'We need to find a way down,' said Max, his eyes searching busily all around.

Eric glanced to his right, past Max, and smiled. 'I really hoped our Scratchling intuition wouldn't lead us to a dead end ... and it hasn't!'

Max followed his friend's gaze and spotted a small gap in the wall. 'Let's hope you're right,' he said, backing away from the edge and scrambling to his feet.

They squeezed through the gap and discovered a path almost wide enough for the two boys to walk side by side. Max took the lead, and they followed it as it wended its way downward. 'Where do you suppose the light is coming from?' asked Eric.

'That's actually a really good question.'

'There's not much of it, granted, but we *can* see, so ...'

'You're right. It must be coming from somewhere.'

'Yes, but maybe ...' Eric tailed off, drawing a deep breath.

'Maybe what?'

'Maybe it's like this because it's waiting to be filled by the *you-know-what*,' said Eric, tapping Max on the shoulder and then pointing to the darkness far above them.

'You could be right. Just as long as it stays all the way up there.'

They walked on, descending on a slight incline for the best part of an hour. During their walk they discussed the possibility of the path not having an end, and just continuing down and down into the earth. The hungrier and thirstier they grew, the more terrifying this possibility seemed, so both were relieved when Eric spotted a change in the rock on their left. 'Look,' he said. 'Up there, there's a gap in the wall.' They stopped walking and Max peered up at it.

'I reckon you're right,' said Max, as Eric squeezed past him.

'Look,' continued Eric. 'There's another gap further down, and this one's lower.'

They stood below this second gap in the stone, which was approximately three metres above them. As Max attempted to get a foothold in the rock, Eric walked on around a corner. 'Max!' he whispered urgently. 'Come here! You'll definitely want to see this!'

Max stepped back down to the ground and hurried around the bend. Eric was staring through a brick-sized gap in the wall, his mouth hanging open.

'What is it? Let me see!' whispered Max, elbowing his friend.

Eric stepped back. 'I knew it! As I live and breathe, she's alive, Max. Ellie's alive!'

Through the hole, about thirty metres away, Max beheld a cage large enough to hold King Kong, let alone one small Scratchling. Sitting cross-legged on its floor, her head buried in her hands, Ellie looked like a toy action figure in a cage big enough to house a band of gorillas. Max glanced at Eric, and the sight of the tears in his friend's eyes brought a tear to his own. The boys shook hands heartily, and then moved back for another look through the hole to make sure they hadn't imagined her. 'You reckon her cage is what we could see from up in the lagoon?' whispered Max.

Eric nodded. 'Come on,' he said, fighting down his emotions. 'We're going to need to find a bigger gap to climb through.'

They were about to move away when Ellie looked up from her hands. They watched her clamber to her feet and back away towards the side of her cage.

'She's *seen* something,' said Eric, as Max tried to look as far right as possible to see what it could be. Moments later, both boys could see what Ellie saw: a wall of darkness that moved with sinister slowness across the cage towards her. The wall of darkness stopped centimetres from Ellie's nose, making her look like a little girl standing face to "face" with a starless night. Max and Eric held their breaths as the Darkness spoke, its voice so deep that they could feel the walls about them vibrate. 'Can it be? Are you truly *Scratchling-born,* child?'

Ellie stood as still as a statue and said nothing.

'It amazes me,' the voice thundered on, 'that something so *small* and *insignificant* could be such a large thorn in our side.'

Ellie raised her chin as though it was very heavy. 'A grain of sand might seem insignificant, but … it takes only *one* to tip even the largest of scales when they're finely balanced.' Max and Eric could hear the tremble of fear in her voice but she still sounded strong somehow.

'You are soon to be removed from those scales, *Scratchling-born.*'

'What are you?'

'Can you not see me with your own eyes?'

'All I can see is *darkness.*'

'Well, then, *Scratchling-born*, your eyes do not deceive you.'

Ellie took a step back without seeming aware of it.

The Darkness moved closer and said, 'The League of Dark Scratchings exists to make *me* stronger, and once the balance shifts in my favour, once there is more darkness than light in the hearts of men, I will finally be able to leave this realm and fill the hearts of *all.*'

'That will never happen,' said Ellie breathlessly.

'Foolish child. You must be aware that capturing you is a significant step in that direction.'

'We rescued the Ninth Scratchling. He'll take my place.'

'Oh, yes. The *Ninth Scratchling.*' The voice dripped with derision. 'He is soon to become the *Eighth,* once you are terminated. What possessed you to come here, *Scratchling-born*?'

'You … you kidnapped Eric Kettle's parents. You stole his parents away from him.'

Eric had been listening intently at the peephole, but he now collapsed to his knees and gasped as though he been punched in the stomach. Max crouched beside his stricken friend and opened his mouth to speak, but words failed him. The Darkness began to laugh, and plumes of dust came away from the walls and drifted down upon their heads and shoulders.

The Darkness stopped laughing. 'It is noble acts such as yours that will lead to the undoing of all your kind.'

'I doubt that,' replied Ellie resolutely. 'The Kettles ... they're innocent in all this. What have you done with them?'

On hearing Ellie's question, Eric reached up, gripped hold of the bottom of the peephole, and used all his might to pull himself back to his feet.

'Your mission was always doomed, *Scratchling-born*,' the Darkness went on. 'And so were the Kettles, the moment their son underwent his Initiation Ceremony. Once sworn to your cause, it was no longer possible to make him one of us.'

Ellie's shoulders drooped. 'And ...?'

'And his parents' usefulness as bargaining tools then came to an abrupt end. They have already been *terminated*.'

Max moved closer to Eric in readiness to catch him, but Eric clung steadfastly to the edge of the hole with whitening knuckles. Max leaned even closer to catch the whispered words of his friend. 'Mother and Father *didn't* leave me?'

Max placed a hand on Eric's bony shoulder. 'No. It seems they were taken.'

'Then perhaps ... perhaps Mother and Father loved me, after all.'

'Of *course* they did!'

'What should we do now?' asked Eric, sounding lost.

'What we came here to do.'

Eric looked through Max as though he wasn't there. 'What did we come here to do?'

He's in shock, thought Max. 'We came here to rescue Ellie.'

At the mention of Ellie's name, Eric's eyes widened. 'She ... Ellie ... risked her life to save Mother and Father?'

'Yes, and now we're going to return the favour. That way it will be *five* Scratchlings against their four. It will be impossible for these monsters to win. It will be payback for what they have done to you, Eric.'

Eric shook his head slowly, dazed. 'Not for what they did to me, but for what they did to poor, poor Mother and Father.'

From beyond the peephole, there came a faraway yet thunderous scraping sound.

'What is that?' said Ellie, peering into the gloom behind her.

'That, *Scratchling-born*, is the sound of your approaching doom.'

'But … but what is it?'

'What you hear is two cages being dragged towards you. Cages that contain giants.'

'Gog and *Magog*?' said Ellie, agog.

'Your knowledge serves you well. The giants' cages are to be joined to your own and, at the appropriate time, a mechanism will join your three cages into one, and they will join you.'

Ellie looked with wide eyes to her left into the darkness where the sound of scraping grew louder. 'What, *both* of them? For one Scratchling? Are you so afraid of me?'

'You can never be too sure when it comes to the likes of *Scratchling-born*. You will be aware that it was your kind – human beings – who betrayed and imprisoned the giants down here three millennia ago. In a short while, they will be able to unleash three thousand years' worth of pent-up hatred on you.' The Darkness began to back away. 'Farewell, *Scratchling-born*.'

Ellie looked to her left. Where the Darkness had receded, two gigantic cages could now be seen, each containing a slouched figure as tall as a ten-storey building, each cage pulled by two Dark Scratchlings. 'Just how strong do those Dark Scratchlings need to *be!*'

Thirty-two
Gog and Magog

'We need to find a way to get to Ellie!' cried Eric. He grabbed Max by his shoulders and shook him as though to persuade him of that fact. Relieved to see that his friend's spirit had returned, Max smiled and nodded his agreement.

With the sound of scraping growing ominously louder, they scrambled further along the path, where they discovered a narrow opening close to the ground. Eric took the lead, crouching down by the gap. 'I think we've found it, Max! A way to get to Ellie.'

Eric laid himself flat on his stomach and wriggled into the opening, up to his knees. Max crawled through the gap and lay beside him, the tops of their heads poking out into the cavern. To their left, fifty metres away, they could see Ellie's cage. The contents of two more cages, not far from Ellie now, took their breath away: the phantasmal green forms of Gog and Magog, dressed in dark leather breastplates and golden helmets. Below their helmets their facial features appeared squashed too close together, and they had long, whiskery moustaches that curled up and resembled deranged smiles. 'They look like monstrous warriors,' gasped Max.

'That's what I was thinking! And just *look* how strong the Dark Scratchlings are.'

'It's a good thing they didn't catch us. Trying to fight them would have been a joke.'

'Even so, I bet you anything Ellie hasn't given up hope,' murmured Eric as they watched her move to the centre of her cage.

The scraping sound stopped. Gog and Magog's cages had halted either side of Ellie's, and they gazed down at the first human being they'd set eyes upon since being imprisoned by them three thousand years earlier. This realisation prompted them to wrap their meaty fists around the bars, which creaked under their iron grip.

'They look like exhibits in the weirdest zoo ever,' whispered Max. 'Angry giant, *girl*, angry giant.'

Ellie looked up at Gog and then at Magog. 'Hello!' she called out, wishing she had a white flag to wave.

Neither Gog nor Magog answered. They just watched her, as did three of the four Dark Scratchlings hovering in front of her cage. The fourth had ascended smoothly up to the top of Gog's cage, where it pulled an enormous lever across the front of Ellie's. The end of this lever contained half a dial and, when the Dark Scratchling retrieved an identical-looking lever from Magog's cage, the two came together to form a clock face at the centre of Ellie's cage.

The ticking started – if you could call it ticking. Each tick was like a metal pole being hit with a sledgehammer, and each tock like a wooden stake taking the same punishment. The countdown to Gog or Magog's cages opening into Ellie's had begun. 'How long do you reckon we've got?' said Eric.

'If the Dark Scratchlings would clear off, we could get close enough to see the clock.'

'What if they don't go, Max?'

'They will. They *have* to.'

The fourth Dark Scratchling had rejoined the other three at the front of Ellie's cage. Two of them were wearing bowler hats, while the other two held theirs to their chests. As they observed Ellie, they switched the positions of their hats several times.

'That's too weird,' shuddered Max.

'You think that could be how they *talk* to each other?'

'Looks like it.'

Ellie suddenly marched forwards to the bars of her cage, as though she had every intention of punching one of the Dark Scratchlings on the nose. Grabbing the bars in her hands, she bellowed, 'Take a picture, why don't you?'

The four teenaged Dark Scratchlings, all dressed as Edwardian bankers, switched their hats again.

'I'm *so* interesting that you've got nothing *better* to do than stand there all day watching me?'

Again they switched their hats.

'If you have something to *say,* then why don't you just say it?' spat Ellie.

They stared back at her, their black eyes glittering lifelessly.

'Don't you have *tongues* in your heads?'

The Dark Scratchlings bared their fangs and darted forwards as far as the bars would allow, and Ellie stumbled back beyond their reach. She could see a gleam of pleasure in their jet-black eyes – enjoyment of her fear. They blinked slowly in unison, switched the positions of their hats again, and then two floated up to Gog's eye-level, the other two to Magog's. The Dark Scratchlings appeared to be communicating with the giants.

'A telepathic link,' murmured Ellie. Apparently satisfied with what was said, the Dark Scratchlings converged in front of Ellie's cage one last time. 'If you think you can get inside *my* head, you've got another think coming!' she shrieked.

By way of reply, they switched their hats, grinned as though to say that was hardly necessary now that Ellie's life expectancy was so short, and began to float away.

'The pleasure was definitely all yours!' Ellie shouted after them. She watched them for a few more seconds, then collapsed onto her backside as though her legs could hold her up no longer.

'She's exhausted,' whispered Max as the four Dark Scratchlings floated past their hiding place.

'The coast's clear. Come on. Ellie needs to know she's not alone, Max.'

Ellie was still sitting on her bottom, her knees hugged to her chest, while the giants gazed down at her in eager anticipation of the timer reaching zero. As the boys drew nearer, they could see that Ellie's eyes were closed.

'I bet she's thinking up a solution,' said Eric as they sprinted the last few metres to her cage. Doing their best to ignore the giants, whose piercing eyes had now swivelled to them, Max and Eric called, 'Ellie!'

Ellie opened her eyes and blinked in their direction. 'I must be hallucinating,' she murmured.

'It's us, Ellie!' cried Eric, waving his arms.

Ellie climbed unsteadily to her feet. 'But it's not *possible,*' she said. 'You can't be here. You *can't!* That darkness … it …'

'Almost got us,' finished Max.

'A gladiator helped us to outrun it,' explained Eric, grinning from ear to ear.

Ellie reached through the bars and grasped hold of Eric's narrow shoulders. 'I'm not seeing things. You're *real!*'

'Ye-ee-ee-ss! I'mmm reeeal!' Eric teeth rattled as his head got whipped around under her hands.

'Are you both mad? You shouldn't have risked coming here! Do you hear me? Either of you. You're much too important!' She tried to sound angry but her voice faltered, and her eyes filled with tears.

Max stepped forward and pulled Eric from Ellie's grasp. 'We *had* to come.'

'But why?'

'Because one good turn deserves another, doesn't it?' said Max.

'Two good turns, Max,' corrected Eric. 'You tried to rescue Mother and Father as well, Ellie.'

Ellie's tearful smile as she gazed back and forth between her fellow Scratchlings said a fervent *thank you!* more than words ever could.

High above them, Gog cleared his throat, with a sound so repulsive that his throat must have been full of several litres of phlegm. He yanked on his bars, grumbling something under his breath. Ellie's smile went from a heartfelt *thank you* to one of possibility and wonder. 'And now to the problem at hand,' she said, flapping a hand up to Gog and Magog. 'As problems go, it's a pretty *big* one.'

'Understatement times two,' agreed Max.

Ellie pointed up to the clock at the top of her cage. 'How long do I have?'

Max and Eric backed up for a look.

'It's impossible to say, *exactly*,' said Max. 'There's only one hand on the dial.'

'And so far it's moved slowly around to the six,' added Eric.

'That suggests half the time has elapsed. Approximately ten minutes have passed since that ticking started, which suggests we have approximately ten minutes to come up with a plan.' Both boys opened their mouths to say something more, but Ellie silenced them with a raised palm. 'Don't speak,' she commanded. 'I'm going to need at least *one* of those minutes to factor you two into a solution.' She turned and began to pace up and down, muttering to herself.

Max and Eric watched her.

Gog and Magog watched her.

She stopped pacing and struck her own forehead with a palm. 'Of course!' she exclaimed. 'Call yourself Scratchling-born!' She hurried back over to Max and Eric. 'Now pay attention,' she whispered. 'To the untrained eye, my cage looks identical to Gog and Magog's, but it isn't.'

'It isn't?' echoed Max.

'No, of course it isn't. These cages have been adapted for the prisoners they hold. Scratchlings are known for their lock-picking skills, so my cage has no locks. It's been soldered shut. *Giants,* on the other hand, are lousy with locks due to the size of their hands. Better still, Gog and Magog's cages have levers on the outside that can open them.'

'Their hands are too big to fit through the bars,' said Eric.

'Exactly.'

'So what are you saying?' said Max. 'That we should set them *free*? They'll tear us apart.'

'Taking the grudge they bear against all human beings into consideration, you're not wrong. That's why I need you to follow my lead and do *exactly* as I say. There's a chance for us all make it back up to the cusp of time in once piece, so let's keep cool heads and seize that chance, Scratchlings.'

Ellie turned, clasped her hands behind her back, and walked with a carefree countenance into the centre of her cage. Once there, she cleared her throat and in the commanding tone of a lawyer in a courtroom said, 'I was there, *Magog*. I was in the Forest of the Isle of Giants the very day you betrayed Gog to King Brutus.'

Magog shook his head, and in a rumbling, grumbling voice that sounded as though he'd been woken from a thousand years of sleep, he said, 'The human lies. They all do.'

'This human most certainly does *not*,' Ellie asserted. 'I was *there,* and I overheard every word you and King Brutus exchanged that day, Magog.'

Magog wiped his forearm across his brow. 'Humans have such pitifully short lifespans. How could *you* have been alive three thousand years ago?'

'Because I am *Scratchling-born,* and Scratchlings are time-travellers. Granted, I wasn't *supposed* to be there. It's not as though my day out was sanctioned, but I like to be prepared for any eventuality and made it my *business* to be there.'

Max and Eric were gazing at Ellie, open-mouthed.

Ellie turned and looked up at Gog. 'I would like you to cast your mind back to the day when you were lured into the trap laid by King Brutus. It just so happens that I paid you a visit on *that* important day, too,' said Ellie, glancing with feigned nonchalance at her fingernails. 'Isn't it the case?' she went on, 'that it was at Magog's suggestion that you took the High Cliff Pass into the forest that day? I recall him saying something about a dam being in danger of bursting its banks.'

Gog turned his steely gaze to Magog. 'She speaks the truth. You said we needed to shore up the southern dam. You were *adamant* that we take the High Cliff Pass.'

'Quite,' said Ellie. 'But you never made it through the pass, did you, Gog?'

'No, we did not.'

'Because you fell into a trap. A giant pit.'

Gog narrowed his eyes at Magog. 'We did.'

'I had good intentions,' sighed Magog. 'King Brutus said he was going to offer us a fair deal: that we could divide the Emerald Isle *fairly* with him.'

'And you never thought to discuss this with me?' boomed Gog.

'You would never have agreed to meet with him.'

'And with very good reason. It seems I have *you* to thank for the last three thousand years in *this* place.'

'What does it matter now?' said Magog bitterly, slumping down onto his backside with an almighty crash that shook the very ground they stood on. 'We are doomed to spend all eternity here. It will seem even longer if we argue.'

'Longer than eternity? There is nothing longer than eternity, Magog. Although it's going to *feel* longer for you when this timer reaches zero and we share a cage.'

'There's no reason why you need to share a cage for eternity. Not anymore,' said Ellie, looking up at Gog. 'You can be free to return to your beloved Emerald Isle this very day. *And* settle your grievances once you get there.'

'*How*? Do not taunt me, human,' boomed Gog, rattling the bars of his cage.

'I wouldn't do that,' objected Ellie. 'Do I have your complete attention?'

'You have! Speak!' said Gog, glaring at Magog.

Magog stood up. 'The human is bluffing. She is as helpless as we are.'

'True. But *they're* not,' said Ellie, jabbing a finger at Max and Eric. 'And they'll release you from your cages if I ask them to.' The giants turned to look at Max and Eric, and then switched their attention back to Ellie as she continued. 'Scratchlings are nothing if not fair. In fact, the pursuit of fairness is one of the main things that separate us from Those Who Leave Much to Be Desired. Therefore, in the interests of fair play, I will instruct my friends to release Magog first, and give him a head start.'

'*Why*?' boomed Gog.

'Not a big one. Just a few minutes. You'll be able to track him easily enough due to the hole he's going to rip through the League of Dark Scratchings in his bid to get to the surface.'

Magog sounded pleased. 'Given your current mood, Gog,' he said, 'that sounds very wise. It would be better to make haste than to quarrel down here. We might alert *them* to our escape.'

'Only too true,' said Ellie. 'Now, obviously, for setting you both free, there's something my friends and I want in return.'

'You need only ask,' said Gog.

'It's not much. All we require of you, Gog, is that you provide us safe passage back to the surface. I'm thinking we might climb inside that ridge on your breastplate?'

'Agreed,' said Gog.

'As do I,' said Magog. 'Now, have your friends free me before they are discovered.'

'There's just one more thing I must ask of you both,' said Ellie.

'Ask it,' said Gog, his voice full of anticipation at seeing his beloved Emerald Isle again.

'I want you to invoke the Pledge of the Ancient Tree Sprites, and use it to *pledge* that you'll stick to your side of bargain and see my friends and I safely back to the surface.'

'How do you know about that?' asked Magog, his eyes opening wide.

'How do you *think* she knows, you lumbering halfwit?' said Gog.

'It's true that my research does tend to be thorough,' said Ellie.

Gog drew a deep, mournful breath and said, 'I pledge by the wisdom and protection of the tree sprites that I shall do as you have asked. I will deliver the three of you back to the surface, where you will be allowed to go free.'

Ellie turned to Magog, who repeated the pledge obediently.

'Good,' said Ellie, rubbing her hands and noticing Eric beckoning to her. Ellie joined them in a huddle through the bars.

'Are you sure about all this?' whispered Eric. 'Only, Caretaker Wiseman took us to Guildhall and told us all about Gog and Magog. He was thanking his lucky stars they were imprisoned down here. In fact, I'd say one of his worst fears is the pair of them getting free.'

'I know,' said Ellie sagely. 'I had the exact same speech from Caretaker Wiseman when I first started. But *look* at them!' she smiled. 'Caretaker Wiseman has no way of knowing that the years have turned them *spectral*. That they're harmless – well, harmless to everyone but us three, obviously. Very few people, if anyone, will even be able to *see* them on the cusp of time.'

'Let's get on with it, then,' said Eric, with a twinkle in his eye.

'Just one more thing,' said Ellie, producing and opening a pen knife. She cut one strip of cloth from her black cape, and then another. 'We're going to need to be disguised when we get back to the surface.'

'Why?' asked Max.

'Trust me.' She ripped a third strip and then cut two slits for eye holes in it.

A couple of minutes later, Max and Eric were making their way to the lever on Magog's cage, wearing the highwayman-style masks that Ellie had quickly fashioned. As they went, Eric raised his voice and spoke to Magog. 'The League of Dark Scratchings took my mother and father, so I'd really appreciate your smashing their HQ to smithereens.'

'You have my word that I shall inflict as much damage on their lair as possible,' said Magog solemnly.

'Good,' said Eric, as he and Max stood beside the lever.

'You can do the honours,' said Max.

'Really? You don't mind?' said Eric, sizing up the lever.

'Not at all. Go for it.'

'Ta very much. This is for Mother and Father,' intoned Eric, pulling down the lever with all his might.

***

Above, in the League of Dark Scratchings, a strange rumbling could be felt. Curious glances were exchanged by bankers as they floated through the vast entrance hall. These glances morphed from curious to frightened as the rumblings escalated into what felt like a major earthquake. Books and files tumbled off desks and crashed onto the marble floor, while crystal chandeliers swung wildly back and forth. Cracks began to appear in the floor – cracks that were promptly obliterated by Magog as he burst up into the lobby like a monstrous jack-in-the-box. Standing fifty metres tall, the top of his head brushed the ceiling as he lurched forwards, arms flailing, and smashed his way through pillars and walls as though they were made of breadsticks and crackers. As he rampaged on, floors that teemed with Those Who Leave Much to Be Desired came crashing down in his wake. Some of these League of Dark Scratchings employees lay trapped and screaming beneath the fallen debris, while others had been instantly crushed. Up Magog leapt, grasping hold of iron beams in his bid to climb up through floor after floor after floor to reach his beloved Emerald Isle …

***

Across the way at the Ancient Order of Wall Scratchings, Mrs O snatched up the receiver of a phone on her desk. 'You need to see what's happening outside,' said a worried-sounding voice on the other end of the line.

'I presume you're talking about the *spectral* outside?' said Mrs O.

'Afraid not, ma'am. There's a big problem occurring on the cusp of time. Over at the Bank of England.'

Mrs O slammed down the receiver and moved so close to the window that her breath steamed it up. 'But this *can't* be happening,' she murmured, as cracks branched out from the bank – cracks large enough for cars to fall into. The area quickly became littered with abandoned cars and buses as drivers and passengers ran for cover. 'And what on earth is *this?*' Mrs O watched in horror as a green mist rose from the cracks. She gasped as the spectral form of Magog climbed out of the ground and dwarfed the surrounding buildings.

'Gog!' she cried.

Behind her, Caretaker Wiseman hurried into her office and joined her at the window. In a voice overflowing with excitement, he said, 'That's not *Gog*. As I live and breathe, that's *Magog!*'

'Gog? Magog? What difference does it make, if he's free?'

'Free, yes! But let's thank our lucky stars he's *spectral*. No one on the

213

cusp of time can even can *see him*. My, isn't he *magnificent!*' enthused Caretaker Wiseman, as Magog strode away.

'I wish I shared your excitement, Caretaker Wiseman. What do you suppose has caused this breach?'

'Need you really ask?' chuckled Caretaker Wiseman.

'Ellie?'

'I sincerely hope Ellie. Who else!' he clapped.

A minute later, Gog climbed up through the same crack as Magog, with the three children hanging on for dear life in the ridge of his breastplate.

'Unless I'm very much mistaken,' said Mrs O, screwing up her eyes to see a little better. 'A certain Masters Hastings and Kettle, *that's* who.'

'Good *lord!*' breathed Caretaker Wiseman.

'Good lord indeed. And while *Gog* might be invisible to those who live on the cusp of time, our three Scratchlings most certainly are not!'

Mrs O wasn't wrong. Those on the cusp of time could see three children huddled together and seemingly hovering forty metres above the ground.

***

'You were absolutely right about us needing these masks,' said Max, peering over the rim of Gog's breastplate at the people gathered at their office windows, taking pictures of them with their phones.

'The first rule of engagement: *always* think ahead,' said Ellie.

'What has become of our beloved Emerald Isle?' said a sorrowful-sounding Gog. He strode forward, casting his gaze around for something he recognised, but there was nothing. He spotted St Paul's Cathedral and made his way towards it, all thoughts of giving Magog a good hiding forgotten. The spring in his step was completely gone.

Gog climbed up and sat astride the roof of St Paul's Cathedral, his back resting on its dome, surveying the city around him. In the distance, the sound of a police helicopter could be heard. 'I'm very sorry, Gog,' said Ellie, raising her voice so that he could hear her.

'What have they done to my beloved Emerald Isle? There's barely any green left!'

'Some people call it progress,' said Ellie gently.

'Progress? The forest I left was filled with potent magic. It's all been destroyed. How can the destruction of so much enchantment be considered progress?'

'It has been three thousand years,' said Max. 'You must have expected a few changes.'

'Changes? I see only annihilation. Is nowhere on the Emerald Isle *emerald* anymore?'

'Absolutely,' said Ellie. 'If you head north, you'll find plenty of unspoiled places.'

'Those that have wrought this destruction are fortunate that I'm a spirit,' said Gog through gritted teeth. 'And look what the cat has dragged in.'

Ellie, Max and Eric saw Magog walking dejectedly towards them. He shrugged and cast his gaze around at all the concrete, glass and steel that covered what was once their beloved forest home.

'The Scratchlings say we will find trees in the north!' Gog called out.

'Be that as it may, human beings are very fortunate that I'm a spirit,' replied Magog, echoing Gog's words. All around St Paul's Cathedral, the streets thronged with people gawping up at the three children apparently suspended in mid-air. The police helicopter was now hovering high overhead.

'You are causing quite a stir, Scratchlings,' said Gog.

'Yes, and it's time we made ourselves scarce,' said Ellie. 'Would you mind putting us down in quiet backstreets? It's best if we separate and make our way back to Mansion House on foot.'

Gog got up and stood astride the great cathedral. 'You have ensured our freedom, and now I will ensure yours, Scratchling-born.'

Thirty-three
Debrief

After being released gently by Gog's giant fingers into three secluded backstreets, Ellie, Max and Eric had whipped off their masks and made their way back to Mansion House separately. Now, several hours later, they were sitting at Mrs O's desk with Caretaker Wiseman. On the desk was a well-thumbed copy of the Evening Standard, a newspaper that came out late in the day, and across its front page was the headline, "LONDON HALTED BY FLOATING CHILDREN AND SINK HOLE."

Caretaker Wiseman leaned forwards in his seat for a closer look at it. 'Cripes,' he said.

'Mrs O has kept us waiting for ten minutes,' said Ellie. 'So she must be positively *champing at the bit* to hear what we have to say. Not to mention give us a ticking off,' she added, tapping the headline.

Eric, who'd been fidgeting for the last ten minutes, glanced sideways at her. 'If she's so keen to talk to us, she's got a funny way of showing it.'

'Annoying, you mean!' laughed Ellie. It was good to see her smiling again.

'So you *really* chatted to Gog and Magog?' asked Caretaker Wiseman.

'Ellie did most of the chatting,' said Max.

'I can imagine,' said Caretaker Wiseman, looking at Ellie.

'I'm not sure if *chatted* is the right word,' said Ellie.

'But you *conversed* with them?'

'At length,' said Max. 'How else was she going to convince them to help us escape?'

'Jeepers creepers, Ellie! Talk about Scratchling nerve! So what were they like?'

'They were actually pretty cool once Ellie convinced them not to kill us,' said Max.

'Pretty *cool*? I'm looking forward to reading all about them in your mission reports. You're not to leave out any details, you hear?'

Mrs O walked in behind them. She sat down behind her desk, removed her spectacles, and looked down at the row of Scratchlings. Her gaze settled on Ellie. 'It is rare that words fail me.'

Unheard of, you mean, thought Ellie. 'Take your time,' she replied politely.

As it turned out, Mrs O didn't require any time at all. 'Let me get this straight. You took it upon your*self* to infiltrate the League of Dark Scratchings, Miss Swanson?'

'It didn't feel like I had a choice. Not once I discovered they had Mr and Mrs Kettle.'

'Thanks again for trying,' sighed Eric.

'About that,' said Mrs O. 'We're all very sorry that the League of Dark Scratchings deprived you of your family, Mr Kettle, but what Miss Swanson attempted was reckless. Plain and simple. As was what you two did in attempting to rescue her.'

'But it's all worked out for the best,' pointed out Caretaker Wiseman. 'All three Scratchlings are back with us safe and sound.'

'By the skin of their teeth,' huffed Mrs O.

'There's a lot to be said for doing things by the skin of your teeth,' said Ellie.

'Be that as it may, the skin of your teeth must be worn very *thin* indeed, Miss Swanson, and helping Gog and Magog return to the cusp of time was not really your decision to make.'

'Calculated risk, Mrs O,' said Ellie.

'Calculated risk?'

'Yes. Not to mention a tactical necessity.'

'Tactical necessity? Calculated risk?'

'Glad you understand, Mrs O,' said Ellie. 'Anyway, they're spectral now, so it's not as though they can do any damage.'

'Maybe not, but are they to become permanent fixtures on the London skyline for those of us who can see them? Like ... like mobile *Big Bens*?'

Max shook his head. 'They prefer the countryside.'

'So they'll be going north in no time,' said Eric.

'I hope you're right. As of three minutes ago, they were sitting side by side on the Houses of Parliament, dangling their feet in the Thames. It's not that I'm ungrateful to have you returned safely to the fold, but unless you take more care it's only going to be a matter of time before your luck runs out.'

'I imagine it's our job to see that it doesn't,' said Caretaker Wiseman.

'There are limits, Caretaker Wiseman.' Mrs O looked at Eric, who still looked shell-shocked. 'Do you still want to spend Christmas with the

Hastings family?'

'Oh, yes, very much!' said Eric, perking up.

Mrs O nodded and sat back in her seat. 'Alright then. Off you all go and enjoy your Christmas. Mr Hastings and Mr Kettle, I'll expect you back here on the first of January to commence your training.' She looked at Ellie. 'As for you, young lady, I suggest you spend your Christmas holidays thanking your lucky stars. And I have a suggestion for your New Year's resolution: no more solo missions without back-up.'

'It's not as though I intend to make a habit of it,' said Ellie, thoughtfully tapping her fingernails on the arm rests of her chair.

Caretaker Wiseman shook his head and sighed. 'Just imagine the adventures the Scratchling Trinity are going to have in the New Year. The people you'll rescue! The wrongs you'll put right! The *incredible* things you will achieve together!'

Ellie cleared her throat and looked first at Caretaker Wiseman and then at Mrs O. 'What exactly *is* this trinity?' she asked.

Mrs O glanced at Caretaker Wiseman. 'It's something to discuss when you return in the New Year. As we speak, our vast underground library is being scoured by our best minds, under the direction of Professor Payne, for further references.'

'And it has something to do with the three of us?' asked Ellie.

Mrs O leaned forward. 'You are the first Scratchlings capable of journeying through time *together,* and the first to be able to communicate *freely* with the spirit world when you get there.' She stood up abruptly. 'That's enough questions for now. Go home, Scratchlings, and have yourselves a very merry Christmas.'

Thirty-four
Christmas Morning

When Max returned home later that day, he introduced Eric to his father. Mr Hastings took an instant liking to the little urchin with the big kind eyes. 'You're very welcome to spend Christmas with us, young man,' he said, squeezing Eric's shoulder. So too did Maxine, who smiled gummily at Eric whenever he asked a question.

As for Mrs Hastings, she treated Eric like she'd known him his whole life, and Eric thanked his lucky stars for that. And also for the handful of presents around the Christmas tree that bore little red cards with his name on. Eric had made a gift for each member of the Hastings family, too.

A week passed by, and it was finally Christmas morning. Eric was lying on his put-you-up bed in Max's room, and it was 6am. They'd been up most of the night talking about the places they'd been, and the extraordinary things they'd seen. Snowflakes fell softly outside the window, bright white against the night sky. Eric sat up in bed and rested his head in his palm. 'Do you think Marcus was reunited with his gladiator pals?'

'Who could say? I hope so.'

Eric sighed. 'Me too.'

'Tell you what, after Christmas is over, we'll go back and look for him at his old haunt.'

'If we can't find him, then he must have been,' said Eric hopefully.

Max nodded and sat up in bed. 'How about we go downstairs and exchange our presents now?'

'Would that be allowed, before your parents are up?'

''Course! It's Christmas morning,' said Max, jumping out of bed. Max and Eric crept downstairs together in their pyjamas. Max wriggled under the tree to switch on the Christmas tree lights, only knocking off two baubles as he did so. Then they sat cross-legged under the tree, with the coloured lights reflected in their excited eyes.

Max handed Eric the present he'd chosen for him. It was a large package wrapped in gold paper and tied with a big red ribbon by Mrs Hastings. Eric reached out and took it with reverence. 'Is this really for me,

Max?'

''Course. It's my gift to you.'

Eric removed the wrapping carefully, intent on leaving the luxurious paper intact. When it fell away to the floor, he turned over the box, and the picture on the front took his breath away. 'It's a *car*.'

'Yes. It's not a real one, obviously, but it's remote controlled so you can drive it, kind of like a real one.' Max opened the box and lifted out the shiny red Ferrari.

'Cor blimey, Max! Are you sure this is *my* car?'

Max handed it to him. 'Absolutely.'

'In all my days, I never thought to own anything like this,' said Eric, holding it up like it was made from eggshells.

'Look. Watch this,' said Max, picking up the remote control. 'Put it down ... other way up ... that's it! Now watch.'

Eric leapt to his feet. 'Blimey! It moves, Max!'

'Yes, you control it with this.'

'As I live and breathe! What I wouldn't give to show it to the lads back at the orphanage. Which reminds me, here's my present to you,' said Eric, reaching for a parcel near his elbow. Max put down the remote control and took it from him. Eric's eyes shone with anticipation as he watched his friend tear off the wrapping paper. 'It's not much. Back at the orphanage we always whittled a present from the firewood we managed to hide away throughout the year. We used to go cold so that we could save it up, but like I always used to tell the lads, what's the point of Christmas without presents?' The paper fell away and Max held up a replica of the Ghost Galleon carved expertly from wood. 'Like I said, it's not much.'

'You *made* this?'

Eric nodded. 'Been working on it whenever you went out.'

'*Not much*? This is *incredible!* It makes my present to you look like nothing. Thank you, Eric. I'll treasure it.'

There was quiet knock at the front door. Max got up, went to the window, and looked askance towards the front porch. 'I don't believe it! It's Ellie and Caretaker Wiseman.'

'No!'

'Yes. Better open the door before they knock again and wake Mum and Dad.'

Max opened the front door. Ellie was standing with Caretaker

Wiseman, who sheltered them both from the falling snow with his umbrella. Ellie was dressed in a smart red coat buttoned all the way up, her normally dishevelled hair up in a bun.

Max looked her up and down. 'What happened to *you*?' he said.

'Oh, this?' she said, looking down at herself and touching her bun self-consciously. 'It's just a disguise.'

'What are you disguised as?' asked Max.

'A normal person.'

'You almost pull it off. What are you doing here?'

'We have something for Eric,' said Caretaker Wiseman mysteriously.

'You do?' said Eric, appearing behind Max and looking at their empty hands.

Ellie nodded. 'Go and put some clothes on, and we'll show you,' she said, barely able to contain her excitement.

A few minutes later, Max and Eric reappeared wearing coats and scarves. They joined Ellie and Caretaker Wiseman at the bottom of the drive and set off in silence down the street, the snow crunching under their feet as they passed under the street lights. Seven houses down on the opposite side of the road, a light was on in a front room. Ellie and Caretaker Wiseman led them up the drive and stopped before the lit window. The net curtains had been pulled open, and the condensation on the inside displayed the fingerprints of someone who must have been standing there, looking out, a short time ago. 'What's going on?' said Max. 'This house has been up for sale for a while now.'

'It's no longer for sale,' said Caretaker Wiseman with barely concealed excitement. 'It was purchased this week by the Ancient Order of Wall Scratchings.'

'But why?' said Max, stepping closer to the window with Eric. Inside, a man and a woman were sitting on a sofa, holding hands and glancing up at a clock on the wall.

'Who are they?' asked Eric.

Caretaker Wiseman placed a hand on Eric's shoulder and tried to speak. Seeing that he was choked with emotion, Ellie said quietly, 'They're your mother and father, Eric.'

Eric drew a deep breath and gazed hungrily inside at the pair on the sofa. He drank in the kind face of the woman, who had a button nose and full lips just like his own. The man next to her had the same fawn-coloured hair and large brown eyes that he saw whenever he looked in a mirror. Eric looked up at Caretaker Wiseman. His mouth fell open, but no words came out.

'I know. And yes. It really is your mother and father,' said Caretaker Wiseman quietly.

Max tore his gaze from the window and looked up at Caretaker Wiseman. 'So Ellie … she saved them after all?'

'In a way, you all saved them,' said Caretaker Wiseman. 'You see, they hadn't been terminated at all.'

'They escaped … through one of the cracks we made outside the Bank of England with Gog and Magog,' added Ellie.

'Yes,' said Caretaker Wiseman, 'and it was fortunate that one of our own people found them huddled on the steps of Mansion House. It was thanks to their Victorian clothing that our keen-eyed employee managed to put two and two together. Come on.' Caretaker Wiseman stepped towards the front door. 'Those poor people have waited long enough to meet you, Eric.'

'But I can't *move*,' said Eric, gazing imploringly at Max and Ellie. They each took an arm and led him to the front door. 'Do … do I look alright?'

'You'll do just fine,' said Ellie, ruffling Eric's hair with affection.

Eric wriggled free and started patting his hair back down again.

'What's more, they know their son is Scratchling-born. Someone *special*,' said Ellie.

Eric froze. 'But I'm not special. I'm not. I'm not even an orphan, which means I'm not much of anything. Not really. *What* did you say?' he asked of his three silent companions.

'The boy's in shock,' said Ellie, reaching for the doorbell. 'Come on,' she said to Max and Caretaker Wiseman. 'Let's go. This should be a private reunion.'

Max, Ellie and Caretaker Wiseman walked slowly down the path towards the garden gate, leaving Eric gazing at them over his shoulder. They turned to watch him wobble on his skinny little legs, and reach out for the door for support. Max and Ellie gave him the thumbs-up, and he turned back towards the door, which began to open …

Eric gazed raptly up into the tear-streaked face of the mother he could not remember but whose shadowy form had often appeared to comfort him in his dreams. His father appeared suddenly by her side, and Mr and Mrs Kettle gazed at down at Eric like he was the most precious thing on earth. They opened their arms wide, whereupon Eric stumbled inside and collapsed into them.

Just beyond the garden gate, Max said, 'They're going to hug the life out of that boy if they're not careful.'

'Only if he doesn't hug the life out of them first,' said Ellie, blowing her nose into a handkerchief.

The End

A massive thank-you to Rebecca Keys for going above and beyond during the editing process!

This book is dedicated to my friend Peter Wiseman, brought back to life as the Caretaker of the Chamber of Scratchings
1924-2012

The Scratchling Trinity will return!
If you enjoyed this book, other children's books by
Boyd Brent for the same age group include:

The Lost Diary of Snow White Trilogy
I Am Pan: The Fabled Journal of Peter Pan
Jack Tracy and the Priory of Chaos
Diary of a Wizard Kid 1 & 2
&
To be published in November 2017
The Fabled Journal of Beauty

The opening pages to The Lost Diary of Snow White Trilogy follow here
...

This diary is the property of Snow White.

Strictly speaking, I'm not supposed to keep a diary. No fairytale characters are. It's *the* unwritten rule of the land. And now I know why: because life here is so unlike anything people in the real world have been led to believe. Once it's finished, I'll have to find a hiding place for it. But if you're holding it now, it means it's been found, and the truth about my life can *finally* be revealed...

Monday

"Mirror, mirror on the wall, who's the fairest of them all?"

"You are Snow White." I've never much cared for this mirror. It's not even supposed to have an opinion – not according to the fairy tale upon which my life is based. It's only my evil stepmother's mirror that's supposed to say what an unrivalled beaut I am. Well, it simply isn't true. I mean, there's pale and then there's PALE. And I'm the kind of PALE that makes me visible from space most nights.

I can't *tell* you what a relief it is to share this secret: you can't believe everything you read in fairy tales. The truth is that all the mirrors in the land (not to mention all the reflective surfaces) are wrong about my fairest-of-them-all status. I caught my reflection in Not Particularly Hopeful's eyes the other day, and his eyes said (you heard me correctly, welcome to my fairytale paradise), "You are without doubt the fairest of them all, Snow White." At this point you may be wondering who Not Particularly Hopeful is. You know there are seven dwarves, and even though you can't name them all, you're pretty certain that none of them are called Not Particularly Hopeful. Yet another misunderstanding about my life. There are *five* dwarves, and contrary to popular belief, none are even remotely Happy. How could they be, with names like Not Particularly Hopeful, Insecure, Meddlesome, Inconsolable and Awkward? According to the little lamb that skips past my kitchen window every morning, the dwarves represent facets of my own personality. Cripes.

That's deep. Particularly for a constantly-on-the-go lamb of such tiny proportions.

Then there's Prince Charming. He wasn't supposed to arrive until *after* my stepmother poisons me, and I've been in a coma for a hundred years. As the story goes, that's when he wakes me with a kiss, and after that we live happily ever after. No pressure, then. But the other day, when the little lamb hopped, skipped and jumped past my kitchen window, it bleated something about a hunky prince on a white stallion coming into my life. "Really?" I replied. "Stop the press. We're talking in a hundred years' time, once I'm fully rested and up to the challenge of living happily ever after."

"No," replied the little lamb. "His arrival is imminent."

"Imminent?"

"Any second now."

"Did you swallow a dictionary? Imminent? I don't think…" And there he was, a hunky prince riding a white stallion. He looked me up and down, smiled and said, "Reports of your beauty have not been exaggerated. You are indeed the fairest in the land." Prince Charming isn't the only one who can look a person up and down. And once I'd made a point of doing just that – minus the smile, of course – I said, "What are you *doing* here? You're over a century early. Please. Leave me alone. I'm not ready to live happily ever after yet."

"Nonsense!" said he. "One so perfect on the outside must also be perfect on the inside. And ready for any challenge. What have you to say to that?"

"That you should never judge a book by its cover," said I firmly.

As Prince Charming rode away on his horse, he called out, "I intend to win you over, Snow."

"But why ever would you want to?"

"So we can live happily ever after."

"Really? No pressure, then!"

The next day as I swept the porch, the little lamb saw me crying. It hopped about in a circle and bleated, "Whatever is your problem?" I rested my chin on the broom handle, and my eyes went up and down as they followed its cute bounce. "My problem? At least I can do stationary. What's with all the bouncing, anyway?"

"I was just written this way: always on the move, and quite unable to slow down."

"Really? Well, I was just written this way."

"What way?" asked the little lamb.

"I suppose I'm insecure. And at times such as these, quite inconsolable."

"Anything else?"

"Well, now you come to mention it, I'm awkward and not particularly hopeful."

"About what?"

"About living happily ever after with the prince."

"Why? Is the prince not charming by name *and* by nature?"

"I presume so. But he doesn't understand me at all."

"Then introduce the prince to your dwarves. The clues are in their names," said the wise little lamb.

I began sweeping the porch again and said, "First of all, they aren't *my* dwarves, and secondly the prince is already well acquainted with them."

"Then he's been blinded by your beauty?"

I nodded mournfully, then shook my head. "He must need his eyes tested. I have seen a three-headed toad fairer than I."

Saturday

Today my evil stepmother invited me to tea. Yes, that's right, the same evil stepmother who has hated me ever since she asked her mirror, "Who's the fairest in the land?" and it lied and told her that I was. And ever since that day, she's been trying to poison me with apples. She's quite the one-trick pony in that way: apples, apples, always apples. My friend Cinderella said I should count my blessings.

"*Blessings*?" said I.

"Yes. That your stepmother has absolutely no imagination when it comes to poisoning you." Cinders also pointed out that I'm related to my stepmother. And that when it comes to our relatives, we must make allowances, even if they do hate us enough to poison us with fruit. Then she reminded me of what she has to put up with with her sisters. Poor Cinders. They give her a dreadful time.

My stepmother sent a sparrow with a message this morning. In between tweets, the sparrow read the following to me: 'I'm so excited about your early engagement! You must come for tea! And a slice of apple pie! I baked it myself only this morning! Especially for you!" As you can see, my stepmother is fond of exclamation marks. In my experience, the more exclamation marks a person uses, the crazier they are. It's really no different from someone shouting all the time for no apparent reason.

I stepped onto the porch, and whistled for Barry the boar. Barry runs a taxi service, and is the fastest boar in the land (ask any mirror). He also has the longest tusks, and they're perfect to hang on to. "Mind that hanging branch, Barry!" said I, lowering my head.

"I see it."

"Appreciate the ride, Baz."

"No problem, Snow. Happy to help out. How are the dwarves? Still whistling while they work?"

"Oh, yes. Of course. It helps to keep their spirits up. It's hard work down that mine."

"If I could, I'd whistle while I worked too."

"Then why don't you?"

"I can't on account of my piggy lips. Whenever I try, I blow raspberries instead."

Barry dropped me off outside the palace, and then trotted off, blowing raspberries (at least, I assume he was trying to whistle). And so it was with a heavy heart that I turned and knocked on the door. The palace is very large and the butler very small. The sun had gone down by the time he let me in... and had risen again by the time we reached the parlour, where my stepmother stood over an apple pie, pastry knife in hand. "Pie?" she asked.

"I'll take a rain check on the pie, thank you."

"Nonsense," said she, cutting an ample slice. "You're such a waif of a thing. You need fattening up."

"Oh," I said, looking at my reflection in one of the parlour's many mirrors. "I'm quite fat enough already, thank you."

My stepmother slammed the knife down on the table. "Fat, are you? If you're *fat,* then what does that make me?" She turned yellow and green with envy (she does that a lot around me), then she remembered her charm offensive and assumed a more plausible colour. "No matter," said she. "How lovely it is to see you! I so look forward to your visits. Come and sit beside me. Tell me all about Prince Charming. He must be awfully keen. Why else would he turn up so early?"

I sat down, and she placed a piece of pie before me on a plate. I watched as apple oozed from its sides.

"What*ever* is the matter? It won't bite," she said.

I pushed the plate away. "I'm too bloated for pie. And what's more, I don't want to marry Prince Charming. Not yet."

"Why ever not?"

"Because I'm not ready to live happily ever after."

My stepmother rang a little bell on the table to summon a servant. "We'll skip the apple pie," she told her servant, "and have apple strudel instead."

I rolled my eyes.

My stepmother did the same, then she lowered her voice to a whisper and said, "Trust me. If you have a slice of my apple strudel, you won't have to marry the prince."

"Oh? And why is that?"

"Because it's an enchanted strudel," she whispered, like she was confiding a secret. *You mean because it's a poisoned strudel,* I thought. I straightened my back and said, "I'm in no need of enchantment at the moment, thank you very much."

"Ungrateful girl!"

"Is my father home?"

"The king is away on state business."

"Will he be back soon?"

"Just as soon as you eat some strudel."

"I won't do it," said I.

"How about a nice bowl of fruit salad?"

"Are there apples in it?"

"Just the one."

"No, thank you."

"Toffee apple?"

"No."

"Apple fritter?"

"No."

"Tart, then."

"Ex*cuse* me?"

"Apple tart?"

"No way."

"Perhaps I can tempt you with a delicious glass of apple cider? Seventy percent proof. Promise I won't tell your father."

I couldn't take any more apple offers, I simply couldn't. So I left.

It was cold and dark, and a long walk back to my cottage. I felt a pang of guilt at not being home to make the dwarves their supper. After all, they had taken me in and befriended me in my hour of need. It seems like only yesterday when my stepmother asked her mirror *that* question, and it lied to her. She told the woodcutter to take me into the woods and make sure that I *never* came back. I promised the woodcutter that if he let me go, I would leave the land for good. And that way, my stepmother's mirror would tell her that *she* was the fairest in all the land. The woodcutter must have been a kindly fellow, for he let me go. I walked for many days looking everywhere for the exit to the land, but the land seemed to go on forever. I grew downcast, and that's when I came upon the dwarves. They were on their way home after a hard day down the mine. "Excuse me," I said. "I have been walking for days, and I'm very tired. I'm looking for an exit to the land. Is it close by?"

Not Particularly Hopeful shook his head (I've since discovered that Not Particularly Hopeful shakes his head a lot), then Inconsolable began to cry. I put my arm around the little fellow, doing my best to console him, but it was quite useless. Awkward went bright red and snorted... awkwardly. He looked at Insecure, who said not to ask him *anything* because he didn't know anything. Not Particularly Hopeful spoke up again, and he said that as far he knew, there was no exit to the land. Not anywhere. That everywhere you went, you found more land. And there you had it. Or didn't. Not if you were looking for an exit, anyway.

I sat down on a tree stump and rested my heavy head in my hands. "Do you mean to say that I've spent all this time looking for something that doesn't exist?"

Inconsolable blew his nose, and said it wasn't like it had stopped anybody before. So why should it stop me? Then he pointed in no direction in particular and said the exit was probably that way.

"It can't be. Not if it doesn't exist. Oh, whatever I shall I do! I promised the woodcutter."

"Can you cook?" asked Meddlesome. "Only, Insecure makes all our meals and he's a terrible cook."

Insecure nodded his head in agreement.

"I suppose I can cook. I won't really know until I try," I said.

"What about housework?" asked Meddlesome. "Only, Insecure does all our housework too, and he's terrible at it."

Again, Insecure nodded.

"I suppose I could do housework. I won't really know until I try."

The dwarves went into a huddle, and they decided that in return for cooking and cleaning, I would be given a roof over my head. Apparently, I was almost exactly what they'd been looking for.

The early hours of Sunday morning…

So anyway, back to the present. As you may recall, I'd just left my stepmother's, and had begun my walk home in the dark through the woods. I was just feeling peckish (for just about anything other than apple) when I saw a trail of breadcrumbs. The trail was long and winding, and once I'd eaten it, I found myself on my hands and knees outside a cottage – not my own cottage, but one made entirely from gingerbread. I said to myself, "*Dessert*? I like gingerbread, but don't think I could eat a whole abode."

I peered in through a kitchen window. Inside, I saw a small boy sitting beside a sweet old lady. The old lady was feeding him marshmallows by hand. *How lovely,* I thought. I heard someone chopping wood close by, and hoped it might be the woodcutter. I felt guilty about breaking my promise to him, and wanted to explain why I hadn't left the land. *The land is absolutely everywhere,* I would say. *And therefore quite impossible to leave. And if you did, you'd end up precisely nowhere. And how dreadful would that be*? Having rehearsed my explanation in my mind, and being happy with it, I was disappointed to see not the woodcutter, but a little girl chopping wood. She had long brown hair and big brown eyes, and said her name was Gretel. As it turned out, Gretel and I had a lot in common: she had a stepmother of questionable character too. Her stepmother had left her in the woods with her brother Hansel, where she hoped they would starve to death.

"That's pretty grim," I said.

She nodded and asked, "Did your stepmother abandon you to starve in the woods as well?"

"Oh, no. She told the woodcutter to flat-out murder me." I glanced over my shoulder at the gingerbread house. "Thank goodness," I said.

"What do you mean?" she asked.

"That you and your brother found a happy ending after all."

"How so?"

"You came upon a lovely gingerbread house. And a kind old lady who feeds children marshmallows by hand."

Gretel shook her head. "She's not a kind old lady. She's a witch. And she's fattening my brother up."

"But why?"

"So there'll be ample meat on his bones when she eats him. Or so she said."

I tutted.

Gretel echoed my tut and said, "The old witch plans to fatten me up too, and then she's going to eat me. But not before she's worked my fingers to the bone." I reached out and squeezed Gretel's shoulder. "Sorry. That's pretty rough. Whatever does a person have to do to get a break in this land?"

"It beats me," said she.

"I won't have it."

Gretel shrugged her shoulders. "What can you do? What can anybody do? It's just the way our story was written."

"I used to think that way too. And then my prince arrived early, and said he couldn't wait to marry me."

"You must have been so happy," sighed Gretel.

I cast my gaze upon the ground and shook my head. "I'm not ready to live happily ever after. Tell me, is there any mention of me in your story?"

"Who are you?"

"Snow White."

"The fairest in the land?"

I shook my head.

"Well, no," said Gretel. "I don't believe there's any mention of Snow White."

I folded my arms and said, "My own story has been changed. And my being here only goes to prove one thing."

"And that is?" asked Gretel.

I raised an arm and brought my thumb and forefinger together. "That we might change it a *teensy weensy* bit more."

"How so?"

My gaze fell upon the axe in her hands, then I looked over my shoulder at the cottage where the witch was fattening up her brother.

"Oh!" said Gretel. "Why ever didn't I think of that?"

Monday

I'm back at home now, and you'll be pleased to know that Hansel and Gretel's story ended happily after all. The same could not be said for the witch. I imagine she had quite a shock when Gretel burst into her kitchen, axe raised above her head, and said the story was about to be altered 'a *teensy weensy* bit more.'

Today Prince Charming invited me to the enchanted lake for a picnic. He seems quite convinced that he can change my mind about marrying him early. His invite said that when it came to wooing the ladies his record was flawless. And that even if he had to make an effort to understand my feelings, that's precisely what he would do. His message said I should *fear not* and *brace myself for falling hopelessly in love*, and that if all else fails, *I should get a grip for once in my life*.

I handed the dwarves their lunch boxes and kissed them goodbye at the garden gate   all except Insecure, who was even more worried than usual about hitting the wrong part of the mine and causing a cave-in. "I'll stay with you today, Snow, that's if you don't mind?" Of all my dwarves, I feel closest to Insecure. "Of course I don't mind. I'm going to meet Prince Charming down at the enchanted lake later."

"Do you mind if I tag along?" he asked.

"You know, I somehow thought you might."

Insecure and I walked up a steep hill, on the other side of which the sun glistened upon an enchanted lake and leaves rustled upon enchanted tress. At the top of the hill, we stopped and looked down upon the scene as just described. The only difference was Prince Charming. He lay on a blanket beneath the shade of a tall tree, his perfect head placed in a perfect palm, a blade of grass turning slowly between his perfect lips. Placed upon his blanket were all manner of tasty treats to tempt me.

Insecure looked up at me and I looked down at Insecure. "The prince will not be at all happy to see me," said he. "Of that I'm quite sure."

"What makes you say that?" asked I.

Insecure sat down and hugged his knees to his chest. "Because nobody is ever happy to see me. I'll keep watch over you from up here."

"If you're sure?"

Insecure nodded.

"Okay then."

As I approached the prince, he got up and told me I grew fairer with each visit. "Come and sit beside me," said he, "and share this delightful picnic."

Prince Charming and I sat cross-legged opposite each another. He took an apple from a bowl of fruit and handed it to me. "The apple's ruddiness is intense, is it not?" said he. I glanced down at the apple in my hand. Indeed, it was the ruddiest apple I had ever seen. The prince smiled and said, "I chose that apple for you especially."

"Why?"

"Because it matches perfectly the colour of your cheeks when you blush."

"Really? Thanks. I think."

"Tell me," said he, leaning closer, "what good and charitable deeds have you performed lately?"

I rubbed the apple against my sleeve to bring out its shine. "What makes you think I've performed any good and charitable deeds?"

"One as fair as you must have charity in her heart."

"Really? Well…"

"Come now, my love, there's no need to be coy about your charitable deeds."

I took a bite out of the apple. As I chewed I said, "I presume my stepmother didn't provide the fruit for this picnic?"

Prince Charming's eyes opened wide, and they filled with wonder. "Not only are you the fairest in the land, you also possess the wisdom of kings."

With a mouthful of apple it wasn't easy to talk, but I did my best. "Are you 'elling me that eye step-um gave 'ou this apple?"

"Yes, my darling. She insisted on supplying all the fruit for our picnic."

I spat out the apple. As I picked bits of it out of his hair and lap, I said, "In the future, if my stepmother offers you fruit… say no."

"But why, my love?"

"She's been trying to poison me with it for years."

"With *fruit*?"

"Apples, to be precise."

"I can't believe *anyone* would wish to harm even a hair on your fair head."

"Believe it."

"I don't want to believe it."

"You must believe it."

"But what if I can't believe it?"

"Then you must try harder."

"But why apples, my darling?"

I shrugged up my heavy shoulders. "Maybe she's just written that way." Prince Charming stood up and hurled the fruit bowl into the enchanted lake. Moments later, a great many fish floated to its surface, all in deep comas from which they would never awaken – well, not unless kissed by a prince who wanted to live happily ever after with a fish. I thought about how unlikely this was, and sighed.

Prince Charming sat down again. "Now," said he, "you were about to tell me of your charitable deeds?"

"But why should I?"

Prince Charming leaned back on the palms of his hands. "I have been led to believe that talking of your charitable deeds will fill you with pride, and make you feel less insecure."

I leaned back on my own palms. "Fat to no chance of that," said I.

"All the same, please indulge me."

"Alright. I helped a brother and sister in the woods yesterday. Does that count?"

"I knew it! One so fair must carry out at least *one* charitable deed every single day."

"If you say so."

"Tell me of these fortunate siblings whose paths crossed your own, my dearest, most charitable darling."

"I simply had to help them."

"Oh, my darling!"

"We had such a lot in common."

"How so?"

"They have a stepmother of questionable character too."

"So how did you come upon the unfortunate brother and sister?"

"Their names were Hansel and Gretel. I came upon Gretel chopping wood. She told me how a witch was fattening her brother for her cooking pot."

The prince looked suitably concerned and said, "Whatever does a person have to do to get a break in this land?"

"Tell me about it."

"So what did you do?" asked the prince.

"Well, I knew I had to change their story, as mine had been changed."

"And?"

"And I considered the options available to me."

"Very wise, my love, very wise indeed. And these options were?"

"Pretty scarce, actually. There was a barn filled to bursting with marshmallows, a well filled with chocolate syrup, and a young girl with a grudge... and armed with an axe."

The prince twirled his moustache and looked very pleased with himself. "Say no more," said he. "It's clear that your plan involved marshmallows and chocolate syrup."

Tuesday

Yesterday, when I described the crime scene that Gretel had created in the witch's kitchen, the prince turned quite pale. I imagined he'd quite fallen out of love with me, but alas, when I asked him if this were true, he looked once again like a love-sick puppy and said, "When faced with evil witches who eat children, charitable solutions are not always possible."

"You're not wrong, and…"

The prince held up a palm. I'm no palm reader, but even I could read that palm. *Pipe down and let me speak*, it said. The prince smiled, and then finished what he was saying using words, "If there had been a way to escape using only chocolate syrup and marshmallows, then you would have found one. Of this I am convinced, my love."

I thought about that for a moment and nodded. "I suppose we *could* have thrown the witch down her well and drowned her in chocolate syrup. Oh! Or we could have locked her up in her barn with *nothing* to eat but marshmallows. She'd have grown fatter and fatter and eventually burst. A proper taste of her own medicine. Or…" The prince raised his other palm, and with both palms now raised, I imagined he wanted to play pat-a-cake. While we played, he told me that while he appreciated my ingenuity, he'd quite heard enough alternative endings for the witch.

Anyway, today I'm going to visit my friend Cinderella. I expect you've heard of Cinders. Her story is as well-known as my own, and like me she is supposed to go through a terrible time before her Prince Charming rescues her. I rode over to her palace on Barry the boar. As Barry trotted through the forest, I said, "Is everything okay, Barry?"

"I mustn't grumble," said he.

"Only you seem slower than usual."

"I never was the brightest boar in the land."

"That's not what I meant. The spring has quite gone out of your trot. It's my fault, isn't it? I've grown fat."

Barry shook his head. "Is Cinderella expecting you?"

"Oh, yes."

"Only she generally has a lot of palace-work to get through," said Barry.

"Don't I know it."

Barry snorted. "I can't imagine Cinderella complaining much if her Prince Charming arrived early and wanted to live happily ever after."

"*What* did you just say, Barry?"

"I said I can't imagine Cinderella complaining if her Prince Charming turned up early. Not with her working her fingers to the bone every day."

"Barry! You've just given me a brilliant idea! The solution to both mine and Cinderella's woes."

"How so?"

"All I need do is get my Prince Charming to fall in love with Cinderella. That way, I'll have time to sort out my issues, and Cinders can live happily ever after right away. Do you think my plan might work?"

"It might. I hear that Cinderella scrubs up pretty well. And one Prince Charming is just like any other. There's a factory that makes them. And I hear they're pretty easy to put together."

"And why is that?"

"Because they're only one-dimensional characters. Gallant and charming."

I yawned. "That sums up my own Prince Charming to a tee, Barry."

"There you have it, then."

"There I have it."

Barry dropped me off at a side entrance to the palace, and I slipped inside unnoticed. I expect you've heard about Cinderella's sisters: ugly by name and ugly by nature. They don't allow Cinderella to have a social life. What's more, the palace is huge, which means there's always a room in need of scrubbing. But in many ways that's quite handy, as all I have to do to find her is follow the smell of bleach. Today I came upon her in the ballroom. The ballroom is very grand, and Cinders looked out of place in her sackcloth and rags. She was halfway along the ballroom's floor on her hands and knees, scrubbing for all she was worth. I took off my shoes and tiptoed up behind her. "Surprise!" I said.

"Argh!" she cried, and fell flat on her face.

"Do not be alarmed," I whispered. "It's only me. Your good friend, Snow."

She sat for a minute with birds circling her head, and slowly her senses returned. "*Snow?*" said she.

"Hello, Cinders."

She glanced about fretfully. "Do my sisters know you're here? Only, if they find out I have a visitor they will punish me."

"Fear not, good friend of mine. Your sisters' carriage was not on the palace forecourt."

This news cheered Cinders no end. She stood up and extended a hand for me to shake. "Why the formal greeting?" I asked.

"I'm just so pleased to see a friendly face. How are you, Snow?"

"Not so good."

"Is it your evil stepmother? Is she *still* intent on poisoning you?"

I shrugged up my hulky shoulders. "You know how it is. And you? Do your sisters still think of you as a horrid blot on their family tree?"

Cinders shrugged up her beautiful shoulders. "Just look at me. So what's new?"

"Glad you asked me that. My own Prince Charming has turned up early, and seems keen as mustard to live happily ever after."

"Oh, you lucky thing! Then why the face like you've spent the morning sucking on a rotten lemon?"

"Think about it, Cinders," said I, looking at my reflection in one of the ballroom's many mirrors. While we waited for the mirror to make its predictable pronouncement, I rolled my eyes. "Without doubt you are the fairest in the land," said the mirror.

"Still don't believe the mirrors?" asked Cinders, scraping some dirt from beneath her thumb nail.

"Not just the mirrors," said I. "It seems to me that all the reflective surfaces in the land need their eyes tested."

"But they don't *have* eyes, Snow."

"That explains a lot. Had they eyes, perhaps they wouldn't talk such nonsense. And that's especially true with you standing beside me."

Cinderella looked at her own reflection: her long blonde hair was dirty and matted, and her face smeared with dirt. "Truly, I am a dreadful mess," said she.

"And still more beautiful than I."

Cinderella began to chew a nail. "How'd you work that one out?"

"You just are. And what's more, you're so patient with your sisters. And so accepting of all the awful things in your life."

"What choice do I have, Snow? It's just the way things are written."

"That's what I used to think, but then my Prince Charming turned up early. And I met Hansel and Gretel in the woods. And neither of these things were in the book."

"What does that prove?"

"That we can change things."

"Not me. But in a year and a bit, give or take, my own Prince Charming will rescue me. And then we're going to live happily ever after."

"What if you don't have to wait a year and a bit for your Prince Charming?"

"But I do."

"But what if you don't? What if my Prince Charming falls for you?"

Cinders cast her gaze the length and breadth of the ballroom. "Is he here?"

"I hope not."

"But why would he fall for me? I'm not the fairest in the land."

"That's just the thing. Barry the boar said there's a big demand for Prince Charmings in stories such as these, and that there's a factory that makes them on demand. One Prince Charming is just like any other, apparently."

Cinders nodded. "Gallant and charming."

"You know, I sometimes think that if my prince was a bit less charming, I'd find him more interesting. I may even think myself more worthy of his attention."

"You mean if he was a bad boy?"

"Whatever is a *bad boy*?"

Cinders lowered her voice. "I sometimes hear my sisters giggling about them. They say they're not in the least bit charming."

"But they are gallant, surely?"

Cinders shook her head. "They are perfectly horrid. I don't understand what my sisters see in them. The worst of all is the Big Bad Wolf. My sisters say he only has eyes for Little Red Riding Hood. I sometimes think they hate her almost as much as they hate me."

"I'm going to arrange a meeting."

"With the Big Bad Wolf?"

"No, silly. Not for me. For you with my Prince Charming."

Cinders looked in a mirror and toyed with her filthy locks. "Do you really think he might prefer me to you?"

"Oh, yes. I'm quite convinced of it."

Thank you for reading! If you enjoyed this sample, *The Lost Diary of Snow White Trilogy* is available from Amazon.

Printed in Great Britain
by Amazon